QUEER AS FOLK
The Scripts

RUSSELL T DAVIES
QUEER AS FOLK
The Scripts

First published 1999 by Channel 4 Books
an imprint of Macmillan Publishers Ltd
25 Eccleston Place London SW1W 9NF
Basingstoke and Oxford

www.macmillan.co.uk

Associated companies throughout the world

ISBN 0 7522 1858 1

9 8 7 6 5 4 3 2 1

A CIP catalogue record for this book is
available from the British Library.

Typesetting and plate section design by Blackjacks
Photographs by Joss Barrett, © Red Production Company 1999
Printed in Great Britain by Mackays of Chatham plc, Chatham, Kent

Queer as Folk: The Scripts accompanies the television series *Queer as Folk*,
produced by Red Production Company for Channel 4.

CAST AND CREW

Stuart Jones .... Aidan Gillen
Vince Tyler .... Craig Kelly
Nathan Maloney .... Charlie Hunnam
Hazel Tyler...................................... Denise Black
Donna Clarke .... Carla Henry
Alexander Perry .... Antony Cotton
Bernard Thomas .... Andy Devine
Cameron Roberts............................. Peter O'Brien
Phil Delaney.................................... Jason Merrells
Janice Maloney.............................. Caroline O'Neill
Romey Sullivan .... Esther Hall
Lisa Levene .... Saira Todd
Rosalie Cotter.................................. Caroline Pegg
Christian Hobbs............................... Ben Maguire
Marie Threepwood...................... Maria Doyle Kennedy
Margaret Jones................................. Ger Ryan
Clive Jones.................................... Ian McElhinney
Dazz Collinson ....Jonathon Natynczyk
Sandra Docherty............................. Alison Burrows
Lance Amponah..............................John Brobbey
Dane McAteer .... Adam Zane
Harvey Black................................. Andrew Lancel
Marcie Finch.................................. Susan Cookson
Siobhan Potter ....Juley McCann
Gareth Critchly ....Jack Deam
Mrs Delaney .... Kate Fitzgerald
Roy Maloney .... Paul Copley
Martin Brooks .... Michael Culkin
Striking Man................................. Lee Warburton
Susie Smith.................................... Sarah Jones

Producer/Executive Producer.................. Nicola Shindler
Co-Producer/Series Creator .... Russell T Davies
Directors.................. Charles McDougall/Sarah Harding
Associate Producer .... Tom Sherry
Designer.. Claire Kenny
Director of Photography .... Nigel Walters
Editors .... Tony Cranstoun/Tony Ham
Costume Designer .... Pam Tait
Make Up Designer............................. David Jones
Sound Recordist............................. Gary Desmond
Composer.................................... Murray Gold
Casting Director............................. Beverley Keogh
Script Editor................................. Matt Jones

FOREWORD

1 INT. MANCHESTER RESTAURANT, NIGHT

The INTERVIEWER sits, drumming fingers, impatient, then looks up as RUSSELL T DAVIES walks in. He's very tall, handsome, dashing, could pass for nineteen.

> RUSSELL: Hi, sorry I'm late, did you sign the contract? The one that stipulates 'handsome, dashing, could pass for nineteen'?

> INTERVIEWER: Yeah, d'you want a drink?

> RUSSELL: Just a mineral water, thanks.

> INTERVIEWER: So, I thought we'd cover the basics for the Script Book. How the series came about, its development, the changes that were made from script to screen, that sort of thing.

Beat.

> RUSSELL: Oh, let's have some wine.

2 INT. MANCHESTER RESTAURANT, 20 MINUTES LATER

CU a bottle of red wine, half of it drunk already, RUSSELL in full flow. INTER-VIEWER still on water.

> RUSSELL: ...the important thing is, no one at Channel 4 said, 'let's have a gay drama series'. They wouldn't be that dull. Catriona MacKenzie in the Drama Department just looked at my work, and I'd been putting gay sub-plots in everything I'd written – I am actually gay, did you know that?

RUSSELL straightens his lycra t-shirt over his washboard stomach. (As stipulated.)

> RUSSELL (CONT'D): It was just a natural development of my work – if I'd been a vicar, they'd have encouraged me to write about God. So off I went. And at first, I did feel this incredible pressure to be representative, to include every single angle of gay life. Lesbians, older gay men, monogamous gay couples, AIDS. And it's just too big, trying to represent an entire world – that's never going to create good drama. God, it would be bland and worthy. And besides, no straight drama has that kind of remit. In the end, I realised I had to focus – to find good characters, good stories, and to hell with representation.

> INTERVIEWER: There's been a lot of criticism that you portrayed gay men as sex-mad –

RUSSELL: – oh my God, look at the arse on that.

A WAITER is walking past. Historic arse. RUSSELL signals.

RUSSELL (CONT'D): 'Scuse me, another bottle of red wine please.

WAITER: Certainly, sir.

RUSSELL: (flirting) We're just discussing my Script Book. Queer as Folk, I'm the writer. Ha ha.

WAITER: Oh, what's that, then?

RUSSELL: (loses smile) Queer as Folk.

WAITER: Is that a documentary?

RUSSELL: It's a drama. I'm the writer. It was very big in March, very big indeed, now fetch the fucking wine.

WAITER goes. Awkward pause.

RUSSELL (CONT'D): He's just kidding. Ha ha.

3 INT. MANCHESTER RESTAURANT, 20 MINUTES LATER

RUSSELL and INTERVIEWER now both eating. The second bottle of wine is half demolished, INTERVIEWER still on water.

RUSSELL: The Script Book's got the original shooting script, printed before filming began. And the script's important – to my mind it's the most important thing, but at the same time, it's just a template. You've got to allow for freedom in filming, and in casting.

INTERVIEWER: Yeah, I noticed in ep.1, Stuart isn't even described as Irish.

RUSSELL: He wasn't Irish until Aidan Gillen walked in to audition. And that's brilliant, you just write around it. Eps 5 to 8 were still being written when filming started, so I was able to build the actors into the later scripts – it takes until ep.7 for Hazel to refer to Stuart as 'Irish boy'. And the first – and only – reference to Donna being black comes in ep.5, after we'd cast Carla Henry.

INTERVIEWER: There's a fair bit of material in the Script Book that never made it to the screen.

RUSSELL: Yeah, and about 95% of it was actually filmed. Only a couple of scenes fell through the schedule and never actually existed – like the Midge school scene in ep.4, and the whole Nathan-persecutes-the-lesbians sub-plot in ep.3. Everything else was filmed, then dropped in the edit.

INTERVIEWER: Was that because the episodes were too long?

RUSSELL: No, never, I think all the episodes came in slightly under their running time. We wanted the whole thing to move fast, and if a scene was holding up the pace and energy, it went into the bin. And sometimes you find that you just don't need a scene – and you can't tell which scenes are needed until they're filmed. The thing is, once you enter the edit, the script's forgotten – you're building an episode out of the pictures and the plot, the stuff you've already got on screen, not the paper version. And it was completely collaborative – director, writer, producer, script-editor, the film editor, Channel 4 people, all of us debating, arguing sometimes, over what to keep.

The INTERVIEWER is staring at RUSSELL, as though fascinated. But reveal that RUSSELL has a line of pesto sauce running from lip to collarbone. He chunters on, completely unaware that he looks a twat.

RUSSELL (CONT'D): We've been asked if there's any chance of restoring the missing material, like a Director's Cut. But there's no way. The transmitted version took weeks of editing, and it's honestly the best, it's the version we all love.

INTERVIEWER: Did the scripts change once you started filming?

RUSSELL: Oh, one or two locations changed, to keep the sched-ule intact. And small line changes as we went along, tiny stuff. I'd be on set every day, and if anyone thought of a better line on the spot, we'd put it in.

The pesto sauce is now trickling down the front of RUSSELL's shirt. INTERVIEWER subtly tries to hint there's a problem, licking lips.

RUSSELL (CONT'D): ...are you flirting with me?

INTERVIEWER: No, um, I, no –

RUSSELL: Cheeky. Course you are. Don't worry, I have that effect. Anyway, the only big script change was at the very start of ep.1. It was assembled in the edit exactly as written, and it was like a thriller. You expected Stuart to take Nathan home and murder him, like an episode of Cracker.

INTERVIEWER: Funny thing is, if it was a thriller, you could've broadcast it on ITV at 9.00. But Stuart doesn't murder him, they just have sex – which means it's banished to 10.30.

RUSSELL: Yeah, don't interrupt. So, we had a big problem, the opening ten minutes of ep.1 were scary and tense. Fortunately, we were still filming, so I was able to go away and write a completely new piece-to-camera for Vince. He becomes your narrator, someone safe, relaxed, smiling, leading you into that world. All written in a panic, it's not part of the actual script, but it ends up as one of my favourite scenes – d'you want a brandy?

INTERVIEWER: Well, we're only halfway through the meal –

RUSSELL: Aah, details – waiter!

4 INT. MANCHESTER RESTAURANT, HALF AN HOUR LATER

Pan across five empty brandy glasses. And the INTERVIEWER'S glass of water. RUSSELL now morose, slurring a tad.

RUSSELL: And I've got to thank them. All those people who pushed, and argued, and inspired. Nicola Shindler, the producer, Matt Jones, script editor, Charles McDougall and Sarah Harding, the directors, Gub Neal and Catriona MacKenzie at Channel 4. And the crew, and that fantastic cast, all of 'em. People think writing's a solitary job – and it is, when you're typing away at four in the morning. (more upset) But at the same time, it's *team* work, you're nothing without good people around you.

INTERVIEWER: Then what's the problem..?

RUSSELL: (sudden anger) Cos I hate them! My first draft script was called Queer As Polk. Polk was a clown, a professional clown, touring the Home Counties in a travelling circus. And every time they stopped in a new town, Polk would save an injured dog from its cruel master. It was brilliant! Circuses, dogs, the public loves 'em. But no, they said, write about poofs. Poofs, poofs, poofs, they're obsessed! Bastards! I loved Polk. I was Polk, Polk was me.

RUSSELL dissolves into tears. The INTERVIEWER signals the WAITER for the bill.

5 INT. MANCHESTER RESTAURANT, 10 MINUTES LATER

INTERVIEWER now alone at the table, RUSSELL is across the other side of the restaurant, sitting with three middle-aged women, scaring them. He's swigging from a bottle of Absinthe, and has butter in his hair.

RUSSELL: I wrote Chucklevision once. I was very big in Children's TV, oh yes. And now it's just poofs, I'm the poof writer, that's me. Oh look, police! Fantastic, I love a man in uniform. Oh good, they're coming over. Hiya. Evening all!

The POLICE grab hold of RUSSELL, drag him from the table. Improvise scuffling, squeals, protests, etc. On the INTERVIEWER. So many questions left unanswered: what about RUSSELL's wife? The lesbian back-lash? And who the hell buys a Script Book anyway? INTERVIEWER catches one last glimpse of RUSSELL as he's carried down the stairs. He's trying to kiss one of the POLICEMEN.

Fade to black.

EPISODE ONE

1/1 INT. BUS STATION, NIGHT 1 0100   1/1
NATHAN

NATHAN MALONEY steps off a bus, a small figure. He's 15, with the potential for good looks, sharp-featured. The bus station's rough at this time of night – a couple of drunks, miserable women. NATHAN keeps his head down, walks out. Terrified of what lies ahead. But he's not going back.

1/2 EXT. CANAL STREET, NIGHT 1 0103   1/2
NATHAN, BERNARD, HAZEL

On the street sign – someone's scrubbed out the C. The Village is alive – gangs spill out of the pubs, on to the street, laughing, couples snogging, transvestites strutting along. The whole place, fearless. NATHAN arrives at the edge of Canal Street. He's been past this street before, but he's never gone *in*. Tonight's the night. He starts the long walk, eyes wide. He passes through the busiest stretch, between Manto's and Metz. NATHAN can see inside the bars – music, light, cigarette smoke. Men. But with bouncers at the door, too scary for him to face. He's come this far, but NATHAN still feels excluded. A police car is edging through the crowd. It's just patrolling, but it's enough to make NATHAN wary; he walks on, towards the Union, head down, lighting a cigarette to calm his nerves.

    A burst of laughter from one group of men nearby unnerves NATHAN; it seems to be directed at him. He's more panicky now, his POV flicking about, from man to man, group to group, building to building. It's like everyone can tell he's 15, a kid, a newcomer.

    As NATHAN's crisis worsens, behind him, a man's walking towards NATHAN, fast. This is BERNARD THOMAS – mid-50s, large, moustache, rough-and-yet-effeminate Welsh accent. He's charging along, having walked out of some argument; we can see, before NATHAN's aware of him, that BERNARD's in a stinking mood. NATHAN's desperate to talk to someone, summoning up the courage, looking round but not seeing BERNARD until the last second. As a result, NATHAN blurts out –

    NATHAN: 'Scuse me, I mean, I'm just looking, but I don't – I mean, what's the best place to go?

BERNARD stops, looks at NATHAN balefully.

    BERNARD: Depends what you're after. If you want bastards, go in there; if you want wankers, go in there; if you want selfish little mincing piss tart dickheads; pick a building, any building, they're full of them.

BERNARD storms off. On NATHAN, crushed. A woman runs past NATHAN – HAZEL TYLER, 45, thin, wiry – though she could be anyone; the focus stays on NATHAN.

    HAZEL: Bernie, don't be so daft, who listens to her? It's just a T-shirt! She's off her head, she's been drinking! Bernie!

NATHAN sits on the canal wall. Defeated.

1/3 EXT. BABYLON, NIGHT 1 0215   1/3
STUART, VINCE, PHIL, MUSCLE MAN, GREEK GOD

The end of the night, people – a ratio of 80% men – spilling out under the neon sign, taxis pulling up.

Through the crowd, we find STUART JONES – 29, beautiful; teeth, hair, clothes, what's called an A-Gay. He's up against the club doorway, snogging a tall, handsome GREEK GOD. But mid-snog, looking over GREEK GOD's shoulder, STUART sees two blokes walking away.

> STUART: Oy, Vince! (To GREEK GOD) Wait there, don't move.

STUART runs to catch up with the two men – VINCE TYLER, 29, unassuming, a less cultivated look than STUART, and PHIL, mid-30s, plump, fast-talking intelligent camp.

> STUART: Where are you going?

> VINCE: You've copped off.

> STUART: I'm just getting his telephone number, that's all –

> PHIL: What did he do, swallow it?

> STUART: I'll be ten minutes, wait for me, wait by the car, you've got to get me home. Wait for me!

He runs back to GREEK GOD (and in B/G, the two of them then wander off). VINCE and PHIL stroll down the street.

> PHIL: So he brings the car, gives you the keys so you can't drink, then he buggers off. Nice system.

> VINCE: I'll give him ten minutes, I don't mind.

> PHIL: He's still looking.

There's a MUSCLE MAN walking parallel at a distance. No great face, but a jacket and white T-shirt over a washboard stomach, fit as hell. He's glancing at VINCE.

> VINCE: He is not.

> PHIL: He is, though.

> VINCE: He's all muscles, I don't cop off with muscles. I mean, what happens? He takes his kit off, Marky Mark, I take mine off, Norman Wisdom.

> PHIL: I had a bloke with muscles once, fabulous. Like being let loose on a bouncy castle. He is looking.

VINCE: (*EastEnders* accent) Shut it.

Pulling out to a wide shot, the complex of streets around Square 1; VINCE and PHIL part of the pattern of men scattering, spreading out, into the night.

PHIL: Shut it.

VINCE: Pat'll go maaad.

PHIL: Shut iiit.

1/4 EXT. RICHMOND STREET, NIGHT 1 0220   1/4
STUART, GREEK GOD

A quiet, dark street. On STUART and the GREEK GOD; they've found a pitch-black doorway behind some bins, but look round, startled, stepping apart as the headlights of a car at the far end illuminate them. The car goes. They grin, then get back to snogging.

1/5 EXT. CANAL STREET, NIGHT 1 0222   1/5
NATHAN, VINCE, PHIL

CU on a cigarette being ground underfoot. Around it, the stubs of ten more cigarettes. Reveal NATHAN sitting there, sullen (he's now on the wall outside the New Union). VINCE and PHIL stroll past – though we don't dwell on them, only catching the drift of conversation. To NATHAN they're just part of the thinning crowd.

VINCE: If you want to wait, I'll give you a lift.

PHIL: Oo, it's not even half past two, it's early. I'm in that sauna mood.

VINCE: Oh you're not.

They pass by, voices trailing off. On NATHAN, alone.

PHIL: Listen! You lose a couple of pounds in sweat with the added bonus of a shag, you don't get that in Weight Watchers.

1/6 EXT. RICHMOND STREET, NIGHT 1 0223   1/6
STUART, GREEK GOD

Getting hotter in the doorway. STUART unbuckles the GREEK GOD's jeans, slides his hands down his arse. Then pulls them out as if he's been bitten.

STUART: What's that?

GREEK GOD: It's a burn.

STUART: What sort of burn?

GREEK GOD: I got burnt. I was a kid, we had this bonfire. It was years ago.

They carry on snogging, but we're on STUART. Kissing a monster. Then he pulls back, starts doing up his trousers, fast, all smiles.

> STUART: Sorry, I should have said, I've really got to go, I've got work in the morning.

1/7 EXT. CANAL STREET, NIGHT 1 0225   1/7
NATHAN, VINCE

NATHAN's smoked his last cigarette, crumples the pack, throws it away. Reveal that VINCE is 50ft behind him, in the car park, waiting next to STUART's car, a black Daihatsu jeep.

CUT TO – VINCE, jangling the keys, waiting.

1/8 EXT. BLOOM STREET, NIGHT 1 0226   1/8
STUART

STUART's walking along, looking at men who walk past him. Hunting. Anyone.

1/9 EXT. CANAL STREET/CAR PARK, NIGHT 1 0227   1/9
NATHAN, STUART, VINCE

On NATHAN. Music in as STUART rounds the corner – a single high chord. Tension, sustaining the moment of connection.
   CUT TO – VINCE, who sees STUART, though STUART doesn't see him. But VINCE automatically assumes STUART's heading for the jeep, gets into the driver's seat, happy again.
   CUT TO – NATHAN's POV. STUART's getting closer. NATHAN glances at him. STUART glances at him, but neither look connects. STUART passes. NATHAN looks at him as he walks away, studying his arse.
   Then STUART looks back round. It's not slow-motion but the *feel* of slow-motion, heightened reality. Eye-contact. On STUART. On NATHAN. On STUART. He stays where he is, just turns round to face NATHAN. The grin. The chord sustains this entire sequence, as we CUT TO –

1/10 INT. ROOM   1/10
STUART

A shadowed neutral background. On MCU STUART, to camera.

> STUART: I lost my virginity in school. Mr Daniels, PE. I was twelve years old. He had this office, with a shower. I had to give him a form or something, and he's standing there, getting his kit off, like it's normal, we're just talking away, football or some-thing, he gets in the shower. He pulls the curtain. Half-pulls it. Then I'm taking my clothes off. I just did. Like it's normal. And stepped in. I must've been scared to death. But I don't remember being scared.

1/11 EXT. CANAL STREET/CAR PARK, NIGHT 1 0228   1/11
CONT. FROM 1/9
STUART, NATHAN, VINCE

STUART's where he was, a distance from NATHAN.

> STUART: Had a good night?

> NATHAN: (Terrified) Yeah.

> STUART: Haven't seen you before.

He begins a slow, lazy saunter to NATHAN.
CUT TO – VINCE, hidden in the interior of the car, watching.

1/12 INT. ROOM   1/12
VINCE

VINCE, MCU to camera.

> VINCE: I was fourteen. Summer holidays, Mum's taken me to
> Penzance. And then one day there's all these vans and lights and
> things, they were filming *The Two Ronnies*. And there's a bit of a
> crowd, I'm standing there, and this bloke walks past, this electri-
> cian. And he looks at me – I'm wearing these shorts, tight little
> shorts, I'd grown out of them. And he says, I can see your thing.
> That's what he said. I can see your thing. Next thing you know,
> he's wanking me off behind the pub in broad daylight. (Beat)
> First thing I did, I went to a phone box and phoned Stuart.

1/13 EXT. CANAL STREET/CAR PARK, NIGHT 1 0229   1/13
CONT. FROM 1/11
VINCE, STUART, NATHAN

VINCE'S POV as STUART saunters to NATHAN.
CUT TO – STUART standing over NATHAN, like a hawk.

> STUART: I'm Stuart.

> NATHAN: Nathan.

Beat.

> STUART: Got somewhere to go?

> NATHAN: No.

Beat.

> STUART: Want to come back to mine?

On NATHAN.

1/14 INT. ROOM   1/14
NATHAN

NATHAN, MCU to camera – the NATHAN we'll see later in the series, no longer scared; only six months older, but more confident, his look – hair, clothes – more cultivated.

> NATHAN: I was fifteen. I did it the first time I went out. I'm quite proud of that. I'm dead proud of that, my first time out. Stuart Alan Jones. He's looking down at me like the face of God.

1/15 EXT. CANAL STREET/CAR PARK, NIGHT 1 0230   1/15
CONT. FROM 1/13
VINCE, STUART, NATHAN, MUSCLE MAN

> NATHAN: ...okay.

CUT TO – VINCE'S POV as STUART and NATHAN walk along together. Only now do we realise that STUART's been aware of VINCE all along, as behind NATHAN's back, he gives VINCE a 'yes!' clenched fist. STUART hails a black cab, gets in with NATHAN.

> VINCE: Bastard.

And the chord cuts dead on a CU of the wheels of the jeep as it reverses, fast.
    CUT TO – VINCE glancing out of the window. The MUSCLE MAN is getting into a car nearby. He gives VINCE *that* look. Hold the look, three, four seconds. On VINCE, jittery as he pulls the jeep round. In the mirror, he can see the MUSCLE MAN's car pull out behind.

> VINCE: (Muttering) Don't follow me, please don't follow me.

VINCE drives out of the car park, turns left. In the mirror, he can see the car following.

> VINCE: Oh shit. Leave me alone, just leave me alone.

The car's still following, headlights in the mirror.

> VINCE: Shit shit shit.

1/16 INT. STUART'S FLAT, NIGHT 1 0240   1/16
STUART, NATHAN

A just-out-of-city-centre apartment block, like Castle Quays. An expensive, spacious flat, gorgeous, design straight out of *Wallpaper*, with a good view of the city.
    STUART strides in, slings his jacket away. NATHAN takes a few steps in, stands there, scared to death. Silence. STUART gets a bottle of water out of the fridge, swigs it down, then stands over the sink and pours the rest over his head, as NATHAN starts wittering.

> NATHAN: Nice kitchen. (Silence) It's great, it's really nice. I never cook, takeaways, that's me, I'm always eating takeaways. Pizza.

Silence. STUART just walks into the bedroom, stays visible in B/G, pulling his clothes off, increasing NATHAN'S terror. Hold the silence, then –

NATHAN: Mind you, I've got to be careful, I can't eat anything. I've got this thing, it's called, like, anaphylactic shock, your throat swells up and everything. Packet of peanuts could kill me.

STUART: You staying out there or what?

Silence. STUART's stripping off his jeans. NATHAN's got no choice – terrified of the bedroom, but drawn to it. He walks towards the door.

1/17 INT. BEDROOM, NIGHT 1 0241   1/17
NATHAN, STUART

NATHAN steps in, STUART now down to his Calvins.

NATHAN: We had this barbeque. Last summer...

And NATHAN just trails off, words gone. STUART looks at him. NATHAN takes a step closer. Then STUART just takes control, grabs hold of NATHAN – a second's clumsiness, NATHAN not knowing what to do, where to put his hands. But as STUART snogs him, it all starts to make sense, and NATHAN'S going for it.

1/18 INT. CAR/EXT. VINCE'S STREET, NIGHT 1 0241   1/18
VINCE, MUSCLE MAN

VINCE lives in a tall, dilapidated house-converted-to-flats in one of Fallowfield's rougher streets. On VINCE, pulling up, the headlights still in the mirror. The car pulls up right behind him.

VINCE: Go away. Please.

He scrabbles in the glove compartment, gets a scrap of paper and a pen, squints in the mirror to read the car's registration, writes down – *If he murders me – CYN 255E*. He gets out. MUSCLE MAN gets out of his car. Silence, the street dark and empty. Tension – both wary, both horny.

MUSCLE MAN: Nice car.

VINCE: Yeah. S'not mine.

MUSCLE MAN: This where you live?

VINCE: Yeah.

Silence.

MUSCLE MAN: I don't normally do this.

VINCE: Nor me.

Silence.

MUSCLE MAN: (Smiles) Look, d'you want me to go?

Pause. VINCE smiles.

> VINCE: Might as well have a coffee.

> MUSCLE MAN: Okay.

> VINCE: ...right.

They head inside.

1/19 INT. STUART'S FLAT/BEDROOM, NIGHT 1 0245   1/19
STUART, NATHAN

STUART and NATHAN, kit off, on the bed, necking away while STUART's wanking NATHAN off.

> STUART: What d'you like doing?

> NATHAN: Um. I like watching telly.

> STUART: What d'you like doing in bed?

> NATHAN: Um. This is fine.

> STUART: Rimming?

> NATHAN: ...yeah.

> STUART: Excellent! Go on then.

Pause, STUART expecting NATHAN to make the move down.

> NATHAN: What d'you mean exactly?

The phone rings. STUART answers it (a cordless phone next to the bed). As he talks, he keeps wanking NATHAN off. NATHAN just lies there, taking it, still scared.

> STUART: Yup? No! *No!* When? When did that happen, why
> didn't you phone me? Of *course* I've been out! What happened?
> (With a tiny, tiny grunt, NATHAN comes. To NATHAN) Oh,
> *what?* Jesus Christ, d'you have to? (Flicking it off his hand. To the
> phone) No, it's just this bloke. (To NATHAN) What's your name?

> NATHAN: Nathan.

> STUART: (Shoves phone against NATHAN) Nathan, say hello to
> Lisa.

> NATHAN: – hello –

> STUART: (Whips the phone back) So where is she? Yeah, right.
> Okey doke.

He hangs up, gets off the bed, walks out of the bedroom.

STUART: Right, thanks for that, got to go.

On NATHAN, completely lost.

1/20 INT. VINCE'S FLAT, NIGHT 1 0248   1/20
VINCE, MUSCLE MAN

The top floor, an attic. VINCE has made his flat a fabulous cave of videos, books and magazines. There's no wall-space visible, shelves of VHSs to the ceiling, magazines and comics stacked five feet high. The only expensive thing in the room is a widescreen TV with satellite attachments. For all its eccentricity, it's a warm, comfortable flat – a tenth the price of STUART's, but without the austerity.

VINCE is standing a good distance from MUSCLE MAN, nervous, horribly aware that MUSCLE MAN's drumming his six-pack torso as he looks at the tapes.

MUSCLE MAN: God, you've got everything. Manga, my dad's
into Manga. Got any porn?

VINCE: One or two, yeah.

MUSCLE MAN: Anything good?

VINCE: American stuff. (Reaches up to one shelf, unlabelled
cassettes, his porn stash) I've got some Cadinot, it's much better,
it's actually got a plot – this one's good, *Service Actif*, I've been
trying to find *Service Actif Deux* but apparently it's been deleted, I
can't... (Realises he's babbling) Um – shall I put it on?

MUSCLE MAN: Haven't got time, really. Can we just get on
with it? (Laughs) Sorry. But it's almost three o'clock.

VINCE: Fine.

MUSCLE MAN starts kicking off his boots. VINCE just stands there, making no move to take his clothes off. Saved by the bell – the phone rings.

VINCE: I'd better just...

MUSCLE MAN: Can't you leave it?

VINCE: I'll, uh... (Picks up the phone) Hello?

1/21 INT. STUART'S FLAT, NIGHT 1 0249   1/21
(CONT. FROM 1/19)
STUART, NATHAN

STUART's hopping round the living room, putting his clothes on.

STUART: Vince! Emergency! I need the car!

1/22 INT. VINCE'S FLAT, NIGHT 1 0249   1/22
(CONT FROM 1/20)
VINCE, MUSCLE MAN

> VINCE: I can't – No! *No!* When? Oh my God, when did that
> happen? No!

The phone call keeps going, VINCE watching MUSCLE MAN. MUSCLE MAN takes off his jacket. Then his T-shirt. Revealing no muscles at all, but body armour shaped to look like muscles, done up at the side with buckles. VINCE keeps talking, mortified, as MUSCLE MAN peels it off, letting his beer-belly flop out. He pats his tum, completely unashamed.

> VINCE: (On the phone) Who phoned you, Lisa? What
> happened, who was there, was she on her own? Right, yeah. God.
> Oh my God. Ohhhh my God.

> MUSCLE MAN: Look, I really can't stay long.

> VINCE: (To MUSCLE MAN) Sorry. Emergency.

1/23 INT. STUART'S BEDROOM INTERCUT
WITH VINCE'S FLAT, NIGHT 1 0250   1/23
(CONT. FROM 1/21 & 1/22)
STUART, NATHAN/VINCE, MUSCLE MAN

STUART now back in the bedroom, finding a shirt, NATHAN quietly putting his clothes on in B/G. Now intercutting between STUART and VINCE.

> STUART: Who's that? You've got someone there!

> VINCE: No, really, it's fine –

> STUART: Sod the car, I'll get a taxi, Vince, you've copped off!
> That's a first!

> VINCE: No, really. Really, I haven't. I'll get the car –

> STUART: Don't you dare! Vince, this is brilliant, well done! I'll
> get a cab, shag him blind then kick him out, I'll see you there –

STUART hangs up. On VINCE.

> MUSCLE MAN: Bad news?

> VINCE: It's my friend, it's his mother, she's in hospital. I think
> it's bad news, I'll have to go.

> MUSCLE MAN: Pity. I was looking forward to that.

> VINCE: Oh, me too.

1/24 INT. STUART'S FLAT, NIGHT 1 0251   1/24
NATHAN, STUART

NATHAN stands in the bedroom doorway, his clothes back on as STUART rushes round.

    STUART: D'you want a taxi? I'll phone a taxi.

    NATHAN: What's happened?

    STUART: Everything!

Silence, STUART rushing about, ignoring NATHAN.

    NATHAN: I'll have to go anyway. I've got college.

Now STUART pays him some attention, amused.

    STUART: College or school?

    NATHAN: Sixth-form college.

    STUART: How old are you?

    NATHAN: Eighteen.

    STUART: What year were you born?

Beat.

    NATHAN: Nineteen eighty one.

    STUART: Bollocks, you had to think, no one has to think about the year they were born; how old are you?

    NATHAN: Sixteen.

    STUART: How old are you really?

    NATHAN: Fifteen.

Pause. STUART grins.

1/25 EXT. HOSPITAL CAR PARK, NIGHT 1 0320   1/25
VINCE, STUART, NATHAN

VINCE is waiting, on edge, next to the jeep as a black cab pulls up. STUART leaps out. Then the next person to step out of the taxi is NATHAN. (VINCE isn't that surprised to see him; this is typical of STUART.) STUART belts towards the hospital, VINCE runs with him, NATHAN tagging along behind.

    VINCE: Where've you been?

STUART: Come on!

VINCE: How is she..? (Running, looks at NATHAN. Back to
STUART) You had to, didn't you?

1/26 INT. HOSPITAL CORRIDOR, NIGHT 1 0322   1/26
STUART, VINCE, NATHAN

STUART and VINCE race along, NATHAN following.

1/27 INT. SIDE-WARD, NIGHT 1 0325   1/27
STUART, VINCE, NATHAN, ROMEY, SIOBHAN, LISA, SUZIE, BABY ALFRED

STUART and VINCE burst in, NATHAN behind them. In bed, a woman, ROMEY.
She's early 30s, bedraggled, tired, smiling. Three women the same age sit around
the room, LISA, SIOBHAN and SUZIE. LISA's a classic lipstick lesbian; SIOBHAN
is bald; SUZIE never says a word. ROMEY's holding a new-born BABY. As STUART
takes control of the room, much of this is played off NATHAN, gobsmacked, out
of his depth.

STUART: Oh my God.

ROMEY: Here he is. This is him.

STUART: Oh my God.

STUART goes forward, reaches out.

ROMEY: Careful. Hold his head. (He takes the BABY) Started
this morning. Ten o'clock tonight, there he was.

STUART: You should've phoned, I was going to be there, I
wanted to see it.

ROMEY: No you didn't. It was like a car crash down there.

STUART: (Studies the BABY) Funny-shaped head. God they're
ugly, aren't they? Doesn't look like me.

SIOBHAN: We weren't talking about names, we really weren't,
cos that's up to you and Romey. But I just looked at him and said,
Frederic.

ROMEY: I quite like it.

STUART: What, in a sort of ironic way?

ROMEY: Yeah.

STUART: Nah, it's not ironic enough. What about Alfred? Then
you still get the Fred bit. Vince, run a check on Alfred.

VINCE: Alf Roberts, Alfie, Michael Caine, Alf, that American

sitcom with the puppet – bit dodgy, but that's forgotten by the
time he's in school, unless they run it on cable, I bet it's on
Bravo. Oh! Alfred's the name of Batman's butler, marvellous.
Good name.

STUART: Alfred. (Turns to NATHAN) What d'you think?

NATHAN: (Aware of everyone looking) ...great.

STUART: (Of the BABY) He's mine.

ROMEY: Aren't you going to introduce us?

STUART: What was your name again?

LISA: Nathan.

STUART: Oh, you've met, Lisa, this is Nathan, you spoke, Lisa
was on the phone when Nathan shot his load all over me.

ROMEY: Oh for God's sake.

And sighs from all, the entire room well used to STUART. STUART just feeds off
others' disapproval.

STUART: Well he did! He's fifteen, aren't you, Nathan?

LISA: So. You've both had a child on the same night.

VINCE: (Mutters to ROMEY) He's brought the trophy cabinet.

STUART: He was there! Nathan was there, the most important
phone call of my life and Nathan was there, I couldn't just leave
him, he wanted to come, didn't you, Nathe?

NATHAN: ...yeah.

STUART sits on the bed, with the BABY, instantly switching to intimacy with
ROMEY.

STUART: (Quiet, serious) Romey. What the fuck have we done?

ROMEY starts to cry a little.

STUART: Oh don't start that, don't.

1/28 INT. HOSPITAL, NIGHT 1 0340   1/28
NATHAN

A tea machine. The plastic cup fills with hot tea.
NATHAN picks it up, trying to carry four cups at once, and clenched in his mouth
he's got three bags of Wotsits and a packet of peanuts from the adjacent sweet
machine. He's a small figure in a wide, echoing corridor; he looks so young. He

walks along, the cups too hot. He drops one, hops about, trying to keep the other cups balanced.

1/29 INT. CORRIDOR OUTSIDE SIDE-WARD, NIGHT 1 0341   1/29
STUART, VINCE, NATHAN, SIOBHAN, LISA, SUZIE

VINCE stands in front of SIOBHAN. She's holding her palms on the side of his neck, staring into his eyes.

> SIOBHAN: Yes. Yes. Yes. (Holds his wrists) Take off your watch.
> (He does so) Yes. Yes. Yes. (Lets him go) You're good, Vince.
> You'll do good things.

> VINCE: Could you tell if I had cancer?

> SIOBHAN: Why would you have cancer?

> VINCE: I always think I've got cancer.

During this, NATHAN arrives. STUART comes out of the side-ward, fast, mobie in hand, LISA following.

> STUART: (On the phone) Oh that's great, she'll love it, thanks,
> see you – (Off the phone) Bloody Ken, he's sending flowers, I
> should've got flowers – Nathan, get some flowers, quick as you can.

He shoves a tenner in NATHAN's hand, walks off, fast, VINCE automatically following. Stay on NATHAN, perplexed, as STUART and VINCE's dialogue drifts off.

> VINCE: You can't use your mobile, you'll switch off the iron lungs.

> STUART: Oh that's a thought, I should have a cigar!

NATHAN's horribly aware of LISA and SIOBHAN, looking at him.

> LISA: (Kind) You don't have to do what he says.

> NATHAN: I don't mind, I'll, uh...

He hurries off. LISA and SIOBHAN exchange a look.

1/30 INT. GERIATRIC WARD, NIGHT 1 0348   1/30
NATHAN, PATIENT

Darkness, just a pool of light at the far end, at the nurses' station. Distant, quiet laughter from two NURSES, going out of sight for a cuppa. They don't see NATHAN creeping in, a thief in the night. He looks round, sees a bunch of flowers in a vase on a bedside cabinet. Ever so quiet, he walks up to the bed, grabs the flowers. Suddenly the overhead bed-light switches on. The PATIENT is propped up – he's at least 90, senile, mouth wet and open, eyes black, scared, staring at NATHAN. NATHAN's terrified. Hold the look, a strange moment as the old man and the young boy just stare at each other. Then NATHAN turns and runs.

1/31 INT. HOSPITAL CORRIDOR, NIGHT 1 0348   1/31
NATHAN

NATHAN, clutching the flowers, runs full-pelt down the corridor.

1/32 EXT. HOSPITAL ROOF, NIGHT 1 0348   1/32
STUART, VINCE

The fire door leading on to the roof is shoved open. STUART walks out, VINCE following. STUART's in a strange mood, troubled, distracted. At times like this, he's unpredictable; all VINCE can do is be with him, and wait for STUART to decide the mood.
    STUART walks over to the safety rail, VINCE follows. Below them, hell of a drop; beyond them, the lights of Manchester. Silence. Then VINCE risks saying something.

> VINCE: It's weird, isn't it? (Silence) I mean he's *real*, just seeing him, it's like... I don't know what it's like, I mean it's brilliant, but it's weird.

> STUART: Most expensive wank I've ever had.

Silence. Then STUART goes over to the rail, leans over it, dangerously so.

> VINCE: Oh that's right, top yourself. They do that in soaps, birth and death in the same episode –

Suddenly STUART turns, takes hold of VINCE, pulls him over to the rail so VINCE is standing in front of him, leaning over.

> STUART: That's it, arms out, *Titanic.*

STUART holds him from behind. All the better if the wind's blowing in their faces. STUART leans both of them forward, calls out to the night.

> STUART: King of the world!

> VINCE: I'm always Kate Winslet.

> STUART: King of the wooooorld!

Beat. They separate, step back, STUART still dissatisfied. They look at each other. Pause, then VINCE gives STUART a great big hug. Still holding STUART, VINCE leans back, looks into his friend's face, happy for him. Then he gives STUART a kiss, a big smacker, on the cheek.

> VINCE: Congratulations.

Both look at each other, sad smiles. Then STUART's smile becomes more sly as he becomes aware of something, shifts his hips forward to grind against VINCE's, to prove his theory.

> STUART: Oh my God, Vince! Hard-on!

VINCE immediately steps away, embarrassed.

> VINCE: I have not!

> STUART: (Loving it) I didn't know you cared. No one's looking, get it out.

> VINCE: Fuck off, it's not for you. Six months since I had a shag, it's like Pavlov's dogs.

> STUART: You sad bastard.

STUART walks away to the edge of the roof to look at the city, the moment forgotten; but not for VINCE. With STUART's back turned, he reaches into his trousers to adjust himself, mortified.

1/33 INT. CORRIDOR OUTSIDE SIDE-WARD, NIGHT 1   0355   1/33
NATHAN, LISA

LISA sits with NATHAN, mid-conversation (the flowers dripping at his side). As he talks, NATHAN wolfs down the packet of peanuts, no side-effects, all that anaphylactic shock stuff in 1/16 a complete lie. As he talks, closer on NATHAN; almost talking to himself, intense.

> NATHAN: I'm sitting there with Donna, that's my friend, Donna, and I'm watching this boy, Christian Hobbs, he goes up to this girl, Anne-Marie. Two minutes, that's all it takes, then he's in there, snogging her, he's eating her. She's not even pretty. And I look round the party, they're all at it, they're all snogging. Couples. I'm just sitting there. No one's watching me. (Beat) So I walked out. Stood up and walked out, on to Palatine Road, got the bus, Canal Street.

> LISA: Won't there be people looking for you?

> NATHAN: My mum thinks I'm staying at Donna's. Donna won't say anything, she's stupid.

> LISA: Thought she was your friend.

> NATHAN: She is.

> LISA: (Beat. Cooler) Yes, you're definitely gay.

1/34 INT. HOSPITAL CORRIDOR, NIGHT 1 0359   1/34
VINCE, STUART, MALE NURSE

VINCE and STUART walk along, STUART searching through his jacket. They pass a MALE NURSE – 20s, handsome. MALE NURSE looks at STUART, smiles as they pass. They walk on, STUART looks back at MALE NURSE, MALE NURSE returns the look. They keep walking opposite ways; STUART now turns to walk backwards, looking at MALE NURSE, who keeps glancing back. Only at this point does

VINCE, walking slightly ahead, notice.

> VINCE: Stuart!

STUART turns back to VINCE, MALE NURSE forgotten.

> STUART: Had him.

> VINCE: Listen, you're going home, you're going to sleep, then you're getting up and going to work and you can work hard for the next twenty years, you've got a kid to look after now.

> STUART: Oh absolutely, I promise. (Finds something in his jacket) Yes! (Plucks out two tablets) Want one? (VINCE rolls eyes to heaven, despairing) Okay. More for me.

STUART swallows both tablets. VINCE walks ahead, glowering, STUART laughing at his disapproval.

1/35 INT. CORRIDOR OUTSIDE SIDE-WARD, NIGHT 1 0400
1/35

NATHAN, LISA, SIOBHAN, STUART, VINCE, SUZIE

NATHAN and LISA now joined by SIOBHAN and SUZIE, his new friends. LISA's been telling the story of the night and they're all in fits of laughter. STUART and VINCE stride into the laughter, STUART lighting a cigarette.

> STUART: Right, Nathan, we're off, it's all getting a bit lesbian in here.

NATHAN jumps up like a puppet, STUART striding through without stopping, NATHAN trotting behind.

> LISA: Vince. (Of NATHAN) Take him home.

> VINCE: Yeah.

VINCE runs after STUART and NATHAN.

1/36 INT. JEEP, NIGHT 1 0410
1/36

VINCE, STUART, NATHAN

Driving through the night, VINCE at the wheel, NATHAN in the back next to STUART. The drugs are kicking in, making STUART's moods wander, though he's conscious enough to use mock-sympathy to pull NATHAN in close.

> STUART: He's a calendar. That kid, he's a clock, a great big stop-watch, staring me in the face. Cos he gets older, that's all he can do, d'you know what that means? I'm getting older. (To NATHAN) Look at me. Is that old? That's not old. (Kisses NATHAN) Can't get rid of him, twenty years' time, he'll still be there. (Hopeful) Mind you. They don't always live. (Giggling) Meningitis, that's a good one.

VINCE: Stuart, what have you taken? That's not E, you only took it five minutes ago, what is it?

STUART: Dunno, it was expensive.

VINCE: Christ, you don't even know what you're taking. You twat.

But the remark's lost on STUART, who just snogs NATHAN. On VINCE. He's pissed off, but can't help watching the couple snog in the mirror. VINCE's POV; a selective shot (we don't want to think VINCE fancies NATHAN); focus on STUART as he moves NATHAN's hand down to his crotch. NATHAN rubs him there, STUART leans his head back and groans.

Sudden beep brings VINCE's attention back to the road, as he swerves to avoid an oncoming car.

VINCE: Shit!

VINCE concentrates ahead, angry with himself. STUART and NATHAN haven't even noticed.

1/37 EXT. STUART'S FLATS, NIGHT 1 0415 1/37
STUART, VINCE, NATHAN

The jeep pulls up, STUART gets out. It's like he's casting a spell on NATHAN, not pulling him out, but leaning back into the car, kissing him, stepping back, kissing him again. NATHAN's torn between VINCE (safety) and STUART (sex).

VINCE: (To NATHAN) I'll take you home –

STUART: He's coming with me, aren't you, sweetheart, come on, come with me – (Kisses him) We haven't even started.

VINCE: I'll take you home, where d'you live?

NATHAN: Didsbury.

STUART: (To NATHAN) I didn't get to come, Nathan, make me come, you want that, don't you? Yes you do, oh yes you do, I want to fuck you.

VINCE: Leave him alone, I'm taking him home –

STUART: (In NATHAN's ear, mesmeric) I'm going to fuck you, Nathan, I'm going to fuck you all night, yeah?

NATHAN: (Panicked by the word 'fuck', but still trapped, to VINCE) I can't go home, I'm staying at Donna's, but she's asleep now, I can't turn up this time of night –

STUART: (Biting NATHAN's ear) Stay with me.

NATHAN makes a sudden decision, gets out of the car.

STUART: Good boy.

STUART leads him towards the flats. VINCE calls out of the jeep.

VINCE: Stuart, go to bed. He can sleep on the settee.

STUART turns back, sharper.

STUART: He hates it when other people cop off. Just cos I won't shag him.

On VINCE, that remark hitting home, suddenly silenced. A look which NATHAN clocks. STUART grins, then leads NATHAN away.
As STUART opens the door to the flats, a shaft of light falls across VINCE as he just watches them go. Then the door shuts, VINCE in darkness.

1/38 INT. STUART'S BEDROOM, NIGHT 1 0425   1/38
STUART, NATHAN

STUART and NATHAN naked; NATHAN's lying on his stomach, while STUART works his way down him, licking his back, descending to a rimming position. NATHAN's not sure what's going on. Then, we can tell STUART's reached the appropriate position as NATHAN just goes *wild*. STUART's head pops back up, grinning.

STUART: No one told you 'bout that, did they?

And STUART plunges back down.

1/39 INT. VINCE'S FLAT, NIGHT 1 0426   1/39
VINCE

VINCE storms into his flat in a foul temper. He pulls off his T-shirt, about to go to bed, then stops. He looks across at his VHS library – at the stack where the porn's kept, as identified in 1/20. Changing his mind, bed forgotten, VINCE starts going through the tapes, looking for one in particular.
CUT TO – a VHS being slotted into the machine.
CUT TO – VINCE, now in his dressing gown, sprawled out on his settee, remote in hand, ready for a good night's entertainment. The second he presses play, CUT TO –

1/40 INT. STUART'S BEDROOM, NIGHT 1 0430   1/40
NATHAN, STUART

NATHAN's on his back. STUART's on top of him, with NATHAN's legs up over his shoulders, a classic fucking position. STUART shifts forward to penetrate him.

NATHAN: (Squirms backwards) Ow!

NATHAN's response is to reach up, grab hold of STUART's head, pull him down for a good snog – NATHAN already exerting a small amount of control, and enjoying the necking just as much as STUART. Then STUART reasserts the fucking position.

STUART: That's it, slowly, that's all of them, all the football team...

NATHAN: All the what?

STUART: (The drugs talking) All of them in shorts and naked and oooh, sprawled out on the grass, easy does it, and the referee's saying yes yes yes, in we go –

NATHAN: Aah, no, slowly, really –

STUART: And in and out and *in* – !

And with that he rams himself into NATHAN. On NATHAN's face, bring in –

1/41 INT. VINCE'S FLAT, NIGHT 1 0440   1/41
VINCE

– the electronic howl of the *Doctor Who* cliffhanger music.
    On VINCE, watching his favourite programme. He's practically hugging himself, he's so happy. A few seconds of the theme tune, then he rewinds, plays, and a sepulchral voice booms from the telly; VINCE says the line with him.

    VOICE/VINCE: I bring Sutekh's gift of death to all humanity!

And the cliffhanger howl repeats.

1/42 INT. STUART'S BEDROOM, DAY 2 0759   1/42
NATHAN, STUART

Daylight. CU on NATHAN. Reveal that he's lying in bed, just looking at STUART, who's asleep. The alarm goes to 0800, starts up. STUART's arm slaps it off. Then he opens his eyes.

    STUART: Ohhhhhh fuck.

And he shuts his eyes, rolls away from NATHAN. NATHAN hasn't moved, stares at him. Worship. Fear.

1/43 INT/EXT. VINCE'S FLAT, DAY 2 0801   1/43
VINCE, KID 1, KID 2

VINCE is fast asleep. In the distance, a car alarm comes on. VINCE stirs, ignores it. Then he remembers he's got the jeep, sits up, wide awake, runs to the window. Down below, two KIDS are at the jeep, pulling one of the windscreen wipers off.

    VINCE: (Bangs the window) Oy!

He grabs his dressing gown, starts running.

1/44 EXT. VINCE'S FLAT, DAY 2 0803

1/44

VINCE

VINCE comes tearing out in his dressing gown.

>VINCE: You little bastards!

The KIDS start running, calling out –

>KID 1: Poofter!

>KID 2: We've seen you, we've seen you!

>KID 1: Fucking queer!

And they're off, down the road. VINCE looks at the car. Oh shit.

1/45 INT. STUART'S BEDROOM, DAY 2 0805

1/45

NATHAN, STUART

NATHAN, as we left him, staring, STUART asleep. So, so carefully, NATHAN shifts himself across an inch, reaches out to rest his hand on STUART. STUART responds as he would to any man in his bed, rolls over and hugs NATHAN, eyes still closed. NATHAN's so happy. Then STUART opens one eye, looking over NATHAN's shoulder at the wall.

>STUART: Oh for fuck's sake!

STUART sits bolt upright, NATHAN now unimportant. The bedroom wall's covered in graffiti, a mess of circles and arrows and blobs and stick men, floor to ceiling. Magic Marker pens lying around.

>STUART: What the hell is that?

>NATHAN: It's a map. You did this map. Of all the places you've had a shag. Started out as Manchester, but that bit at the top's Denmark, and then you went to New York –

>STUART: All right, I know, why didn't you stop me? Shit! I'll have to get it painted again, it's the pens! Get rid of the pens! Right, got to go.

He runs out of the bedroom.

1/46 INT. STUART'S FLAT, DAY 2 0806

1/46

STUART, NATHAN

STUART runs to the fridge, gets out two teaspoons, holds them under his eyes. NATHAN appears in his shirt and underpants.

>STUART: God, the state of me. What happened to the car?

>NATHAN: Vince took it.

STUART: Good, that means he's bringing it back.

NATHAN: Can I have a shower?

STUART: Hurry up, then. Oh what is *that*?

All the chairs have been piled on top of the sofa.

NATHAN: It's the Millennium Dome, you said you met that bloke in charge of it and you both ended up –

STUART: That wasn't ecstasy, that fucking Anita, I know her, I bet she sold me dog-worming tablets again. Go on then! Shower!

NATHAN hurries away. STUART starts taking chairs down.

STUART: I'm such a twat, I'm such a twat...

1/47 INT. BATHROOM, DAY 2 0810   1/47
NATHAN

NATHAN looks at himself in the mirror. Then he looks at the shelf. One tooth-brush, STUART's. NATHAN picks it up, studies it. He puts it in his mouth, runs it over his teeth, really slowly.

1/48 INT. STUART'S FLAT, DAY 2 0812   1/48
STUART

STUART's got the room back in a reasonable state. He's calmer now, looks round the room. He sees the light blinking on the answerphone, presses a button.

ROMEY V/O: Now Stuart. Don't panic. I'm in hospital, it's half past six Thursday night, the contractions have started, it's not a false alarm but don't worry –

On STUART, horrified.

STUART: Fuck! I've got a baby!

1/49 INT. BATHROOM – SHOWER, DAY 2 0813   1/49
NATHAN, STUART

NATHAN's in the shower, letting it pour over his head, losing himself in the heat. The shower curtain whips back, STUART steps in, more or less talking to himself as he grabs hold of NATHAN.

STUART: Why doesn't anyone stop me? It's not my fault, they should stop me –

He starts snogging NATHAN.

1/50 EXT. STUART'S FLATS, DAY 2 0827   1/50
VINCE

VINCE at the wheel, now in his grey suit, Harlo's name-badge pinned on. Keep on a mid-shot so we can't see the full damage to the jeep, as he pulls up outside STUART's, beeps the horn.

1/51 INT. STUART'S BEDROOM, DAY 2 0827   1/51
NATHAN, STUART

NATHAN's in the bedroom. STUART's clothes from the night before are scattered around (he's wearing a completely new outfit today). NATHAN sees STUART's discarded Calvins. He picks them up; inhales them.

     STUART: He's here!

On impulse, NATHAN stuffs the Calvins in his pocket, hurries out.

1/52 EXT. STUART'S FLAT, DAY 2 0830   1/52
VINCE, STUART, NATHAN

VINCE on a mid-shot, standing in front of the jeep jeep largely OOV, though VINCE is holding the windscreen wiper. STUART's heading towards him, NATHAN trotting behind.

     STUART: (Of the jeep) Oh excellent, well done, Vince.

     VINCE: Then don't give me the car, I've warned you before, on that road. It was those kids from round the corner –

     STUART: Doesn't matter. Company car. (Gets in the driving seat) Now, let's get our little lad to school.

NATHAN and VINCE clamber in, STUART mutters to VINCE.

     STUART: What's his name again?

VINCE just looks at him.

1/53 EXT. SCHOOL, DAY 2 0850   1/53
DONNA

Crowds of kids piling off buses, wandering in to school. On DONNA, who's standing there, on edge, looking round. DONNA's 15, lanky; the sort of girl who, if she had a bit more gumption, could be hip; as it is, she just looks awkward, hair badly dyed, a bit of a loner. NATHAN's natural friend. She's carrying two Head sports bags, one hers, one NATHAN's. She looks at her watch, worried.

1/54 INT. CAR, DAY 2 0851   1/54
STUART, VINCE, NATHAN

Racing along, with STUART at the wheel, music on loud, passing crowds of kids as they near the school. NATHAN's a scared little face in the back.

VINCE: Pull in here!

STUART: He's going to school!

VINCE: Pull in here!

STUART: I'll take him to the door!

VINCE: Stuart, they'll see the car!

STUART: So?

1/55 EXT. SCHOOL, DAY 2 0852   1/55
STUART, VINCE, NATHAN, DONNA, CHRISTIAN, BOY IN CROWD

On DONNA as the jeep speeds up to the school, horn blaring, kids scattering. As
it approaches, the jeep looks normal, but STUART executes an arc in the middle
of the road so the jeep swings round to face the other way. Revealing that, down
one side, the KIDS have painted, in big white letters, a single word:
   QUEERS
   Loads of schoolkids are watching, lads laughing, taking the piss, as NATHAN
has to get out in front of them. He's mortified; but shame doesn't matter, he's got
to talk to STUART.

STUART: Thanks, then. Off you go, first lesson, Home
Economics.

NATHAN: (Quiet, desperate) Can I see you again?

VINCE: Let's just go.

NATHAN: Can I see you again?

STUART: You can see me now.

DONNA's running over.

DONNA: Nathan, where've you been?

NATHAN: (Hisses at DONNA) Piss off!

DONNA's stopped in her tracks, doesn't come too close.

STUART: Aww, now, your little friend.

NATHAN: I could meet you tonight –

STUART: God knows where I'll be tonight, I could be anywhere,
I could be in Ipswich –

BOY IN CROWD: Come on, boys, give's a kiss.

STUART: (At the BOY, savage) I'll give you a fuck, you tight little virgin, you won't be laughing then.

VINCE: We're going! *Now!* Stuart, just shut your face and drive –

1/56 INT. ROOM   1/56
VINCE

On VINCE, to camera, as though the speech is continuous from 1/55.

VINCE: He was a one-night stand. And with Stuart, they really are one-night stands, one night, that's all they get. But *this* one. (Beat) This one came back.

1/57 EXT. SCHOOL, DAY 2 0854   1/57
(CONT. FROM 1/55)
STUART, VINCE, NATHAN, DONNA, CHRISTIAN, BOY IN CROWD

Hard cut into the engine roaring, STUART revving up, NATHAN desperate.

NATHAN: Can I see you, though?

STUART: Oh, you'll see me. Can't miss me.

With that, the jeep accelerates away, and we go with them. On STUART, NATHAN instantly forgotten, as he jacks up the volume on the music, loud, abruptly cutting to the silence of –

1/58 INT. ROOM   1/58
STUART

On STUART, to camera.

STUART: I don't care what people think of me, people are *dull*. So he's fifteen, I was drunk, fuck off.

1/59 EXT. SCHOOL, DAY 2 0856 –   1/59
NATHAN, DONNA, CHRISTIAN

DONNA's now with NATHAN, and she's given him his sports bag containing his uniform. He's changing into his school shirt (though he keeps his T-shirt underneath, he wouldn't strip to the waist in front of kids). DONNA's quiet, solemn, not understanding what's happened. CHRISTIAN HOBBS calls out from the crowd – he's 15, tall, a hard bastard, the God of NATHAN's class.

CHRISTIAN: Who's the bloke then, Maloney? Your boyfriend?

NATHAN stops, looks him in the eye, cool. He'd never have dared say this yesterday.

NATHAN: What if he is?

CHRISTIAN's thrown, wasn't ready for that. Lost for a reply – and not really believing NATHAN – he just sneers, turns away. Even DONNA's standing back, as NATHAN calmly gets into his uniform.

1/60 INT. ROOM   1/60
NATHAN

The older NATHAN looks at camera, so much more confident, certain, in control. In a word – *out*.

> NATHAN: I was just a shag, I knew that. S'pose I fell in love a bit. Like you do. I'm not stupid, I thought, I'll never see him again. How was I to know? Stuart Alan Jones. (Smiles) Six months later, he was *begging* me to stay.

Hold on NATHAN.

EPISODE TWO

2/1 INT. SCHOOL CORRIDOR, DAY 3 1220   2/1
NATHAN

The opening three scenes are on CU faces, the locations unclear at first; all these people could be in the same space. Soundtrack – Air, 'Sexy Boy', loud, intense.

CU NATHAN. He's keeping his head down, walking along. But his eyes are keen, darting about. Searching.

His POV – CU various faces going past. Glimpses of the unimportant – girls, kids – only pausing on a good-looking lad. Then a blur of faces until finding another lad. Then another. None of them looks at NATHAN.

NATHAN keeps going. Hunting. We're barely aware that the location has changed as we CUT TO –

2/2 INT. HARLO'S FOOD HALL, DAY 3 1220   2/2
VINCE

CU VINCE. He walks past faces, his eyes darting about, discounting the women, pausing on men, just like NATHAN.

He stops, consulting an OOV clipboard, then looks round. His POV; CU on a long lens, indicating a BLOKE some distance away. The BLOKE's mid-20s, deep in thought, not looking at VINCE. VINCE's eyes flick away, as though he shouldn't be looking. Beat, then he looks back. Again, no immediate sense that we've changed location as we CUT TO –

2/3 INT. THRIVE FOYER, DAY 3 1220   2/3
STUART, MAN

CU STUART, on the move. His POV as he pushes through a sea of faces, moving past a bloke in his 50s, one in his 40s, one in his 30s, dismissing them, until he reaches a MAN, early 20s, best-looking of the lot. CU on the MAN, looking up. Eye contact. A nervous smile as he sees STUART approaching. STUART grins. Like a wolf.

2/4 INT. SCHOOL CORRIDOR, DAY 3 1221   2/4
NATHAN

All three locations clearer now, a little more of real sound bleeding in – NATHAN, VINCE and STUART members of a secret society.

NATHAN is walking along the corridor of his comprehensive school, kids in uniform going to and fro in the changeover between lessons. NATHAN is alone in the crowd. His eyes are still darting. A YEAR 12 BOY is heading the opposite way. On NATHAN, eyes flicking, with the innate skill of one who doesn't want to be seen looking. His POV; the YEAR 12 BOY's face. Then darting down to the crotch. Then back to the face.

Then they've passed each other. NATHAN executes a well-practised routine, finding a way to casually stop, looking at his watch (*Oh, forgotten something*), then turn around (*Where did I leave it..?*), looking back the way he came (*Should I go back..?*). The real purpose of this is to sneak a look at the YEAR 12 BOY's arse.

2/5 INT. HARLO'S FOOD HALL, DAY 3 1221   2/5
VINCE

Revealing VINCE's location, the aisles of HARLO'S. VINCE is in the uniform of assistant manager, checking shelves, ticking things off on his clipboard.

He's still sneaking glances at the BLOKE, who's shopping. Then a SECOND BLOKE approaches the first, puts something in his trolley, both talking. The SECOND BLOKE's more obviously gay. All the signs that they're a couple.

VINCE looks at them for a few seconds. A bit jealous, a bit wistful. Then he's back to his job, unseen.

2/6 INT. THRIVE FOYER, DAY 3 1221   2/6
STUART, SANDRA, MAN

Location clearer, now – the foyer of a city-centre PR company, *THRIVE*. Modern, minimal design; framed stuff on the walls indicating that *THRIVE* handles cutting-edge accounts, Manchester indie record labels, etc.

STUART and two female colleagues are meeting a group of five men – clients, for a fashionable jeanswear account AKYA JEANS. They're being greeted and shown through to a conference room.

STUART hangs back, so that he's alongside the MAN. Indicates 'after you'. The MAN smiles, goes in, STUART openly studying his arse. He then catches the eye of one of his colleagues – SANDRA, 40, STUART's PA, the woman who holds his life together. STUART nods towards the MAN, i.e., 'I'm in here'. SANDRA rolls her eyes to heaven. As he goes into the room, STUART's digging something out of his pocket.

2/7 INT. CONFERENCE ROOM, DAY 3 1222   2/7
STUART, SANDRA, MAN

A big, long table ready for the conference, pens and paper laid out, coffee, flip charts, carpet samples. STUART strides in, pinning on a badge. He makes sure he's sitting opposite the MAN. The MAN's POV, nervous as he glances across at STUART, catching the badge – an AIDS red ribbon, a posh one, metal.

Then STUART's POV as his eyes dart over the man. Flicking down to the MAN's hands. He's wearing a wedding ring. Which makes STUART smile all the more.

2/8 INT. CLASSROOM, DAY 3 1225   2/8
NATHAN, DONNA, CHRISTIAN, TEACHER

NATHAN is sitting at the back of the class, an English lesson, the TEACHER droning on (sound still distant, vague), everyone taking notes, bored. He's sitting next to DONNA. She's head down, scribbling away, not noticing that NATHAN is staring across the room.

Next row, two seats ahead, sits CHRISTIAN HOBBS. NATHAN isn't taking notes. CU on his exercise book. He's sketching CHRISTIAN.

NATHAN's POV; CHRISTIAN, then the sketch. He's scribbled his head, his back, the back of his chair. Closer and closer in, the moment becoming more intense. NATHAN draws the curve of CHRISTIAN's arse, then the line of his thigh.

Now NATHAN is just staring down at the drawing, losing the real CHRISTIAN. He goes back over the lines, making them stronger. So close we can see the ink-line spreading on cheap paper. NATHAN is 15; he's burning up. On DONNA – unseen by NATHAN – who glances across, sees the sketch, looks at CHRISTIAN. Then back to her notes, keeping shtum.

2/9 INT. HARLO'S FOOD HALL, DAY 3 1225   2/9
VINCE, MARCIE

VINCE at work, clearing another aisle. He sees the GAY COUPLE walk past. Two women working on the shelves – MARCIE and JILL, both large, mid-40's – have clocked the couple, giggling, shushing each other. MARCIE catches VINCE's eye, indicates the COUPLE, a little gesture meaning 'poofs'.

VINCE smiles, joins in the joke. Then he sees that the COUPLE have looked back, have seen him join in the mockery. An acid look, then they move on. VINCE loses the smile, awkward, pretends he's busy.

2/10 INT. CONFERENCE ROOM, DAY 3 1230   2/10
STUART, SANDRA, MAN

The room now in darkness, all illuminated by the light of a projector, images shining on one wall. The bloke in his 50s is leading the conference, droning on as we flick through a number of slides, all dull, statistics, pie charts, etc. STUART keeps glancing across at the MAN, though now the MAN's studying the projections, studiously ignoring STUART.

Then they click to the next photo. It's an advert, a beautiful, moody photograph, male torso, jeans hanging loosely on his hips. The MAN can't help it, his eyes dance from the photo, to STUART, back to the photo, to STUART. STUART's loving it.

2/11 EXT. SCHOOL, DAY 3 1300   2/11
NATHAN, CHRISTIAN, DONNA

On NATHAN. Kids passing foreground; on his eyes, darting to and fro, still searching. Widen to reveal he's sitting on a wall outside the school, dinnertime. Some distance away, CHRISTIAN HOBBS is with his mates, joshing about, laughing. Music out as DONNA arrives, sits next to NATHAN.

> DONNA: I could have a sandwich and a Snickers, but if I skip the Snickers I'm one step closer to them Caterpillar boots.

NATHAN appears to ignore her, keeps watching CHRISTIAN; but he's nervy, burning up, actually very focused on DONNA, building up to the moment. Faced with silence, DONNA babbles on.

> DONNA: Here's some news, now Christian Hobbs over there, Mandy said that Nicola Gooch is chasing him, I said that is *so* wrong it makes you look subnormal, just don't *say* it again. Cos Nicola Gooch boned off with that new bloke, proper couple an' everything, they went to Chinatown, *and* it was a Thursday, she wouldn't look at Christian Hobbs, not if you paid her.

> NATHAN: I'd give him one.

Beat. It's the first time he's said anything like this. She's flustered, scared, looks anywhere but at him, keeps talking to change the subject. NATHAN just looks at her, a smile spreading across his face – he's said it.

> DONNA: Cos. I dunno, it might be Nicola Blake, she likes him. But she never goes out, her dad's blind, she has to sit and read him books. Or he's in a wheelchair, something like that, I dunno.

> NATHAN: (Intense, right at her, forcing a reaction.) I would, though. I'd give him one.

Now she looks at him. Both exposed, on edge, excited, a confession. Hold, then both burst out laughing.

> DONNA: You'd never!

> NATHAN: Watch me! I'd give him one, I'd shag him right now, in front of you. I've met a bloke called Stuart, Stuart Jones. Had sex.

> DONNA: No!

> NATHAN: Shagged till five in the morning!

Both still laughing, shocked, right in each other's faces.

> NATHAN: What?

> DONNA: Nothing.

> NATHAN: You surprised?

> DONNA: No.

> NATHAN: Why not?

> DONNA: Dunno. (Beat. Quieter) You never said.

> NATHAN: Just said it, didn't I?

> DONNA: You seeing him again?

> NATHAN: Oh *yeah.*

Pause. Then DONNA's howling with laughter.

> DONNA: Nathan, that's just brilliant!

> NATHAN: (Gleeful, savage, his new catchphrase) I'd give him one!

> DONNA: I'd give him one. 'Cept I haven't got one to give him.

Which just destroys them with laughter.

Suddenly, they're on their feet, raw energy, running through the crowd, laughing like idiots. Wide shot as they run away. In amongst the mass of kids, there's something exultant about NATHAN and DONNA, the only ones full of life.

2/12 INT. THRIVE CORRIDOR, DAY 3 1330   2/12
STUART, SANDRA, MAN

In B/G, the meeting's broken up for coffee, all standing round, chatting. Foreground, STUART's standing in the doorway. His POV – the MAN, walking away, down the corridor. He goes through a door at the far end. STUART starts to follow. His mobile rings, he answers.

> STUART: What?

> SANDRA: His name's Michael.

He looks back down the corridor. SANDRA's taken his place in the conference room doorway, on her mobile.

> STUART: Thank you, but the information isn't relevant.

2/13 INT. SCHOOL YARD, DAY 3 1331   2/13
NATHAN, DONNA

Close on NATHAN and DONNA, sitting in a deserted part of the yard, an alleyway by the bins.
Part of DONNA loves being NATHAN's confidante, but at the same time, so much of this is outside her knowledge. Silent – only in those moments when she's looking at him but he's not looking at her – she feels as if she's losing her best friend.

> NATHAN: He's on top of me, right. And he's like in there, he's...
> *up* there, and it's killing me, I'm telling you, it's like being stabbed
> by a stick, and it's fantastic. It's brilliant, cos it's him. And he's
> looking down at me, I'm right in his eyes. I can feel him now, I
> really can, it's like – it's like he's left a space. He's still there.

2/14 INT. TOILET,
INTERCUT WITH THRIVE CORRIDOR, DAY 3 1331   2/14
STUART, MAN/SANDRA

The MAN's at the urinal, looks round to see STUART enter, still on his mobile. The MAN looks away, awkward. Intercut with SANDRA in the corridor.

> STUART: (On the phone) Anyway, thank you, Sandra, that'll be
> all, the matter's in hand.

> SANDRA: I'll string out the coffee as long as I can, good luck.

> STUART: Don't need it.

SANDRA folds up her mobile, shakes her head in resignation as she goes back into the conference room.

CUT TO – STUART, going to the urinal right next to the man – which no straight man would do, since there are other urinals to choose from. STUART's perfectly at ease, takes a piss. Silence. The MAN's staring ahead, trying to ignore him. STUART cops a look. Nice. Pause, both pissing. Then the MAN can't help it, he has to glance down at STUART. *Very* nice.

2/15 INT. SCHOOL YARD, DAY 3 1332   2/15
NATHAN, DONNA

Close on NATHAN and DONNA.

> NATHAN: And I know what he's like, he's had dozens of blokes, he's had hundreds. He told me everything. We talked and talked, five in the morning, he's telling me his entire life. Cos he said. He said, it's the most important night of my life. And he spent it with me.

2/16 INT. TOILET, DAY 3 1332   2/16
STUART, MAN

The MAN's now at the wash-basin. STUART zips up, relaxed, saunters over to the adjacent basin, washes his hands. The MAN keeps washing and re-washing. Now STUART's openly looking at him, which freaks the MAN out, he looks anywhere but at STUART. Though he doesn't leave. STUART's smiling away – this is easy.

2/17 EXT. SCHOOL YARD, DAY 3 1333   2/17
NATHAN, DONNA

Even closer on NATHAN.

> NATHAN: He's coming, right, he's coming, because of me, and I'm looking up, his face, it's just amazing. And he said it. He said he loved me.

2/18 INT. TOILET, DAY 3 1333   2/18
STUART, MAN

The MAN's drying his hands, still nervous. STUART saunters over, but instead of joining him at the dryer, he just looks directly at the MAN, smiles.

> STUART: Don't know about you, but that meeting's boring me rigid.

> MAN: Yeah.

Then just silence, as STUART looks at the MAN, transfixes him, grins, utterly confident. Grinning like a wolf.

2/19 INT. SCHOOL YARD, DAY 3 1333   2/19
NATHAN, DONNA

> NATHAN: I'm not stupid, he was off his face, he'd say anything. But he meant it. Just for that second. He loved me.

2/20 INT. TOILETS, DAY 3 1334   2/20
STUART, MAN

CUT TO – the cubicle door slamming shut.
CUT TO – the bolt being slammed into place.
CUT TO – STUART and the MAN inside the cubicle, frantic, STUART tugging at the MAN's shirt, his belt, his zip, the MAN terrified. Hands all over the place, STUART starts to kiss him, the MAN pulls back.

> MAN: (Whispered) I don't kiss.

> STUART: Oh *sure.*

STUART snogs him, hard. Then he drops out of frame, kneeling, going down on him.

2/21 INT. HARLO'S FOOD HALL, DAY 3 1600   2/21
VINCE, MARCIE, ROSALIE

VINCE at work with his clipboard as MARCIE comes up to him, pushing a trolley of produce, which she puts on the shelves throughout the dialogue.

> MARCIE: Seen that new piece, Rosalie Cotter, started Monday.

She's indicating, at a distance, ROSALIE – 23, small, stacking shelves.

> VINCE: What about her?

> MARCIE: Can't stick her. Walking round like she's it, I *said*, I said there's no room for Jackie Onassis in this shop, love.

> VINCE: Oh don't start, she's all right, I had to talk her through the roster, she's nice.

> MARCIE: D'you think?

> VINCE: Yeah.

> MARCIE: You think she's nice?

> VINCE: Yes, I do.

> MARCIE: (Instant change to gleeful) That's brilliant cos she fancies you, and she's that lovely, Vince, you'll get on a storm, right, in the pub, end of shift, I'll have her waiting, be there and brush your teeth. I knew it!

And she hurries off. VINCE, trapped, looks across at ROSALIE, who sneaks a glance in his direction, shy, knowing that MARCIE's setting them up. On VINCE – oh shit.

2/22 EXT. HOSPITAL CAR PARK, DAY 3 1750   2/22
STUART

Location unclear at first, on STUART in the stationary jeep (the vandalism now gone). He's on his mobile.

> STUART: Well just don't go.

2/23 EXT. STREET (CLOSE TO LAMB & FLAG)
INTERCUT WITH HOSPITAL CAR PARK, DAY 3 1750   2/23
VINCE/STUART, ROMEY, LISA, SUZIE

VINCE is walking along, downcast, on his mobile (one of those Orange 2-for-1 phones, bought by STUART).

> VINCE: We need a codeword, if I phone you up and say a certain word, you come and get me. Think of a word.

> STUART: Twilight.

> VINCE: How the hell am I supposed to get twilight into a sentence?

> STUART: Then don't go!

VINCE has arrived outside the Lamb & Flag.

> VINCE: Oh my God I'm here, straight pub! I'm going in, I can't stop.

> STUART: What's it like?

2/24 INT. LAMB & FLAG,
INTERCUT WITH HOSPITAL CAR PARK, DAY 3 1751   2/24
VINCE, MARCIE, ROSALIE, BOB/STUART, LISA, SIOBHAN, ROMEY, SUZIE, BABY ALFRED

VINCE walks in. It's a big Manchester pub, big enough so that VINCE can keep talking on the phone, with the Harlo's lot over the far side, well out of earshot, though VINCE keeps his voice a whisper, like he's a spy. (CUT TO STUART occasionally during this speech; a chance to see that VINCE can really make him laugh).

> VINCE: It's all true. Everything we've ever been told. Oh my God, flock wallpaper. Ohh, and the people! There are people talking in sentences that have no punchline and they don't even care. Can you believe it, they've got toilets in which no one's ever had sex.

As STUART talks, the passenger door opens behind him and LISA, SIOBHAN and SUZIE start to get in.

STUART: Vince, it's been lovely, but this is goodbye. We'll have a candlelit vigil in your memory, I'll put a patch on the quilt.

VINCE is now looking across the pub – MARCIE and JILL are with ROSALIE and six others, including five LADS from the store. MARCIE waves at him.

VINCE: I've changed my mind, twilight!

STUART: Tough, the baby's here.

STUART hangs up. His POV – reveal the hospital, ROMEY with ALFRED, at a distance, saying goodbye to a nurse.

STUART: (To the back seat) What's taking so long? Those women who nick babies from maternity wards, takes 'em thirty seconds flat. -

2/25 INT. LAMB & FLAG, DAY 3 1753   2/25
VINCE, MARCIE, ROSALIE, BOB

VINCE approaches the gang. ROSALIE's looking down, shy.

MARCIE: That's right, you've already met, you two, Rosalie, Vince, Vince, Rosalie. Park yourself, we've saved you a seat. (Opposite ROSALIE)

VINCE: No, I'll, uh, get the drinks. Anyone?

2/26 EXT. HOSPITAL CAR PARK, DAY 3 1800   2/26
STUART, LISA, SIOBHAN, ROMEY, SUZIE

ROMEY's now in the passenger seat with ALFRED, who's asleep, LISA leaning forward to fix ROMEY's seat belt.

ROMEY: Now you be careful, just for once, take it slowly. You don't overtake, you don't cut corners, you don't start a race, you don't take your eyes off the road cos you're cruising boys on the pavement, all right?

STUART: God, you think I'm such a twat.

He guns the ignition. As the jeep comes to life, the radio blasts out, full volume. Everyone leaps to switch it off, but ALFRED's awake, wailing.
STUART feels the full glare of four lesbians staring at him. Which makes him giggle like a kid.

2/27 INT. LAMB & FLAG, DAY 3 1810   2/27
VINCE, MARCIE, ROSALIE, BOB

Everyone else has cleared away, MARCIE and JILL watching from the bar, VINCE sitting opposite ROSALIE. Pause.

VINCE: So, where d'you live – ?

BOB – 35, slobbery, lardy – grabs his jacket, leers –

> BOB: Watch out, Rosalie, he looks normal then he rips off his face and there's a lizard underneath, that's your kind of thing, in't it, Vince?

> VINCE: Wrong programme, actually.

> BOB: What's he called then, Stavros – (Walking away) We will exterminate!

> ROSALIE: What was that?

> VINCE: Nothing. I just sort of like science-fiction stuff.

> ROSALIE: *Doctor Who?*

> VINCE: Yeah.

Pause.

> ROSALIE: I never really watched it.

> VINCE: Well. No.

Pause.

> ROSALIE: They moved it opposite *Coronation Street*, I mean, no chance, sorry.

Conversation warming up now –

> VINCE: No, fair enough, God, I remember that, '87 to '89, I had to tape one and watch the other –

> ROSALIE: D'you watch the *Street*, then?

> VINCE: Course I do, yeah.

> ROSALIE: Cos my mother, she's given up watching, she says it's full of kids now, but it's not, Wednesday, it was all Alec Gilroy, past fortnight it was non-stop Rita, it's just not true, the old ones are just as important.

> VINCE: God, you *really* watch it, don't you?

> ROSALIE: Love it. (Dreads asking) D'you like *EastEnders?*

Beat. VINCE takes a deep breath.

> VINCE: Load of Cockney nonsense.

> ROSALIE: Oh and me! Vince, we're the only ones left! On the house, love, that's all they ever say, on the house! Sorted!

VINCE: Oh, bloody 'sorted'!

CUT TO – MARCIE and JILL, watching VINCE and ROSALIE laugh. MARCIE clinks her glass with JILL, success, a 'told you' look.

2/28 INT. ROMEY'S LIVING ROOM, DAY 3 1820   2/28
STUART, SIOBHAN, LISA, ROMEY, SUZIE

A big, old three-storey Didsbury house, like Fitz's in *Cracker* but undecorated, ramshackle throughout, comfortable, big windows. STUART sitting (baby alarm in evidence), SIOBHAN handing out tea, LISA and SUZIE also there as ROMEY hands STUART a sheaf of papers.

ROMEY: I thought you could have a look at this, it's a first draft, nothing's set in stone, it's called a Security of Provision contract. I know we agreed the monthly payments and I trust you, Stuart, I trust you absolutely. But Alfred's going to be there for the rest of our lives –

STUART: (Edgy, keeping cool) Why would I stop paying? He's my kid.

ROMEY: And, there's some stuff at the back, about insurance.

STUART: Insurance for what?

ROMEY: Anything could happen, you could get run over tomorrow.

LISA: Watch out for a Ford Mondeo.

ROMEY: And, you know, you could get... ill, I mean, I'm not penniless, I'm not starving, but if you were out of work I'd need something, it's for Alfred, not me.

STUART: (Knowing full well) Why would I get ill?

ROMEY: ...it covers anything.

STUART: Like what?

ROMEY: I don't know, anything.

LISA: Stuart, we're not talking mumps. We had you tested but that was nine months ago. Thirty six weeks ago. Two hundred and fifty-two one-night stands ago.

ROMEY: (Warns her, peacekeeping) All right. (To STUART) It's for Alfred, really it is. We've got to be sensible.

STUART: Fine. Whatever you want. Of course, I'll have to run it past a solicitor.

ROMEY: I've done that already.

STUART: Is he any good?

LISA: Yes, I'm fully qualified, thanks.

ROMEY: You don't mind, though?

STUART: No it's fine. Fine.

2/29 INT. STUART'S JEEP, DRIVING, DAY 3 1830   2/29
STUART

STUART, driving fast, on his mobile.

STUART: The fucking bastard cunts!

2/30 INT. LAMB AND FLAG,
INTERCUT WITH INT. STUART'S JEEP, DAY 3 1830   2/30
VINCE, MARCIE, ROSALIE/STUART

VINCE on his mobile, standing apart from ROSALIE, who's sitting politely, waiting.

VINCE: What did they say?

STUART: First of all they want my money, then they want me dead! Vince, you've got to come out, you're supposed to be my friend –

VINCE: I'm sort of busy – (Whispers) She's really nice.

STUART: Oh for fuck's sake, tell her you take it up the arse and get out!

VINCE puts his hand over the receiver, to ROSALIE –

VINCE: It's my friend. His mother's in hospital.

2/31 EXT. LAMB & FLAG, DAY 3 1835   2/31
STUART, VINCE

STUART's jeep screeches up, VINCE runs out, gets in.

CUT TO – int. jeep as STUART drives off, fast. Both just stare dead ahead.

STUART: It's the exact opposite of childbirth. First you have a baby, *then* you get fucked.

VINCE: In some parallel universe, I just met my wife.

2/32 INT. NATHAN'S BEDROOM, DAY 3 1840   2/32
JANICE

A picture of a penis. Then the pages are skimmed over, to two naked men, wrapped round each other. (This is *Euroguy*, soft-porn, no erections.)

CUT TO – the woman studying the magazine – JANICE, 42, smart-ish, not too mumsy. The magazine's part of a stack spread across the floor – the other magazines harmless, *Smash Hits*, *Judge Dredd Megazine*, etc. JANICE is calm, little emotion, only a certain sadness. It's not the first time she's found something like this. Then, under the magazine, she finds a drawing – well-drawn, by a teenage hand – of a male model, copied out of *Euroguy* but with an addition; the man's jeans are unbuttoned, an erection thrusting out.

JANICE pauses over this. Just for a second. Then it's as if she's gone too far. Quickly, she tidies up the magazines – and we see that the stack has toppled over from inside a wardrobe, JANICE now shoving everything back where it was. Then she puts two shirts on hangers inside the wardrobe – her original intention in opening the door.

She walks out, fast (we only catch a glimpse of the bedroom – average-sized room, semi-detached house, middle-class family; there's a CD, portable TV, all the bog-standard stuff, but the room's got a fair bit of style, like Ferris Bueller's bedroom). JANICE leaves.

2/33 INT. MALONEYS' KITCHEN/HALL, DAY 3 1842   2/33
JANICE, NATHAN, DONNA, HELEN

JANICE walks from upstairs, down the hall towards the kitchen, revealing NATHAN and DONNA (and only now, we realise JANICE is NATHAN's mother). NATHAN and DONNA are shoving plates into the sink, then grabbing jackets, etc., JANICE's arrival having cued their departure. Also sitting there is HELEN, NATHAN's 10-year-old sister, playing with a Geostation. JANICE acts as though all's normal, no hint of what she's seen upstairs.

> JANICE: I was going to phone for a pizza –

> NATHAN: We had the cheese, we're going round to Sally
> Colasanto's and I'm staying the night at Donna's, see you –

> JANICE: Is that all right with your mother, Donna?

> NATHAN: No, like I didn't ask.

> DONNA: Thanks for the cheese, bye!

NATHAN and DONNA run out, a whirlwind, slamming the front door. Pause, silence. Hold for a few seconds on JANICE, as she busies herself; a lingering worry about NATHAN, about where he's going.

2/34 EXT. WILMSLOW ROAD, NIGHT 3 2040
(TWILIGHT)   2/34
NATHAN, DONNA

NATHAN and DONNA wait for the approaching bus. Now we can see NATHAN properly; he's done up for a night in the Village, best shirt. Small but vital changes to his appearance – it's a bit more thought-out, hair gelled to death. Perhaps some small imitation of STUART in his image. But unintentionally, the overall effect is to make him look even younger.

> NATHAN: (Excited, energised) You see that lot in school, all those couples, Robert Coles and Cathy Broderick and that lot, but half of them's never done it, they haven't, Robert Coles was saying. He's desperate, they have a snog and a bit of a thing and that's it, he goes home and has a wank. (Bus arrives, he gets on) Town, please. (Back to DONNA) They're just kids, they're just talking. I'm *doing* it! I'm really doing it.

DONNA watches the bus pull away, NATHAN runs to the back seats, looks out of the back window, points at himself, mouths 'I'm doing it', gleeful. Then he sits, turns away.

On DONNA, watching the bus go. Sadly, left out of things, she turns, starts the walk home.

2/35 EXT. CANAL STREET, NIGHT 3 2100   2/35
NATHAN

On the Canal Street sign. No C, and now no S.

CUT TO – NATHAN, standing outside the Union, watching men go in. He's nervous as hell, all the confidence he showed DONNA gone; a fast, manic display as he checks his hair, straightens his eyebrows, rubs a finger along his teeth, digs in his nostrils to make sure he looks all right. Then deep breath, and he heads in – his first entry into a gay pub.

2/36 INT. NEW UNION, NIGHT 3 2101   2/36
STUART, VINCE, PHIL, NATHAN, HAZEL

The New Union's a big, old-fashioned pub, packed to the rafters, gay and lesbian, maybe 70% men, all types, all ages, though the Paradise-type clubbers like STUART are in the minority.

Follow NATHAN in, his checking-of-his-hair now almost a twitch as he looks at all the men around him. Handsome is in short supply in the Union, so there's nothing to distract NATHAN in his quest. His eyes flick about as he pushes through the crowd, hunting down STUART.

CUT TO – STUART, VINCE and PHIL, standing around one of the tall tables. As they talk, VINCE and PHIL keep glancing around the place, measuring up who's in, a constant tick throughout every pub/club scene. STUART does this in spades, barely paying attention to VINCE and PHIL.

> STUART: D'you know why they chose me? Cos I'm rich, and cos I'm handsome as fuck! And that's all! She said so, that fucking Lisa. I'm just a gene pool to them, I'm just spunk!

> PHIL: (Like STUART hasn't spoken) Now, there, him with the collar, that's the one Jason Black went out with. Burst into tears, said his mother was dead, said she died on the *Herald of Free Enterprise*, two days later she turns up, she's been walking the Peak District. Mad as a moose.

STUART: They get benefits, don't they, single mothers? Or have they stopped that now? I bet they've gone and bloody stopped it.

VINCE: (Quiet, delighted) Oh stand by your beds, have you seen, have you seen? Twelve o'clock.

Their POV – NATHAN in the crowd. And in that second, NATHAN sees them, heads towards them.

STUART: Shit.

VINCE: Behave. Stuart, behave.

PHIL: What?

VINCE: The chicken has landed. (To STUART) His name's Nathan, all right?

NATHAN arrives. VINCE and PHIL dying to laugh, STUART amused but remaining aloof. NATHAN's scared, transfixed on STUART; now he's there, he doesn't know what to say.

VINCE: Hiya.

NATHAN: Hi.

Silence. All exchanging looks.

NATHAN: How's the baby?

STUART: Ask my solicitor. (Suddenly bright) Nathan, d'you want a drink?

2/37 EXT. NEW UNION, NIGHT 3 2107   2/37
STUART, VINCE

STUART walks out of the main entrance, smiling, glad to be out. He saunters along, heading for Manto's. But VINCE has anticipated this, has run across the Union and emerges via the fire exit door, right in front of STUART.

VINCE: Oh no you don't.

2/38 INT. NEW UNION BAR, NIGHT 3 2110   2/38
STUART, VINCE, PHIL, NATHAN

Drinks being handed over to STUART, VINCE with him. (NATHAN with PHIL visible in B/G, not talking.)

VINCE: First time we came here, we were sixteen, older than him, and how long before anyone talked to us? Ages. Go on, be nice to him. But I don't mean shag him.

STUART: Oh, give me some credit. (Looks at NATHAN, winding VINCE up) On the other hand. He's quite sweet, don't you think?

VINCE: I don't know, I haven't licked him.

2/39 INT. NEW UNION, NIGHT 3 2112   2/39
STUART, VINCE, PHIL, NATHAN, HAZEL

On the stage – a line of men and women, old, young, fat, thin, miming the actions to Rolf Harris's 'The Ladies of the Court of King Caractacus' (an old crowd-pleaser). From the crowd, HAZEL clambers up, elbows her way into the middle, joins in.
     CUT TO – STUART and VINCE joining PHIL and NATHAN.

PHIL: Just in time, would you look at that old slapper?

STUART: She needs locking up.

VINCE: Some people have no shame.

NATHAN: (Trying to join in) She's like a twat, isn't she?

STUART: That's Vince's mother.

NATHAN: (Thinks it's still a joke) Yeah, like, imagine if she was, a proper twat like that.

CUT TO – HAZEL. She sees the boys, waves.

HAZEL: Vinnie!

VINCE: Mum.

NATHAN's horrified. STUART pretends to be cold, offended.

STUART: Just be careful, next time.

VINCE: I don't mind, honestly, she's off her head.

PHIL: We don't see your mother down here, Stu. Funny, that.

STUART gives PHIL a scathing look, which PHIL loves. During PHIL's next speech, on NATHAN, plucking up the nerve; he's finally found something to which he can contribute, and a way to earn sympathy after his gaffe.

PHIL: How are they, Mr and Mrs Jones? Still waiting for Golden Boy to get married?

NATHAN: (Suddenly) Cos like my mother, she'd kill me if she knew I was here, like we're watching *Emmerdale* and Zoe Tate was having that lesbian wedding, and my mother stood up and turned it off.

PHIL: That's not homophobia, that's good taste.

VINCE: Phil. (Meaning, listen to him)

NATHAN goes into one of his anaphylactic-shock self-dramatisations, to make himself seem more important, more adult. During this, VINCE shoots a look at PHIL, both smile, remembering what it's like to be 15.

NATHAN: If she saw me here, she'd hate it, she'd kill me, she'd chuck me out – cos they're all like it, my family, I've got this cousin, I've never even met her but she's a lesbian, they threw her out. She went to London, she never came back, I heard Mum say she's probably dead now –

STUART slams down his empty pint, breaking any attention NATHAN might have held.

STUART: What about me? I've given my son a lesbian mother! I bet all those women queue up at her breast to drink the milk – I'm sick of this place, can we go?

2/40 EXT. CANAL STREET, NIGHT 3 2130   2/40
STUART, PHIL, NATHAN, VINCE, DANNY

The street busy, STUART and PHIL walk along, NATHAN and VINCE trailing behind. NATHAN keeps his eyes on STUART.

VINCE: It's just a bit dodgy, your mum thinks you're at Donna's, Donna's mother thinks you're somewhere else; where are you going to spend the night? (Cautious) It might not be Stuart's.

NATHAN: I *know.*

In a tone of voice that says, leave me alone. They keep walking, VINCE stuck for anything to say.
CUT TO – STUART and PHIL, walking ahead.

PHIL: You fucked him, he's your responsibility, don't you dare go swanning off –

STUART: Everyone's having a go at me! Listen, I have to spend every single day living with me, so I know for a fact, I'm lovely, I'm completely lovely – (Sudden smile) Danny, how's things?

DANNY's 30, fit, walking in the opposite direction. They talk on the move, passing. DANNY despises STUART.

DANNY: Not so bad.

STUART: How's Peter?

DANNY: Still dead.

STUART: Oh shit, sorry, forgot. (DANNY walks on. STUART can't help laughing, to PHIL) Oops.

PHIL just despairs.

2/41 INT. VIA FOSSA, NIGHT 3 2145   2/41
NATHAN

Via Fossa's a big, successful pub, labyrinthine, Gothic design, all wood, more fashionable than the Union. Music pumping out, loads of people. At the bar, it's literally like that Caffrey's advert, a tight crowd at the bar heaving to and fro with the beat. In the mayhem, NATHAN's struggling along, carrying four pints of Stella.

2/42 INT. VIA FOSSA SEATED AREA, NIGHT 3 2200   2/42
STUART, VINCE, PHIL, NATHAN

All seated around a big farmhouse-kitchen type table.

STUART: I should give London another go. I look round this place, I've had them all.

PHIL: Oh, I'm haunted by that problem.

VINCE: You haven't had me.

STUART: There was the once.

PHIL: No! When?

It's STUART's way of being in control; showing off in front of NATHAN, and taking the piss out of VINCE. CUT TO – NATHAN throughout this, a spectator.

STUART: We're in his bedroom, we must've been fourteen, and Vince has got the *Radio Times* –

VINCE: Oh don't tell this story, don't!

STUART: And we come to this photo and we're both going phwoaaarh, guess who it was? Barry Sheene! On his motorbike!

PHIL's howling with laughter.

VINCE: In his leathers, God, I'm shamed –

STUART: Not even black leather, it was red and cream, and we're going, cor, look at him, then we're sort of groping ourselves, then Vince gets it out, not bad either –

VINCE: Oh fuck off –

STUART: I said give's a go, so I'm giving him a wank, nice and slow, we're looking down at Barry Sheene –

PHIL: Oh my God, you've had each other!

STUART: No, I'm just about to unzip when his mother comes back, he's jumping up, shoving it back in! And that was it.

VINCE: See, that's not sex, it's not sex if you don't come!

Next speech, STUART OOV as VINCE catches NATHAN's eye. A cold, fixed moment; VINCE is caught in mid-laughter, he's unnerved by NATHAN's stare, looks away.

STUART: When Barry Sheene broke his legs, Vince went to W.H. Smith and bought a card and sent it to Barry Sheene, London. He was the saddest man on earth.

PHIL: Giving yourself away, Barry Sheene, showing your age.

NATHAN: (Blurts out) How old are you?

STUART: How old d'you think I am?

NATHAN: Thirty-three?

PHIL and VINCE just explode laughing, STUART's ridiculously pissed off.

STUART: Fuck off.

NATHAN: What?

STUART: I'm twenty-nine.

PHIL: Not for much longer! Six months to go, then it's straight into the bladder-control clinic.

STUART: Then I'd better go for a piss, while I still can.

STUART walks off. NATHAN's mortified, VINCE distracted.

VINCE: It's not that funny, I've only got three months left.

PHIL: Yeah, but you don't count.

VINCE: Sad but true.

2/43 EXT. CANAL STREET CAR PARK, NIGHT 3 2205   2/43
STUART

On the jeep – headlights blaze, music blares out, the engine roars. STUART's free at last. The jeep pulls away, leaving us behind.

2/44 INT. VIA FOSSA, NIGHT 3 2210   2/44
PHIL, VINCE, NATHAN

PHIL's crossing the pub as VINCE runs to catch up with him.

>VINCE: Phil, don't leave me with him –

>PHIL: There's been a hundred bloody Nathans and we always get stuck with them, this is typical Stuart, I'm not cleaning up his mess. It's a Friday night, I'm not wasting it on little boy Nathan –

>VINCE: Oh thanks, so he's my problem.

>PHIL: Stuart's your problem. Sorry.

No pause, instant switch from a near-argument to the old banter –

>PHIL: Oo fab, my luck's in, Dave the Builder, don't mind me –

>VINCE: You don't fancy him.

>PHIL: I need shelves putting up.

PHIL heads off. Follow VINCE back to NATHAN.

>VINCE: He always does this, he never stays in one place.

>NATHAN: Has he gone?

>VINCE: He never stays. (Beat) It wasn't you.

Silence, NATHAN mortified, VINCE trapped.

2/45 INT. STUART'S FLAT, NIGHT 3 2220   2/45
STUART

STUART strides in, goes straight to his PC. He does a double click on an Internet icon, the phone starts doodling.
    CUT TO (compressing the time it would take) – the 'gaymanchestersex' IRC Chat Room. Down the right hand side of the screen is a list of those talking – BUMBOY, CHARMER, WELLHUNG, GOODFUK, BLKDUDE, 9INCH, GORGEOUS. (STUART's name is just STUART; he considers that enough.) Grinning, STUART selects GOODFUK.

2/46 EXT. CANAL STREET/MAIN ROAD, NIGHT 3 2221   2/46
VINCE, NATHAN

VINCE is on the main road, trying to flag down a black cab. NATHAN stands a few feet away, ashamed, upset, not wanting to show it. A taxi whizzes past.

>VINCE: Turn your light off, then!

Pause, VINCE keeps signalling. But at the same time, he looks at NATHAN, wanting to help.

> VINCE: You'll be all right, it's only half ten, you'll get into
> Donna's, won't you? (Silence. Quiet, kind) Look, he's not your
> boyfriend. (Silence) He's... He just doesn't think, he's -- he just
> has a laugh. He's never had a boyfriend, he doesn't do
> boyfriends, he's... (Pause) Nathan, he's a cunt. He doesn't give a
> toss about anyone. Ah!

Taxi pulls up. NATHAN heads towards it, sullen, VINCE gets out a fiver.

> VINCE: That'll get you home.

At the taxi door, NATHAN stops, looks at VINCE. He's more in control now, already that bit older.

> NATHAN: You slag him off, yeah? But then you follow him round
> all the time.

> VINCE: We go back years.

> NATHAN: You're friends with a cunt.

> VINCE: Yeah.

Beat.

> NATHAN: Never got to finish that wank, did you?

Silence. On VINCE, unnerved. Then, quiet, cool.

> VINCE: All right, chicken. Fuck off home.

Knowing he's won, NATHAN gets in the cab, it drives off. VINCE walks away, disturbed by NATHAN's knowledge.

2/47 INT. STUART'S FLAT, NIGHT 3 2231   2/47
STUART

On STUART, on the IRC, grinning. The screen's full of the usual chat, statistics, etc., and a picture of GOODFUK is being downloaded. It's from the neck down, great body, pierced nipple (he would be erect, if we can show that).

> STUART: Oh *yes.*

On the screen, we see STUART type in --
apartment 16 mariner's court

And then GOODFUK's reply --
on my way ; -)

2/48 INT. HAZEL'S HOUSE, NIGHT 3 2250   2/48
HAZEL, BERNARD, VINCE

One of those faceless modern terraces along Brunswick Street, near the Apollo. A mess inside, though not dirty; it's stacked with boxes of Christmas crackers, the components of which are strewn about. VINCE is just walking in with HAZEL and BERNARD, mid-conversation. He's in quiet mood, HAZEL and BERNARD bustling about.

> HAZEL: Kettle on, look at me, sweating like a pig –

> VINCE: He's a wanker, though, Stuart. Every time! Every time he does it, I get stuck –

> HAZEL: What shift you on tomorrow? We'll need a hand with the boxes, I've had Pied Piper on the phone, nagging for these.

> BERNARD: (Of the crackers) You seen? We've been upgraded!

> HAZEL: They're deluxe, they've got jewellery inside, look, I nicked one, it's metal, it's nice. You don't get these in newsagents, no, they're in Kendals, this lot –

> BERNARD: Vince love, I meant to say, you couldn't shift some of your stuff in the bedroom, could you? I mean, I'm sort of permanent now –

> HAZEL: The odd couple, she's calling us next door, I said more of a dog's home, waifs and strays –

> BERNARD: I'd like to put me plants in, you don't mind, do you?

> VINCE: No, I've been meaning to give you some space –

> BERNARD: Vince, you're a star –

> HAZEL: What's that about Stuart? What's he done this time?

> VINCE: ...nothing.

2/49 INT. VINCE'S OLD BEDROOM, NIGHT 3 2255   2/49
VINCE, HAZEL

CU on old photos, pinned to the wall –many of them STUART and VINCE as schoolboys, and in their 20s.
    CUT TO – VINCE, looking at them. Around him, the bedroom's full of his old teenage stuff, with BERNARD's clothes, etc., thrown about. VINCE starts to shift boxes of his things as HAZEL comes in, carrying a mug of coffee.

> HAZEL: I'm not buying that coffee again, it's like dust.
> (VINCE takes it. Pause) Still your room. He's just the lodger.
> (VINCE smiles. Then brisker, HAZEL's not one for sentiment)
> Anything for the car boot sale, shove it on the landing.

HAZEL goes. VINCE sits down with one of the boxes, scrabbles through it, knowing what he'll find at the bottom. He pulls it out. It's the ancient, yellowed photograph of Barry Sheene.

2/50 INT. STUART'S FLAT, NIGHT 3 2256   2/50
STUART

The buzzer goes, STUART goes to the intercom.

> STUART: Come on up.

He presses the door release, then grinning, confident, strides into the bedroom.

2/51 INT STUARTS FLAT - BEDROOM, NIGHT 3 2256   2/51
STUART

STUART looks at himself in the full-length mirror, checks his packet, adjusts it to look his best, loves what he sees, walks out.

2/52 INT. STUART'S FLAT, NIGHT 2257   2/52
STUART, NATHAN, GOODFUK

A knock at the door, STUART already walking towards it. He opens the door – It's NATHAN.

> STUART: *No.* You can't do this, I won't have it, Nathan, go home.

> NATHAN: (Plaintive) I'm not – I just want to talk, and –

> STUART: I said *go* –

> NATHAN: (Desperate) I know you don't want to – and I'm not – I mean I sort of really like you, and, and, I'll go in a minute, I will, but can't I just sit here for a bit? I mean, like, I'll just –

> STUART: Oh shit.

He's seen GOODFUK coming up the stairs behind NATHAN. He's 23, tall, skinhead, denim and DMs, dead hard (and much nicer than he looks).

> GOODFUK: (Wary) Aye aye. Door was open, your neighbour was, uh... What's this about, then?

> STUART: No, he's just going – (To NATHAN) I'm busy, okay?

> GOODFUK: S'not a threesome, is it?

> STUART: No – (Looks at NATHAN) Is it? (Thinks better) No.

> GOODFUK: I don't mind, but he's a bit young.

> NATHAN: (Hostile) Who's he?

STUART: Nathan, this is... (Starts to laugh) ...this is Goodfuk... (Really laughing) ...Goodfuk, this is Nathan.

GOODFUK: My name's Colin.

STUART: Colin Goodfuk.

NATHAN: (Realising, at STUART) You don't even know him.

STUART: (Stops laughing, in control) I'm going to take Goodfuk inside and check out that name, so if you don't mind running along, thanks.

NATHAN's on fire, shame, humiliation, jealousy; he turns and runs.

STUART: Sorry 'bout that. He's my stalker.

GOODFUK: How old is he?

STUART: Dunno, fifteen.

GOODFUK: What's he doing, walking home? This time of night?

And GOODFUK gives STUART *such* a look.

STUART: (Sighs) All right – (Grabs his jacket) There's whisky by the fridge and there's porn by the television, tapes on the left. And don't nick anything.

STUART runs after NATHAN.

2/53 EXT. STUART'S FLAT, NIGHT 3 2300   2/53
NATHAN, STUART

NATHAN's sitting on the wall, miserable, but when he sees STUART coming out of the door, he starts to hurry away. /

STUART: Oy! D'you mind? I've left my flat in the hands of Goodfuk the stranger all cos of you, so don't you dare go running off!

NATHAN stops, some distance away. STUART walks up to him.

STUART: (Quieter) I'll get you a cab. (Dials his mobile, mutters) Everyone has a go at me, *everyone*. (To NATHAN) Call it a lesson learnt. Don't turn up outside my door – (On the phone) Hi, it's on account, Stuart Jones. Number 42601. Yeah, home address, quick as you can. Cheers. (To NATHAN) On its way –

NATHAN's just been staring at STUART, emotion building up –

NATHAN: You'll have *anyone*. He's nothing, he's no one, he's *ugly*. I was *there*, I was there all night, and I really like you – he

doesn't even *know* you, what did I do wrong? (more helpless) Did
I do something wrong? Tell me what I've done and I won't do it
again, I promise. What is it, what's wrong with me?

STUART: Nathan.

And STUART looks at him; not hostile; this one sentence genuinely sums up his
attitude, his entire life.

STUART: I've had you.

NATHAN holds his look. Then he simply bursts into tears.
    Wide shot of the two of them in the street, NATHAN crying like a kid, turned
away from STUART, ashamed, STUART not knowing what to do, not unaffected
by this.
    CUT TO – a Mantax black cab pulling up.
    CUT TO – NATHAN getting inside, STUART still there.
    CUT TO – the taxi driving off. NATHAN, still upset, looks out of the back
window. STUART watches him go, for once troubled by the effect he's had.

2/54 INT. STUART'S FLAT/BEDROOM, NIGHT 3 2310   2/54
STUART, GOODFUK

STUART walks back in. The bedroom door's open, GOODFUK's naked on top of
the duvet. STUART doesn't go in.

GOODFUK: Thought I'd get ready.

STUART: Yeah. (Pause) Maybe not, eh?

GOODFUK: Maybe not what?

STUART: Another time.

GOODFUK: Oh, thanks for nothing.

GOODFUK gets out of bed, starts to dress. STUART sits on the sofa, facing away
from the bedroom, GOODFUK just a figure in B/G as STUART stares ahead. He's
both disturbed *and* unrepentant.

GOODFUK: Fucking waste of time, I didn't have to come here. I
had all sorts of offers. Thought I was on a promise.

STUART: (More to himself) I never promised anyone anything.

Hold on STUART, absolutely still as GOODFUK, shoes in hand, storms out of the
bedroom, heading for the door.
    Then STUART stands on the sofa, literally flings himself through the air,
jumping on GOODFUK, pulling him down to the floor, hungry, wild. They tumble
out of sight behind the furniture.

EPISODE THREE

From titles, into black, and the caption:

SATURDAY

MIX into:

3/1 INT. AIRPORT, DAY 4 1600   3/1
VINCE, PHIL, ALEXANDER, DANE, LEE, BABY ALFRED

Bring up caption: 1600
    VINCE is waiting with PHIL, VINCE carrying ALFRED in one of those basket-like carry-cots.

> VINCE: Thing about Alexander, he's a bit camp, but he's nice –
> mind you, saying he's a bit camp is like saying Hitler's a bit
> naughty – but he's nice, you'll like him, and he's been single for
> ages, he's dying for a boyfriend. Just ignore the voice. And the
> volume. And don't get him drunk. And if he does get drunk, run
> for the hills – (Big smile) Hiya!

He's seen ALEXANDER and DANE. Both late 20s, fit, dressed very London scene. ALEXANDER's permanently hyper, Manchester accent, DANE's permanently glum, London accent. Trailing behind – not obviously with them, at first – is a tall, thin, very cool Japanese boy, LEE. Choruses of 'hiya' (all of them sending up 'hiya'), then fast, overlapping:

> ALEXANDER: Look, this is the jacket, twenty quid! Bargain! Miss
> Corke's wardrobe by Kamizole. (Kisses him) Vince, you look
> dreadful –

> DANE: I thought, fly up from London, bit more exclusive, but
> no! You get anyone, you're sitting there with kids and people
> with back yards.

> VINCE: This is Phil – Alexander, Dane, Dane, Alexander, Phil.

More hiya's, etc.

> ALEXANDER: Vince, nice handbag.

> VINCE: This is Alfred. So it's no smoking.

> DANE: He's a little baby Stuart, ohhh, I bet I'm infertile.

> VINCE: (To ALEXANDER) Now Phil's the one I told you about,
> he's the one met David Beckham –

But LEE's about to wander off, ALEXANDER grabs him.

ALEXANDER: Oy, come here, this is Lee, isn't he beautiful?
Cheekbones! Lee, this is Vince, and what was it?

PHIL: Phil.

ALEXANDER: Vince and Phil.

LEE's all smiles, speaks only in Japanese. (And a glance between PHIL and
VINCE, realising ALEXANDER's taken.)

LEE: *warui kedo – kane ga irundayo. koko ni kitara kaneo kurerutte
ittadaro.*

ALEXANDER: Perfect boyfriend, shags like a rabbit and he can't
understand a word I'm saying, he's fab, isn't he? It's a love job,
we met in the club.

VINCE: What club?

ALEXANDER: Mile High.

3/2 INT. STUART'S FLAT, DAY 4 1615   3/2
STUART

STUART on the phone. (Keep flat in B/G hidden.)

STUART: Can't you get rid of them?

3/3 EXT. STUART'S FLAT, INTERCUT
WITH INT. STUART'S FLAT DAY 4 1615   3/3
VINCE, PHIL, ALEXANDER, DANE, LEE/STUART

VINCE in the jeep, parked outside the flats, ALFRED's cot strapped in beside him.
In B/G: PHIL, ALEXANDER, DANE and LEE reaching the front door. (All the
better if STUART's got a balcony, looking down at VINCE and OTHERS.)

VINCE: Stuart! You invited them!

STUART: I was drunk. Can't they stay with you? (His buzzer
goes) Tell them I'm busy or something.

VINCE's POV: the boys at the intercom, 'hiya!', 'Stuart!'

VINCE: (Starts to drive off) Tell them yourself. I'm taking Alfred
to the lesbians.

3/4 INT. MALONEYS' FRONT ROOM, DAY 4 1616   3/4
NATHAN, JANICE, HELEN

NATHAN's slumped in front of the TV, not looking at JANICE as she talks.
HELEN's visible in the hall, in party frock, carrying a birthday present.

JANICE: If the man phones about the roof, tell him the only day I can get time off is Thursday, or your dad can see him Friday, all right? Nathan?

NATHAN: Yeah.

JANICE: Thursday or Friday, got that? Helen! Don't unwrap it, it's not for you, come on. Party time.

JANICE goes to HELEN, they leave. The moment NATHAN hears the front door slam, he leaps up, full of energy. He sees JANICE and HELEN going down the path, then leaps to the phone, excited, dials.

NATHAN: Hi, yeah. This is Stuart Jones.

3/5 INT. STUART'S FLAT, DAY 4 1617
ALEXANDER, DANE, PHIL, STUART, LEE

3/5

ALEXANDER, DANE, PHIL and LEE are spreading around the flat, helping themselves to drinks. LEE's excited, talking to the others and pointing at STUART, who's on the phone.

LEE: *aitsu to yaru no kai? yaru hou ga kane yori mashi dayo. ore ga sakida.*

STUART: (On the phone) D'you hear that? There must be someone who can translate, he's driving me mad.

3/5A INT. HARLO'S INTERCUT WITH STUART'S FLAT, DAY 4 1619
SANDRA, GEORGE/STUART, ALEXANDER, DANE, PHIL, LEE

3/5A

SANDRA's struggling along with a full trolley and her son, four-year-old GEORGE, on her mobile.

SANDRA: I never even managed O-Level French. (To GEORGE) George, leave it alone! See, that man's looking, he's looking at you! (On the phone) What d'you expect me to do? It's Saturday, I'm off-duty, leave me alone!

STUART: If I have a bad weekend I'll take Monday off, I'll have to, then the entire schedule gets behind.

SANDRA: (Sighs) I'll see what I can do.

STUART: Sandra, I love you.

SANDRA: Oh piss off.

GEORGE: Piss off! Piss off!

SANDRA: (On the phone, weary) Thanks for that.

3/6 EXT. ROMEY'S HOUSE, DAY 4 1630

ROMEY, VINCE, LISA, BABY ALFRED

ROMEY opens the door to VINCE, on his mobile.

> VINCE: You've got Canada Dry, Stuart, there's a bottle by the
> fridge, there is. (Gives ALFRED to ROMEY) He's a bit tetchy, he
> didn't get much of a sleep. (On the phone) All right, I'll go to
> the offy.

LISA's in B/G, calls down the hall:

> LISA: Did he spend a single second with his own son? He left
> him with you, didn't he?

> VINCE: Got to go.

> ROMEY: Thanks, Vince.

> LISA: You're more of a father than he is.

VINCE runs to the jeep as LISA joins ROMEY, watching him.

> VINCE: Port? Who the fuck's drinking port? All right, I'll get
> some, do they sell port in Thresher's? Well I don't know! (Sotto)
> Is it just me, or do those women have a way of staring at you?

3/7 EXT. DONNA'S HOUSE, DAY 4 1650

DONNA, NATHAN

Front door opens, revealing DONNA.

> DONNA: I'm not ready.

> NATHAN: No rush. It'll wait.

He indicates the black cab, parked outside.

> DONNA: Whose is that?

> NATHAN: Mine.

3/8 INT. TAXI, DAY 4 1652

NATHAN, DONNA

The taxi speeding into town, NATHAN and DONNA sitting there like royalty.

> NATHAN: Stuart's got this account, he said, use it. I've been all
> round, I went to that pen shop in Heaton Moor, it's all on him.

> DONNA: God, he must really love you, how much have you
> spent?

NATHAN: Like it says, seventeen forty.

DONNA: Blimey, I thought that was the time. (NATHAN laughs)
I did!

DONNA laughs, then for precious little reason they're both falling about laughing. Like you can only laugh when you're 15, with your best friend.

3/9 INT. STUART'S FLAT, DAY 4 1700 · 3/9
ALEXANDER, DANE, PHIL, STUART, LEE

ALEXANDER, DANE and PHIL have got champagne/tequila slammers lined up.
All go 'one, two, three', slam them, knock them back. React!
CUT TO – LEE, other side of the room, on the phone, STUART beside him.

LEE: *kane o kurerutte ittadaro. kane o dasu to yakusuko sita janaika.*
kane no tameni yattandazo irelando ni iru aneki no tokoro ni ikanakya
naranainda – ferrydai toka de – kane zembu tsukkachimattayo –

3/10 INT. 'THRIVE' OFFICE,
INTERCUT WITH STUART'S FLAT DAY 4 1700 3/10
SANDRA, GEORGE/ALEXANDER, DANE, STUART, PHIL, LEE

The office is deserted. In B/G, GEORGE is unpacking and destroying SANDRA's
shopping. SANDRA's on two phones at once – one to LEE, one to a translator –
juggling that with writing down notes.

SANDRA: (To the translator) *Car-nay zemboo tussookachee* – (To
LEE) What was it?

LEE: *kane zembu tsukkachimattayo.*

SANDRA: (To the translator) *tussookacheemattayo…* right… (To
LEE) Put Stuart back on, *Stuart*, okay?

LEE hands the phone to STUART.

STUART: So?

SANDRA: He thinks he had sex with – who is it, Alexander? He
had sex for money.

GEORGE: Who did?

SANDRA: Hush. He wants £200, he's – well, he's selling himself.

STUART keeps an absolutely straight face, LEE at his side.

LEE: *Yappari – kane.*

ALEXANDER: (Calls across) What's that mean, *kane*, he keeps on
saying *kane*.

STUART: So what's *kane?*

SANDRA: (To the translator) What's *kane?* (To STUART) Money.

STUART: (Grins, to ALEXANDER) It's the Japanese for love.
He's completely in love with you.

3/11 INT. STUART'S FLAT, DAY 4 1730   3/11
PHIL, VINCE, STUART, ALEXANDER, DANE, LEE

PHIL opens the door, VINCE runs in, excited, waving a VHS.

VINCE: Found it! This is the one!

3/11A INT. STUART'S FLAT, DAY 4 1740   3/11A
VINCE, PHIL, ALEXANDER, DANE, STUART, LEE

The flat now in darkness, curtains closed. VINCE, PHIL, ALEXANDER, DANE
and LEE all illuminated by the light of the TV. Solemn music from the speakers.
DANE's crying. STUART sits apart from this, busy on his PC; it's too camp for him,
but CUT TO him at some point, laughing with the others' reactions. Pause, then:

PHIL: Which end's her feet?

VINCE: This end.

PHIL: There's so many flowers on the coffin, you can't tell.

VINCE: It's *this* end.

DANE: I met her once, that charity thing.

ALEXANDER: But if it's this end, they carried her in feet first,
you'd go head first, royalty.

DANE: I'd like to think, at the moment she died, her entire life
flashed before her, and she caught a glimpse of me.

ALEXANDER: Oh fast forward, let's have a look at Elton's
eyebrow.

3/12 INT. TAXI/EXT. DIDSBURY VILLAGE, DAY 4 1740   3/12
NATHAN, DONNA, ROMEY, LISA, BABY ALFRED

Bring up caption: 1740
    NATHAN and DONNA in the cab. Then, urgently:

NATHAN: Could you pull in, please? Could you pull in here,
please?

DONNA: What is it?

NATHAN: It's them.

NATHAN's POV: ROMEY and LISA, walking along with ALFRED.

DONNA: Who's them?

The taxi pulls up, NATHAN runs out, DONNA follows.

3/13 EXT. DIDSBURY ROAD, DAY 4 1744   3/13
ROMEY, LISA, NATHAN, DONNA, BABY ALFRED

ROMEY and LISA walk along a leafy road, NATHAN and DONNA a long, long way behind, like two spies.

DONNA: So if that's his kid, and he's your boyfriend, that makes you... sort of stepfather, oh my God, you're a stepfather! (Silence, NATHAN sullen) Why don't we just go and say hello?

NATHAN: He hates them. It's like they had the kid and then they took him off, they won't let Stuart even see him. Imagine doing that to someone. He really hates them.

3/14 EXT./INT. ROMEY'S HOUSE, DAY 4 1830   3/14
ROMEY, LISA, PIZZA BOY

ROMEY opens the door to a CHECKERS' PIZZA BOY.

PIZZA BOY: Three Vegetarians, two Häagen-Dazs. Having a party?

ROMEY: We didn't order pizza.

PIZZA BOY: Romey Sullivan?

ROMEY: Um. That's me, yeah –

PIZZA BOY: Forty pounds eighty-seven, thanks.

At that moment, a Chinese-delivery-man walks up with two big carrier bags, says 'Romey Sullivan, meal for six?', just as LISA joins ROMEY at the door.

ROMEY: What the hell's going on?

LISA: I don't know how, I don't know why, but the word 'Stuart' comes to mind.

3/15 INT. MALONEYS' FRONT ROOM, DAY 4 1831   3/15
NATHAN, DONNA

NATHAN's flicking through Yellow Pages, excited. DONNA's watching him, only half-smiling, wondering what's going on here.

NATHAN: Look, they deliver bags of cement, brilliant –

DONNA puts her hand on the phone to stop him dialling.

DONNA: You gonna tell me or what?

3/15A INT./EXT. MALONEYS' HOUSE, DAY 4 1840   3/15A
NATHAN, DONNA

NATHAN and DONNA sit on the back doorstep, smoking, taking great care throughout the scene to waft smoke away from the door. NATHAN quieter now, sad, being honest.

NATHAN: He finished with me. Didn't even finish, we weren't even started, I looked a complete mong. And he laughed in my face.

DONNA: But what have the lesbians done wrong?

Pause, then very quiet, ashamed:

NATHAN: They still get to see him.

Pause.

DONNA: When my boyfriend chucked me, I didn't sit moping. I went straight out looking for the next one.

NATHAN: What boyfriend?

DONNA: It was Infants school. (Both laugh) You said, Canal Street, it's choc-a-block. You're that nice-looking, you'll find a bloke, no time.

NATHAN: He'll be there. Laughing.

Pause.

DONNA: Would they let me in?

NATHAN: Course they would, yeah.

DONNA: There you are, I'll come with you! I'm not pretending I'm a lesbo, mind, I've seen Kate Moss on that advert, I felt nothing.

NATHAN: (Excited)We could go tonight!

DONNA: I'll wear my new top!

They hear the front door slam, leap up, throwing away the fags and wafting smoke away.

3/16 INT. VIA FOSSA RESTAURANT, NIGHT 4 2130   3/16
STUART, VINCE, PHIL, ALEXANDER, DANE, LEE

Bring up caption: 2130

STUART, VINCE, PHIL, ALEXANDER, DANE and LEE at a table (all having changed clothes for a night out). They've just finished a meal, lots of drink, all smoking except DANE, laughter.

STUART: Go on, prove it!

ALEXANDER: It's absolutely true! What's it called, it's like a muscle, the ejaculation muscle. Like any muscle, it gets worn out. Like when you're twenty, you can shoot it over your shoulder, thirty, you're lucky if it fills your belly button.

VINCE: Oh my God, that's true!

DANE: We're so old.

STUART: I can still get it over my shoulder.

ALEXANDER: Yeah, well, that's an athlete's muscle.

VINCE: I read this thing in *Attitude*, on the problem page it says, is there any way to make your cock bigger? And the answer says, just lose weight, for every thirty pounds, you gain one inch, a whole inch for thirty pounds of fat.

The WAITER appears, says 'Anyone for dessert?'

STUART/VINCE/PHIL/ALEXANDER/DANE: No thanks.

3/17 INT. CANAL STREET, NIGHT 4 2140   3/17
STUART, ALEXANDER, DANE, VINCE, PHIL, LEE

All now walking to the next pub, Canal Street crowded on a Saturday. STUART, ALEXANDER, DANE and LEE are ahead, laughing, while VINCE and PHIL are lagging behind, a quieter conversation. Throughout, every so often, they nod or say hello to blokes they know, and eye up blokes they don't know, without interrupting the conversation.

VINCE: Pity, though. I've said for ages, you and Alexander, then he turns up with Fu Manchu.

PHIL: Dane's quite nice.

VINCE: Oh d'you think? And he's rich.

PHIL: Is he?

VINCE: Stinking rich, richer than Stuart. He invented this software – hiya – he did this program, Microsoft bought it for 300,000 quid.

PHIL: No! And look at him!

VINCE: Worth a try, Phil.

PHIL: I don't stand a chance. He's all tight T-shirts and thin, I'm eating for two. No chance. (Beat) Is Dane the one shagged Stuart and wet the bed?

VINCE: No, that was David. Damp David.

PHIL: Would you shag him? Stuart?

VINCE: Oh get off! Imagine the next morning, wouldn't be able to look at each other.

PHIL: What, cos you've had sex?

VINCE: Yeah.

PHIL: So having sex means you can't look someone in the eye?

VINCE: Can do, yeah.

PHIL: So this way, you get to look at him all the time – Barney! What a shirt! Get an outside aerial, you could fix that.

PHIL stays with BARNEY, VINCE walks on, disconcerted by the conversation.

3/18 EXT. CANAL STREET, NIGHT 4 2200   3/18
NATHAN, DONNA

Bring up caption: 2200
    A black cab pulls up at the Rembrandt, NATHAN and DONNA – changed into night-out clothes – get out (and don't pay, it's on account).

NATHAN: If there's blokes kissing, right, don't stare at them, and if you see men who look like women don't stare at them either, and if you see Stuart, right, don't even look at him – that's if he's there, he won't be there, prob'ly, just don't look.

3/19 INT. NEW UNION, NIGHT 4 2220   3/19
STUART, VINCE, PHIL, ALEXANDER, DANE, DONNA, NATHAN, BERNARD, HAZEL, LEE, STUNNING MAN

STUART, VINCE, PHIL, ALEXANDER, DANE and LEE all standing round, the Union very busy, Roxy Hart on stage. PHIL's trying DANE, now.

PHIL: What d'you think? Feeling lucky?

DANE: Manchester, it's the dregs of humanity, I wouldn't shag one of 'em.

PHIL: ...no, s'pose not.

STUART: Jesus Christ, look at that.

All turn, their POV: A MAN. He is *beautiful.* Lots of people staring.

ALEXANDER: Oo, I'd stick my head up his arse and wear him like a hat.

LEE: *Nante kakkoii yatu.*

Bring up subtitle: 'I'd give him one!'

STUART: Well that's my night sorted, what are you lot going to do?

HAZEL: This place, they let anyone in!

She's greeting ALEXANDER and DANE, knows them of old.

ALEXANDER: Call security, the bitch has got free! Guards, restrain her!

HAZEL: Come here, put your arms around a woman for once. (Laughing, hugs him)

CUT TO – NATHAN and DONNA, hidden across the pub. They've got a drink. NATHAN's just staring at STUART, sullen.

DONNA: Oy, you said don't look. He's not that nice anyway, thought he was taller. You could do much better –

Suddenly, NATHAN's moving across the pub, not towards the BOYS. DONNA has to follow. He's on a path to intercept HAZEL, who's left the BOYS and is going back to BERNARD's table. NATHAN and DONNA arrive at the same time. (BERNARD doesn't remember NATHAN at all.)

NATHAN: Hello.

HAZEL: Who the fuck are you?

Which makes BERNARD laugh and laugh.

NATHAN: Right, I'm a friend of Vince's, I was in with him, me and him and Stuart, in here, the other night. (Beat) I'm Nathan, this is Donna.

HAZEL: You've met Bernard, then?

BERNARD: (Still laughing) 'Who the fuck are you?' Hazel, what are you like?

HAZEL: (Laughing at BERNARD laughing) I don't hang about, me. Nathan love, park yourself or shift yourself, you're spoiling the view, I've bet Bernie ten quid he won't cop off.

CUT TO – STUART. He's playing to his audience of VINCE, PHIL and DANE (ALEXANDER and LEE are now permanently snogging in front of everyone), STUART staring at the MAN, who's some distance away. Intense concentration.

Every time the MAN turns his head, about to get eye contact, he turns back again. Chat in B/G:

> PHIL: Listen, Stuart doesn't have the copyright on shagging, get in there first.

> VINCE: I wouldn't stand a chance.

> PHIL: Oh shut up, if you could just see yourself –

> VINCE: What is this, have-a-go-at-Vince night? (Suddenly sees:) I don't believe it, Stuart!

Turning STUART's look 180 degrees, to see NATHAN and DONNA, returning to HAZEL and BERNARD with drinks.

> VINCE: It's that Nathan, he's talking to my bloody mother, what's he doing?

> STUART: Nothing to do with me.

> VINCE: This always happens, I always get the shit. You shag him and he ends up stalking me.

> STUART: Leave him alone, he's all right.

VINCE does a big, mock-staggered reaction, to PHIL, then back to STUART.

> VINCE: He's all right? *He's all right?* I beg your pardon, he's what?

> STUART: Oh button it. (Spins round to see that the MAN has gone) Shit! Fuck, where's he gone? Shit! That bastard Nathan!

> VINCE: That's more like it.

3/19A INT. NEW UNION, NIGHT 4 2330   3/19A
VINCE, ROSALIE, STUART, PHIL, ALEXANDER, DANE, DONNA, NATHAN, BERNARD, HAZEL, LEE

VINCE at the bar, waiting to be served.

> ROSALIE: Oh my God, Vince! What are you doing here?

He turns, mortified to see ROSALIE. She's a bit pissed, friends in B/G.

> VINCE: …hi.

> ROSALIE: I'm here with Lucy, she's getting married next week, she said, come and have a look – what's it like, this place!

> VINCE: Yeah, I'm just looking, first time I've, uh – bit of a shock, isn't it?

ROSALIE: All those pretty boys, you watch yourself. They'll try and turn you!

VINCE: Yeah, I'm sick of it, really, I've seen enough.

ROSALIE: Oh go on, have a drink with me –

VINCE: No, I'm going, thanks, nice to see you –

ROSALIE: See you then –

And inspired by alcohol, she gives him a little kiss on the cheek. VINCE smiles, embarrassed, and goes. Follow him back to the BOYS. He keeps his voice down, tries to look as if he's not with them.

VINCE: Work alert, we're going, see you outside. (To STUART) It's that bloody Rosalie, this place is getting so straight.

STUART: Hang on.

VINCE watches, horrified, as STUART crosses over to ROSALIE.

STUART: 'Scuse me, it's Rosalie, yeah?

ROSALIE: That's me!

STUART: Friend of Vince's. Just wanted to say. (He leans in, like a kiss, whispers) He really likes you.

CUT TO – VINCE, watching. He can't hear, but he can guess, especially as ROSALIE looks over to him, delighted.

VINCE: Bastard.

VINCE smiles weakly at ROSALIE, grabs his jacket and goes.

CUT TO – NATHAN watching VINCE go, STUART crossing back to PHIL, ALEXANDER, DANE and LEE, all grabbing their jackets, about to follow. Under this, DONNA's chatting to HAZEL and BERNARD.

DONNA: Cos school, right, they all go to this pub on the corner, like it's clever, and they all sit there drinking cider, like it's so grown-up, they haven't got a clue, they'd die in here –

NATHAN: (Suddenly stands) Right, we'd better go, s'pose they're all off clubbing. (Beat. Casual) Where does Vince go?

HAZEL: Saturday night, that's Babylon.

NATHAN: Yeah. Might go there.

BERNARD: Got membership?

NATHAN: ...d'you need membership?

BERNARD: (Digs out his key-ring) Have it, keep it, I'm sick of it, sod them. Show it at the door, you can sign her in. If they ask, your name's Bernard Thomas.

3/20 INT. BABYLON DOORWAY, NIGHT 4 2344   3/20
NATHAN, DONNA, MAN AT DESK

CU on the key-ring bar-code being passed under a scanner.

MAN AT DESK: Name?

NATHAN: (Nervous, DONNA at his side) Bernard Thomas.

MAN AT DESK: (Looks at computer) Date of birth, 1946, looking good, Bernard. Eight quid.

3/21 INT. BABYLON, NIGHT 4 2345   3/21
NATHAN, DONNA, STUART, VINCE, PHIL, ALEXANDER, DANE, LEE

As NATHAN and DONNA walk down the stairs, bring up caption: 2345
     NATHAN's wide-eyed, seeing Babylon in all its glory (a big, wide club, packed out, 75% men, music a good mix of Hi NRG and chart-orientated house). As they reach the bottom of the stairs, a WOMAN slaps a label on them, a shag-tag, NATHAN 975, DONNA 976. NATHAN barely notices, transfixed by men, all around, handsome, fit, available. He's in sensory overload (though equally, scared of all this). DONNA's more interested in watching NATHAN, then:

DONNA: Drink?

NATHAN: ...yeah.

DONNA: Coke?

NATHAN just nods. She goes to the bar. NATHAN keeps looking all around, then looks at the dance-floor. STUART's dancing with VINCE, laughing, both on poppers. (STUART's the only one not wearing a shag-tag; no need.)
     On NATHAN. Just staring.
     CUT TO – ALEXANDER, making his way through the crowd, looking for LEE, heading from the front of the club to the back. DANE and PHIL are heading the opposite way, alarmed to see him.

ALEXANDER: You seen Lee anywhere? I've lost him, he's wandered off.

DANE: He's not down here.

PHIL: Try over there, come with us.

ALEXANDER: (Pushes past them) He can't speak English, he'll get lost –

Suspicious of DANE and PHIL's alarm, ALEXANDER presses on, turning the corner to the alcove where the cloakroom is. ALEXANDER stops dead. He sees LEE, snogging madly with some BLOKE. On ALEXANDER, horrified.

3/22 INT. SANDRA'S BEDROOM, NIGHT 4 2352   3/22
SANDRA, NS HUSBAND

Darkness. We should have no idea where we are; just a phone, ringing in the foreground. Behind that, a man and a woman are having sex, heaving under the duvet. But the phone keeps ringing, and eventually a body emerges from the duvet. As she picks up the phone, she simultaneously switches on a table lamp, and we see that it's SANDRA.

    SANDRA: Yes?

3/23 INT. BABYLON, NIGHT 4 2352   3/23
ALEXANDER

ALEXANDER's distraught (using STUART's mobile).

    ALEXANDER: What's the Japanese for slut??

3/24 INT. BABYLON TOILETS, NIGHT 4 0020   3/24
STUART, VINCE

In a cubicle, which shudders with the bass line, pure noise. STUART snorts a line of coke, steps back, VINCE takes his place. (Moments like this, close, happy, STUART's intimate with VINCE, rubs his back; casual, tender gestures.)

    STUART: Oh, nice.

    VINCE: It's off Mickey Blake, he can get anything, he got me
    speed an all – (Snorts) And he got me episode three of *Planet of*
    the Daleks in colour, the BBC's only got that in black and white
    cos they burnt it, but Mickey Blake, you just have to ask, he said
    he can get episode four of *The Tenth Planet*, that's a classic, no
    one's seen it since 1966.

STUART's smiling; he loves VINCE when he's like this.

    STUART: There are no words for how sad you are.

3/25 INT. BABYLON, NIGHT 4 0030   3/25
DONNA, NATHAN, STUART, VINCE, PHIL, ALEXANDER, DANE, LEE,
BEAUTIFUL MAN, STUNNING MAN

DONNA at the shag-tag board, collecting messages for 975.
    CUT TO – DONNA arriving back at NATHAN's side.

    DONNA: Look, you've got two, this one's filthy, you're not
    meeting him! But look at this one - 975, can I buy you a drink?
    From 373. Go on then, find him!

NATHAN: (Looking for STUART) I'm not bothered.

DONNA: S'what you came for, innit? 373 might be our age, that Stuart, he's ancient. Go on!

Reluctantly, NATHAN takes the message, heads off.

CUT TO – NATHAN's POV. His eyes flick from chest to chest, number to number, a blur of men. And then we stop, on 373. Look up to 373's face, who's already looking at NATHAN, expectant. A nice, smiling man. But 50, *huge*. NATHAN's frozen, mortified. Then he turns, walks away, fast, ripping off his number. He hurries back to DONNA, whispers in her ear, indicates 373, and both burst into fits of laughter. On poor 373, trying to turn away with dignity.

CUT TO – STUART, VINCE, PHIL, ALEXANDER and DANE together at the side; we're on STUART, looking round, radar at work, dialogue in B/G.

ALEXANDER: Bastard fucking Jap, I'm taking out economic sanctions, that Yoji suit is going straight back. I'm copping off tonight if it kills me.

STUART: Yes!

CUT TO – the BEAUTIFUL MAN's on the dance floor, incandescent in the light. A vision. CUT TO – STUART watching, the BOYS grouped around.

VINCE: Oh shit, he's back again. (NATHAN and DONNA far off, watching STUART) He really is stalking us, this is getting creepy.

PHIL: What, cos he goes to Babylon? Oh yeah, that's so unusual.

On STUART, watching the BEAUTIFUL MAN.

ALEXANDER: Oh my God look, there's a better one.

Across the dance floor – far away from the BEAUTIFUL MAN, nothing to do with him – is a STUNNING MAN, dancing with some bloke. STUART walks forward (to the rail, if there is one), leaving ALEXANDER, to look at STUNNING MAN. VINCE walks forward so he's standing next to STUART – PHIL, ALEXANDER, DANE still present but B/G. And it's at this point, two old friends looking at a STUNNING MAN, that the scene begins to become magic. The intensity of the moment is such that the music falls away; VINCE doesn't need to speak above the noise of the music as he would in a normal nightclub scene. His voice can be soft, even regretful, connecting with STUART even though he's not looking at him, both staring at STUNNING MAN. A profoundly private moment between the two of them. Like they're at the eye of a storm.

VINCE: Sometimes you see these men. You can see them, and you think, that's it, that's *him*. You don't even talk to him, you never see him again. He doesn't even know you exist. But you think about that man for the rest of your life.

STUART looks at VINCE; a gentle smile. Hold the look. And then, it's like STUART is doing this *for* VINCE; STUART gives VINCE a kiss on the forehead, then starts his walk. (The club music's at its best, epic and holy, like a cathedral interior (maybe O.T Quartet, 'Hold That Sucker Down', Builds Like A Skyscraper mix); but at the same time, imperceptibly at first, a chord of incidental music is rising above the club tracks, lifting the moment, heightening it. Our focus on the characters is changing, like CUs on a long lens. The sheer magic of clubbing; dialogue hushed, reverential. STUART walks forward, on to the dance floor, the only one not dancing. He goes up to STUNNING MAN. From VINCE's POV: STUART talks to STUNNING MAN, touches him lightly on the arm; all those tiny copping-off gestures. And STUNNING MAN's smiling too. On VINCE. PHIL, ALEXANDER and DANE stay B/G, just audible, part of the crowd. VINCE pays them no attention, transfixed, somehow knowing that STUART hasn't finished yet.

ALEXANDER: Bastard.

PHIL: He doesn't even have to try.

But their cynicism falls away as they watch STUART's next move. All from their POV: STUART gestures towards the BEAUTIFUL MAN, 'come here'. BEAUTIFUL MAN hesitates. STUART just smiles. And BEAUTIFUL MAN walks over to STUART and STUNNING MAN.
CUT TO – VINCE, PHIL, ALEXANDER and DANE watching. Gobsmacked; not comedy reactions, genuinely overawed, falling into the spell.
Their POV: STUART talking to BEAUTIFUL MAN and STUNNING MAN, achieving an instant intimacy, whispering. Voiced hushed:

ALEXANDER: He's not.

DANE: He can't.

VINCE: (utterly calm) He can.

CUT TO – NATHAN and DONNA, and their POV of STUART; caught in the same suspension, people witnessing a miracle.

DONNA: He's not having them both…?

NATHAN: (Calm) You don't understand.

CUT TO – their POV of STUART, BEAUTIFUL MAN and STUNNING MAN. He's putting his arm round one, then shifts to the other. All smiling.
CUT TO – the BOYS, and their POV of STUART. And now, there's a light creeping in; literally, a golden light, surrounding them, other colours slowly bleaching away. PHIL joins VINCE, quiet.

PHIL: What does he say to them…?

VINCE: If we knew that. If we knew the magic words. But he says them for all of us.

CUT TO – their POV of STUART. He leans in, kisses BEAUTIFUL MAN on the cheek, then STUNNING MAN.
CUT TO – CU NATHAN (losing DONNA). He's staring, no jealousy, just awestruck.

CUT TO – his POV of STUART, BEAUTIFUL MAN and STUNNING MAN, all three laughing, intimate, like they're lovers already.

CUT TO – even closer on NATHAN, the light around him intensifying, colours bleaching as we MIX TO:

3/25A INT. STUART'S FLAT, EP.1 NIGHT 1 0500   3/25A
STUART

Not a real flashback, an idealisation. The camera is NATHAN's POV on that night, MCU on STUART above us, staring down, intense, like we're actually in mid-fuck. The image shines with the same light that's filling the club scene, so there's barely any transition between locations. His voice is solemn, hypnotic.

> STUART: No one. No one else has nights like this. No one else has a life like this.

MIX TO:

3/25B INT. BABYLON, NIGHT 4 0130   3/25B
(CONT. FROM 3/25)
DONNA, NATHAN, STUART, VINCE, PHIL, ALEXANDER, DANE, JONATHAN, O'HAGAN, LEE, BEAUTIFUL MAN, STUNNING MAN

CU NATHAN, the light intensifying, STUART cont. as V/O:

> STUART V/O: ...Home, and work, and family, they're nothing. Just nights like this, night after night after night.

CUT TO – NATHAN's POV of STUART, BEAUTIFUL MAN and STUNNING MAN.

V/O continues, build the light, club music falling away as the chord grows stronger, binding them all together. As we cut back to the club, the BOYS are now so immersed in the moment, they're dancing, joyous. It's as if the magic's spreading out, all of them copping off.

CUT TO – CU VINCE. He's dancing, happy, looks across the dance-floor.

CUT TO – VINCE's POV. JONATHAN, 32, not that handsome but nice. Dancing, smiling at VINCE. VINCE smiles back.

CUT TO – CU ALEXANDER. He's dancing, happy, looks across.

CUT TO – ALEXANDER's POV. O'HAGAN, tall, strong, dancing. He catches ALEXANDER's eye, then turns.

CUT TO – O'HAGAN's POV. DANE, dancing, happy for once. O'HAGAN seems to be happy with DANE *and* ALEXANDER.

CUT TO – CU NATHAN.

> STUART V/O: Hundreds of boys. Thousands of boys. The world is wide and wild and it's turning so fast, all we can do is hold on tight. Take hold of them all. All those beautiful boys.

MIX TO: STUART, BEAUTIFUL MAN and STUNNING MAN as the light finally burns, floods the screen, white out, the words falling away into the void:

> STUART V/O: A world of beautiful boys...

From white, MIX TO:

3/26 EXT. CANAL STREET, NIGHT 4 0210   3/26
NATHAN, DONNA

Bring up caption: 0210
    Dissolving into a wide-shot of the street, to get us back to normality, men heading off into the night (nothing raucous; everything seems calmer, now).
    CUT TO – NATHAN and DONNA sitting on the canal wall. The previous sequence has made NATHAN grow up a bit: he's quiet, a faint smile.

> DONNA: He cops off with anyone, that Stuart, he'll be riddled. You're better off without.

> NATHAN: You saw him. He's the best. (Looks at her, smiles) I've had the best. (Beat) Let's go home.

> DONNA: Naah, let's get chips.

They walk off. As they walk, NATHAN takes DONNA's hand.

3/27 INT. HALLWAY O/S STUART'S FLAT, NIGHT 4 0230   3/27
STUART, BEAUTIFUL MAN, STUNNING MAN

STUART's snogging one man, then the other, then back to the first, all the time trying to get his keys out and open the door. Finally, he manages it, kicks the door open, shoves them through, follows, grinning.

3/28 INT. VINCE'S FLAT, NIGHT 4 0231   3/28
VINCE, JONATHAN

VINCE leads JONATHAN in.

> JONATHAN: Nice place, what's this again? Fallowfield?

> VINCE: Yeah.

> JONATHAN: Don't know my way round yet, I've only been here two months, I'm at the BBC.

> VINCE
> Oh, doing what?

> JONATHAN: Director, on the *Travel Show*. It's not bad, I've just spent two weeks in South America with Duffy from *Casualty*.

> VINCE: Oh fantastic! Brilliant! Oh my God! Um, drink?

> JONATHAN: Uhh, got a gin and tonic?

> VINCE: Yup! Sit yourself down.

VINCE hurries to the cupboard, chuffed. Success!

3/29 INT. O'HAGAN'S STAIRWELL, NIGHT 4 0235   3/29
DANE, ALEXANDER, O'HAGAN

A dank stairwell in a miserable house-converted-to-flats. O'HAGAN leads the way; he now seems more grim and brutish (and not Irish at all). ALEXANDER and DANE follow him up the stairs, muttering to each other.

> ALEXANDER: Oh for fuck's sake, stop your moaning. If you fancy a threesome at this time of night, you can't start getting choosy about which particular three. We'll cope. We can cope. So long as we don't touch each other.

> DANE: Never mind touching, I don't want you even looking.

> ALEXANDER: I've got to look, I might end up sucking the wrong cock. And don't you suck mine.

> DANE: I've no intention.

3/30 INT. O'HAGAN'S FLAT, NIGHT 4 0237   3/30
ALEXANDER, DANE, O'HAGAN

O'HAGAN, without a word, shows ALEXANDER and DANE in. On their reaction: the flat is a tip. Filthy. A cooked chicken carcass on top of the TV. They turn as O'HAGAN locks the door behind them. Big bunch of keys; one lock, then another, then another, then a chain, then the bolts, and a final lock. ALEXANDER and DANE look at each other. Terrified.

3/31 EXT. OXFORD ROAD, NIGHT 4 0238   3/31
PHIL, HARVEY

PHIL's hailing a taxi. One stops – not a black cab, a private hire car. He runs for it, but another bloke thinks it's his, also goes for it. This is HARVEY – 20s, denim, a bit rough but still sexy.

> PHIL: Sorry, was that yours?

> HARVEY: (Laughs) Dunno.

> PHIL: Have it.

> HARVEY: (Smiles, looks at PHIL, copping off) Saw you in Babylon. Where you going?

> PHIL: Withington.

> HARVEY: And me. Go halves?

And on that, we're on CU HARVEY, unnaturally close, and then CU PHIL, the moment heightened; PHIL's fate decided in this small, casual moment.

> PHIL: ...okay.

3/32 INT. VINCE'S FLAT, NIGHT 4 0245   3/32
VINCE, JONATHAN

JONATHAN and VINCE sitting together, finishing their drinks. Awkward silence, both smiling. It's that moment, for VINCE, when you're not quite sure if you *have* copped off. But then JONATHAN leans in, kisses him. Nice, quick kiss, then JONATHAN leans back.

> JONATHAN: Sorry, got to piss.

> VINCE: S'okay.

JONATHAN runs off, VINCE is straight on to his mobile. It rings, answerphone, he waits, excited, then:

> VINCE: (Whispers) You're not going to believe this!

3/33 INT. STUART'S FLAT, NIGHT 4 0245   3/33
STUART, STUNNING MAN, BEAUTIFUL MAN

VINCE's voice on the answerphone, as a naked STUART comes out of the bedroom (we can see the men, naked on the bed). He pays no attention to VINCE's V/O, goes to a cupboard, pulls out a camcorder and tripod, hurries back to the bedroom, slams the door on us.

> VINCE V/O: He's really nice, he's nice-looking and everything, and he works in telly! He's met Ruby Wax, he's got her home telephone number and he's not lying, he's for real!

3/35 INT. O'HAGAN'S FLAT, NIGHT 4 0250   3/35
ALEXANDER, DANE, O'HAGAN

ALEXANDER and DANE sitting on the manky settee, terrified of O'HAGAN. He's in an armchair opposite; he talks right at them, intense, staring. Halfway through this, he knocks his coffee over. But he keeps talking; the coffee runs off the table, on to the floor, he makes no move to pick it up. ALEXANDER and DANE transfixed with horror.

> O'HAGAN: Cos you stitch the mouth up, but the *eye*. The eye opens. The eye on a corpse falls open. The relatives, they're in the Chapel of Rest, they want dignity. So you get this contact lens. It's got spikes, sharp little spikes on the surface. You put in the lens. Slap down the eyelid. Spikes dig in. Sticks it shut. (Looks at his watch) Right, I'll wash me knob.

He walks out. ALEXANDER and DANE, frozen.

> DANE: He's Fred West.

3/35 INT. PHIL'S HOUSE, NIGHT 4 0251   3/35
PHIL, HARVEY

PHIL and HARVEY walk in. The house is nicely done out, though middle-aged, a hint of antimacassar. PHIL's a bit nervous, HARVEY at ease – we can see he's a bit rougher than he seemed at first. Wired.

> HARVEY: Hey. You've done all right.

> PHIL: Well, I work from home, so. I like it to be nice. D'you want a drink?

> HARVEY: I'll have water. What d'you do, then?

During this, PHIL takes off his jacket, puts his wallet on the fridge, as he always does, while HARVEY sits at the table, starts rooting through his pockets.

> PHIL: Oh it's boring, really. It's like editing, it's this project, co-ordinating market aspects of third-world debt. Boring.

> HARVEY: (Takes out a paper wrap) Don't mind, do you? It's good stuff.

> PHIL: ...no, fine.

> HARVEY: Can I stay the night?

> PHIL: Yeah. (Beat) Um. Right, water. I'll have a beer.

PHIL goes to get the drinks; he feels so middle-aged, out of his depth, but won't show it.

3/36 INT. VINCE'S FLAT, NIGHT 4 0252   3/36
JONATHAN, VINCE

JONATHAN and VINCE, heavy snogging on the settee. Both pause to pull their shirts off, fast, laughing, get back to snogging. JONATHAN negotiates himself on top of VINCE. JONATHAN's jeans are already undone, VINCE starts to slide them down his arse. JONATHAN hoists them back up. Snog. VINCE slides them down again, JONATHAN slides them up. JONATHAN stops snogging, looks down at VINCE, serious.

> JONATHAN: I'd better warn you. (Pause) If you ever go to Brazil. If you find yourself in Brazil and you go to the beach, sit on a towel.

> VINCE: ...right.

> JONATHAN: Cos they've got these things. (Beat) They've got parasites that live in the sand, and they... *burrow*, they burrow up through the sand, and they, sort of... burrow themselves into you. I mean, you can kill them, with this ointment, but it takes a while.

> VINCE: So...?

> JONATHAN: So I've got Brazilian beach parasites living in my arse.

Silence. Then both with sad smiles:

JONATHAN: Shall I get a taxi?

3/37 INT. O'HAGAN'S FLAT, NIGHT 4 0253   3/37
ALEXANDER, DANE, O'HAGAN

ALEXANDER and DANE trying to open the window, frantic.

ALEXANDER: It's locked –

DANE: We're two floors up, anyway –

They hear the bathroom door, turn round sharpish, pretend innocence.
O'HAGAN lumbers back in.

O'HAGAN: Let's get on with it, I'm burying a bride and groom
at ten.

DANE: Yes! I'll just, bathroom, can I?

O'HAGAN: Hurry up, then.

DANE runs to the bathroom. ALEXANDER smiles at O'HAGAN. He doesn't smile
back.

3/38 INT. O'HAGAN'S BATHROOM, NIGHT 4 0254   3/38
DANE

DANE, desperate, tries the bathroom window. It opens! He climbs out, fast as he
can.

3/39 INT. O'HAGAN'S FLAT, NIGHT 4 0255   3/39
O'HAGAN, ALEXANDER, DANE

O'HAGAN's just standing in front of ALEXANDER.

O'HAGAN: Make a start.

O'HAGAN starts to unbutton his jeans. As he does this, he leans his head back,
eyes closed, groans, keeps unbuttoning, nice and slow.
ALEXANDER's POV: behind O'HAGAN, he can see DANE, outside the
window, shuffling along some sort of ledge. Trying to hold on, DANE frantically
gesticulates and mouths to ALEXANDER, 'bathroom', 'window'.
From O'HAGAN's gesture, we can take it that he's just got his cock out.
ALEXANDER looks down at O'HAGAN's crotch.
He can't believe his eyes.
He looks at DANE, at O'HAGAN's crotch, at DANE, at O'HAGAN. Then he
smiles, flicks his hand at DANE, meaning 'go away'.
On DANE, horrified.
ALEXANDER kneels in front of O'HAGAN.
DANE topples back, a soundless scream, drops out of sight.

3/40 INT. VINCE'S FLAT, NIGHT 4   0310   3/40
VINCE

VINCE now alone. He's reverted to sitting in his dressing gown watching some
American porn – which he's ignoring, on the phone:

>VINCE: Bastards, all of 'em! Not just bastards, diseased bastards!

3/41 INT. STUART'S FLAT, NIGHT 4 0310   3/41
STUART, BEAUTIFUL MAN, STUNNING MAN

Footage on the TV: grainy camcorder stuff of bare, writhing flesh. STUART's face
surfaces: he's coming. Then he disappears back into the skin.
  CUT TO – STUART and the men, draped across the settee, and each other.
Still idealised; like some classy photo-shoot, naked but entwined with a silk sheet,
etc. All three exhausted, blissful. They just watch the TV, VINCE as V/O on the
answerphone.

>VINCE V/O: You're not going to believe what he told me! I've
>had some stories, but *this* one! Bastard! (Sadder) Oh and he was
>*nice*, he was really nice, he's like the bloke I've been waiting for.
>He was lovely. All of him was lovely. The entire colony.

3/41A INT. VINCE'S FLAT, NIGHT 4 0311   3/41A
(CONT. FROM 3/40)
VINCE

VINCE switches off the telly. Alone, a little plaintive.

>VINCE: Anyway. Bet you're having a good time. Give us a call.
>Lots of love.

He hangs up, just sits there.

3/42 INT. PHIL'S HOUSE, NIGHT 4   0311   3/42
PHIL, HARVEY

PHIL and HARVEY at the table. PHIL's had a beer, delaying him, but now
HARVEY's lined up the white powder for snorting, a generous line for PHIL. It's
heroin; PHIL has no idea, presuming it's coke, tries to act as though he does this
all the time.

>HARVEY: Thaaat's it... (Hands PHIL a tube of rolled-up card) Go
>on, have a go. You paid for the taxi.

>PHIL: Okay, yeah. (He hesitates)

>HARVEY: Jake sold it me, he's a top lad, Jake. Quality.

>PHIL: Good old Jake.

He snorts it.

HARVEY: Thaaat's it.

PHIL sits back.

HARVEY: How's that?

PHIL: S'okay.

HARVEY: Yeah? (Watches PHIL) Should do more than that. If he's sold me shit –

PHIL: Ged some water – (Stands) Woah –

He staggers across the kitchen. Because in an *instant,* he's sweating, tons of cold sweat pouring off him, and he's shaking like mad. HARVEY's on his feet, unsurprised, goes to PHIL at the sink.

HARVEY: All right, mate, first time, s'always like this –

PHIL: Juss – water.

PHIL suddenly collapses to the floor, a dead weight. HARVEY goes to help him, but PHIL's neck is floppy, his eyes rolling around.

HARVEY: (Frightened) Jesus Christ, what you doing? Come here, it's all right, mate, it's all right –

He tries to help him up, but PHIL's suddenly worse. It's a hypoxic fit – for five seconds, his body tenses up completely, then 20 seconds of shuddering violently, PHIL jerking like some kid's toy, out of control, now beyond speech. HARVEY tries to grab hold, terrified.

HARVEY: Shit, shit, shit, what you doing, what the fuck you doing – ?

Then PHIL subsides, lies there, small twitches, little choking noises. HARVEY just stands there, scared to death. He stares. Then HARVEY moves fast. He grabs his stuff, his jacket, runs out. Hold on the empty kitchen, small convulsions from PHIL. Then HARVEY comes back. Still scared, acting off adrenalin. He goes to PHIL's wallet, takes out the cash, stops, thinks, leaves a fiver in there, runs out. We hear the slam of the front door. On a wide shot of the kitchen,
MIX TO: black. Bring up the caption: SUNDAY
MIX TO:

3/43 INT. VIA FOSSA, DAY 5 1150   3/43
STUART, VINCE, ALEXANDER, DANE

Coming straight in on STUART, VINCE, ALEXANDER and DANE in Via Fossa, having breakfast, all laughing. DANE's got his arm in a sling. Which they find hysterical.

DANE: It's not remotely funny, you're all bastards.

ALEXANDER: And I swear! Cock like a baby's arm! He sprained his wrist, I sprained my arse!

STUART: Dane, you're such a twat.

VINCE: That is brilliant, that is so brilliant!

They're just hooting with laughter.

3/44 INT. ROMEY'S HOUSE, DAY 5 1359   3/44
ROMEY, BABY ALFRED

ROMEY, carrying ALFRED, hears the doorbell ring, goes to answer it.

3/45 EXT. ROMEY'S HOUSE, DAY 5 1400   3/45
ROMEY, BABY ALFRED

ROMEY, with ALFRED, opens the door, but there's no one there. Just a box of chocolates on the step, a 2lb box of Milk Tray. She picks it up, puzzled. No message.

3/46 EXT. DIDSBURY ROAD, DAY 5 1405   3/46
NATHAN

NATHAN runs down the street, fast as he can – not running away, just getting the exhilaration of running. He's happy and he's young; sunlight on his face.

3/47 INT. AIRPORT, DAY 5 1600   3/47

STUART and VINCE waving as the boys walk through to the departure lounge. Then they walk off together, glad that their guests have gone.
     MIX TO: black. Bring up the caption: MONDAY
     MIX TO:

3/48 INT. PHIL'S HOUSE, DAY 6 0930   3/48
PHIL

Unchanged, PHIL lying there. The beep of the answerphone, then a woman's voice, HARRIET, 40.

HARRIET V/O: Phil, it's me. Listen, you promised that stuff first thing, can you e-mail it, Jamie's going mad. And Carolyn needs a copy, you'll have to fax it, she's working from home. Soon as you can, thanks, give us a call, bye.

MIX TO:

3/49 EXT. PHIL'S HOUSE, DAY 6, 0931   3/49

The MILKMAN leaves a bottle outside PHIL's house.
     CUT TO – two houses down. A more run-down house than PHIL's, evidently a student house, posters in the front windows. Two STUDENTS, a man and a woman, come out of the house, slope along.

The MALE STUDENT looks around, grabs PHIL's bottle of milk, goes on his way, swigging it down.

MIX TO: black. Bring up caption. TUESDAY

MIX TO:

3/50 INT. HARLO'S FOOD HALL, DAY 7 1000   3/50
VINCE

VINCE at work. Trying not to be seen by a supervisor, he's on his mobile.

VINCE: Oo Phil, lots of beeps, you're popular. You gone to London? Listen, if you're back tomorrow, it's that charity thing at Via Fossa, should be a laugh, we'll be there about nine, see you!

MIX TO: black. Bring up the caption: WEDNESDAY

MIX TO:

3/51 INT. PHIL'S HOUSE, DAY 8 1400   3/51

On the corpse.

MIX TO: black. Bring in the caption. THURSDAY

MIX TO:

3/52 INT. VIA FOSSA, NIGHT 9 2100   3/52
VINCE, STUART

VINCE and STUART in the thick of it, with a crowd of friends. VINCE's mobile rings, he recognises the number, answers.

VINCE: Philip Delaney, where the fuck have you been?

3/53 INT. PHIL'S HOUSE, NIGHT 9 2240   3/53
MRS DELANEY

MCU MRS DELANEY, on the phone. She's trying to hold on, to be normal.

MRS DELANEY: Is that Vince?

3/54 INT. VIA FOSSA INTERCUT WITH PHIL'S HOUSE, NIGHT 9 2241   3/54
VINCE, STUART/MRS DELANEY

VINCE moves to get some quiet, the crowd behind him. Intercut as and when.

VINCE: Yeah, who's that – sorry, that's Phil's number, isn't it?

MRS DELANEY: It's his mother.

VINCE: Oh, right, sorry – how are you? I thought – is Phil there?

As MRS DELANEY talks, we see a wider shot of the kitchen. It's now bare, the body gone, discovered hours ago, the room bare, things taken away for forensics. In B/G, a uniformed WPC is making tea, MRS DELANEY's only companion. MRS

DELANEY's speech is fractured, all over the place.

> MRS DELANEY: It's the phone. He's got numbers programmed into the phone. I thought I'd better start …

> VINCE: (Worried) There's nothing wrong, is there…?

> MRS DELANEY: They phoned me this morning. The police. (It hits her. She starts to cry, like she can't breathe) They're saying it was days ago.

> VINCE: What is it, what's happened…?

And now we stay on VINCE, as she tells him.

Hold on VINCE. Hold and hold and hold. His face.

Suddenly STUART dives into shot, running up from behind and grabbing VINCE, who's unresisting, stunned, still on the phone. STUART's full of life, off his head, gives VINCE a great big kiss on the cheek, and on that, mid-action –

Freeze.

EPISODE FOUR

PRE-CREDITS SEQUENCE

4/1 EXT. VILLAGE, DAY 9 1100   4/1
STUART, VINCE, OLD MAN

It should feel like we're in a different series; the crossroads at the centre of a quiet village in the south of England. Not too pretty, a bit run-down.

To one side there's a village pub. An OLD MAN, with his dog, carries his pint out to sit at one of those wooden bench-tables. As he sits, we get a good look at him; late 70s, shabby, tired. A miserable old sod. He's lived here all his life, never done anything or been anywhere.

We hear the music first, a distant beat. Getting louder. The OLD MAN looks up, sour-faced as the music resolves into Pulp's 'Common People', now surging to full volume, blasting out.

The OLD MAN's POV: a black jeep screeches up to the crossroads, stops. It's paused in the middle of the road while the two men inside work out directions. The OLD MAN stares, music still thundering away. The driver of the jeep is a handsome young man, his passenger and navigator a more ordinary bloke. The driver's laughing at some complaint from his passenger, ruffles his hair to annoy him further. Then the driver leans across to give the passenger a great big kiss on the cheek. The passenger's trying to be cross, but he's laughing.

The image is beautiful: two young men, shining and sharp. Urban creatures.

Then the jeep roars into action, turns, about to pass the OLD MAN. The driver's seen him, fixes on him. The OLD MAN can feel his stare, even from behind sunglasses. As the jeep passes, the driver grins, blows him a kiss.

Stay on the OLD MAN, his eyes never leaving the now OOV jeep as the music recedes, the village settling back into silence. There's no anger. He's shaken, eyes shining, transfixed by this fleeting vision. And for all his regrets – the things he never did, never said – he breaks into a smile; as though seeing those boys has made him somehow... *better.*

  CUT TO:

OPENING TITLES

4/2 EXT. CREMATORIUM CAR PARK, DAY 9 1120   4/2
STUART, VINCE, BERNARD, HAZEL

A wide, open space set aside for cars some distance from the crematorium; countryside all around, rolling hills. The jeep pulls up, STUART and VINCE get out, VINCE clutching two sheets of paper, his speech. STUART immediately starts pulling off his clothes, his black suit on a hanger in the back of the jeep. As if VINCE hasn't got enough to think about today, the speech is knotting him up.

> VINCE: Why's it got to be me? I didn't even know him that well, only went to his house twice. And I mean, who plans their own funeral, it's mad.

> STUART: You've done it.

VINCE: Like I said, it's mad.

The beep of a horn as a battered old MG arrives, BERNARD's pride and joy, BERNARD at the wheel, HAZEL his passenger, calling out:

HAZEL: Blown to buggery, would he put the roof up?

As the MG parks further down, VINCE turns to look at STUART, still undressing, not caring who sees him. He's taking off his jeans. VINCE cops a look. As he always does.

4/3 EXT. SCHOOL YARD, DAY 9 1121   4/3
CHRISTIAN, NATHAN, DONNA

Location unclear at first. On CHRISTIAN HOBBS, walking across the yard (if possible, not obviously in school uniform, he could be anywhere). He looks amazing, a fantasy, shot in slow-motion, sunlight behind him. Camera unashamedly travels down his body; lingering on the chest; then the crotch; back to the face. Then reveal the location as the school (other KIDS in B/G) as we CUT TO NATHAN and DONNA. Awestruck. They've been grading boys out of ten, so:

DONNA: Ohh, *ten.*

CHRISTIAN walks past (oblivious of their looks). Their POV lingers on his arse. They make each other laugh, deliberately childish.

NATHAN: Twenty.

DONNA: Twenty million!

NATHAN: Twenty billion!

The school bell rings, they grab their coats, bags, making each other laugh, deliberately childish.

DONNA: Infinity!

NATHAN: Infinity plus one!

The bell's swamped by the sound of a massive horn, blaring.

4/4 EXT. CREMATORIUM CAR PARK, DAY 9 1130   4/4
VINCE, STUART, HAZEL, BERNARD, ALEXANDER

VINCE, STUART, HAZEL and BERNARD – and other MOURNERS have arrived – all turning to look as they hear the horn, and an almighty engine.
    CUT TO – a huge pantechnicon, the biggest you can get, roaring up. The hiss of hydraulics as it brakes. ALEXANDER, in black suit, clambers down from the cab. STUART and VINCE head over, not at all surprised.

ALEXANDER: Don't ask! Disaster! Exit twelve of the M25, car stops dead, all the wheels fall off, thanks Shirley! Saved me life! See ya!

SHIRLEY's the driver, a 50-year-old butch woman in a baseball cap. She waves, sounds the horn, and the lorry heaves away.

> ALEXANDER: She's fab, worked as a bodyguard for the Aga Khan, took a bullet in '76, thought sod this for a game of soldiers, took to the road, never been home since, she's on the missing persons register, I think she's a man. Right, where's the do?

4/5 EXT. CREMATORIUM, DAY 9 1140   4/5
STUART, VINCE, ALEXANDER, BERNARD, HAZEL, MRS DELANEY

STUART, VINCE and ALEXANDER join the gathering of MOURNERS near the crematorium entrance. In front, the hearse has pulled up and the coffin's being carried in. Behind that, immediate family follow. MRS DELANEY's as composed as she can be. MR DELANEY's 60, a kindly, bluff man, desperately upset; she has to help him along. During this:

> VINCE: (Studying his papers) He has to pick on me, it's like he wanted me to look a twat.

> STUART: Not many people, I'm having thousands.

> VINCE: That's nothing to do with him, it's just the way he died. Car crash, cancer, everyone tips up. Heroin, it's all – (Draws air through teeth, 'dodgy') Like he's an addict or something.

> ALEXANDER: 90% pure, mind, what a way to go, fabulous – Oo, Colin! Thought I'd been to yours! (Goes to join COLIN)

The DELANEYS are just passing, and MRS DELANEY catches VINCE's eye. A sad smile between them and she walks on. But VINCE is unnerved – there's a certain conversation he's got to have with her today, which he dreads. As MRS DELANEY goes in, HAZEL and BERNARD appear.

> HAZEL: She's a bit luggage in advance.

> BERNARD: Very golf club.

> VINCE: It's her son's funeral, d'you mind?

> HAZEL: Good luck.

She gives VINCE a kiss on the cheek, which he shrugs off, awkward. HAZEL and BERNARD follow the MOURNERS into the crematorium, ALEXANDER going past.

> ALEXANDER: Come on! Get good seats!

VINCE and STUART are left alone.

> STUART: That's three of them. Magic Martin, John Baxter. Now good old Phil.

VINCE: Three of them what?

STUART: Three men I've shagged have died. Not a bad ratio, all things considered. Come on.

They head off. On VINCE: no visible reaction, just the amount of time we stay on him tells us that he's thrown by this. As they go, STUART's mobile phone rings, he answers.

4/6 INT. CREMATORIUM, DAY 9 1145   4/6
STUART, VINCE, HAZEL, BERNARD, ALEXANDER, MRS DELANEY, HANDSOME MAN

STUART and VINCE walk down the aisle – STUART on the phone, unabashed. VINCE follows, head still reeling from what STUART said. This is accompanied by soft organ music.

STUART: I can't, I'm at a funeral. I am! Sandra, listen, organ music, funeral, now don't bother me –

At that moment, the organ music is replaced by disco music over the PA system – something old and fabulously cheesy. Warm laughter from the congregation, getting the joke, STUART pissed off.

STUART: Course it's not a party, it's a bloody funeral, I can't help it if he was cheap. It's on my desk, cope without me – I *can't*, write it yourself! (Hangs up)

STUART and VINCE take their seats. In the pew in front, STUART clocks the eye of a HANDSOME MAN. HANDSOME MAN smiles, turns back to face front. STUART sits immediately behind him, and uses the rest of the dialogue in this scene to cop off with HANDSOME MAN, focused on the back of his head (and VINCE is well aware of this, is used to it).

STUART: I'm getting buried. People cry more at burials, I want them sobbing their guts out.

VINCE is casual, though he *has* to know. (And for all his dismay, he finds STUART so *horny* when he talks like this.)

VINCE: So when d'you have Phil, then?

STUART: That party, I told you. May the first, election night.

VINCE: Didn't think he was your type.

STUART: He's not, he was half lard. I was having that boy whatsisname, Winston, then everyone starts joining in, must've been six of us, Phil just threw himself on top.

VINCE: Phil never said. Thought he hated you.

STUART: He was all over me, he was snogging me, I was going, get off. Big Bob was in there somewhere.

VINCE: You've had Big Bob?

STUART: (Aimed right at HANDSOME MAN) If that's what he calls big, I'm colossus.

VINCE: Is there anyone you haven't had?

4/7 INT. SCHOOL CHANGING ROOM, DAY 9 1200   4/7
NATHAN, CHRISTIAN, MIDGE, PE TEACHER, MATE

Hard cut from VINCE's last remark to MCU NATHAN. He's almost fully dressed after a swimming lesson, packing his sports bag, BOYS all around doing the same, background chat. A weedy swot-boy, MIDGE, is next to NATHAN, packing his own bag and wittering away.

MIDGE: Y'know that homework, that Sealink ferries brochure thing – Sally Colasanto said they've got it in Thomas Cook, same brochure, it's on the shelves, you just walk in and pick it up. It's already in English, it's exactly the same, she checked it, it's like they've done the translation for us, we're laughing. I'm going into town, I need new lenses, I'll get you a copy.

But to NATHAN, this is just so much background chat; he's in a world of his own, sneaking glances across at CHRISTIAN HOBBS through the wire mesh of the changing-room divider (though NATHAN feels anything but sexy; it's the scariest, most risky place to catch a glance, and yet genetically impossible not to look). During MIDGE's speech, NATHAN stares as CHRISTIAN gets into his shirt, quickly looks down as CHRISTIAN glances his way. Their eyes don't meet, but there's a tiny, tiny hint that CHRISTIAN knows NATHAN is watching. CHRISTIAN carries on, and NATHAN's eyes return to him as CHRISTIAN turns his back, tucks his shirt in, his hands down around his arse. Then he turns round, almost as if he's showing NATHAN the sexiest moment of all, CHRISTIAN pulling up his zip.
    Suddenly – spoiling the moment for NATHAN, and silencing MIDGE – one of CHRISTIAN's mob starts messing about, laughing, shoves CHRISTIAN. A bit of a mock-fight, CHRISTIAN grabbing his MATE in a head-lock. NATHAN keeps watching, all this a flurry of action through the wire mesh. Like they're separated from him, in a cage. CHRISTIAN grabs a wet towel, is flicking his mates when the PE TEACHER walks through. The action stops abruptly, but CHRISTIAN's been caught with the towel. The TEACHER says 'Christian' (the millionth time he's been caught) and summons him to his office.

CHRISTIAN: Aw give over, we're just messing, sir –

TEACHER says right now. CHRISTIAN, pissed off, follows. NATHAN watches him go.

4/8 INT. CREMATORIUM, DAY 9 1205   4/8
STUART, VINCE, HAZEL, BERNARD, ALEXANDER, MRS DELANEY, MINISTER, HANDSOME MAN

All singing the closing lines of 'The Day Thou Gavest Lord Has Ended', and then they sit.

> MINISTER: Now at Philip's request, a reading by Mr Vincent Tyler.

VINCE stands, hating this – he's not one of life's public speakers – and he has to make the long walk to the podium, all eyes upon him. He feels such a fraud. Even a smile from HAZEL doesn't help, he's in a sweat as he mounts the pulpit, fiddles with the sheets of paper.

> VINCE: Right, uh... I've been asked to do this, Phil wanted, uh, he wanted a reading, um...

He sees STUART lean forward, whisper something to HANDSOME MAN. The fact that STUART's barely listening makes VINCE think: sod it. He gets more into his stride.

> VINCE: Cos it was last Easter, Phil found this bruise on his leg, he said, that's it, I'm dying, I'm off, wrote all this down. His last request. Turns out he bumped his leg on a stepladder. But he chose this, he wanted something ... appropriate. (Reads, unsure at first) D.I.S.C.O, I say, D.I.S.C.O. She is D, desirable...

The congregation starts to laugh, getting the joke (especially the 'she'), some crying at the same time. And VINCE warms up, like it's Shakespeare.

> VINCE: She is I, irresistible, She is S, super-sexy, She is C, crazy crazy, She is oh, oh, oh, I say, D.I.S.C.O.

Everyone's loving it, in just the way PHIL intended. But VINCE sees MRS DELANEY looking at him. She's not laughing; she's bewildered, *lost*. Like the congregation knew her son better than she did.

4/9 INT. SCHOOL CHANGING ROOM, DAY 9 1255   4/9
CHRISTIAN, NATHAN

CHRISTIAN in the empty changing room. It's his punishment, mopping the floor, pissed off – the hard man of the class, reduced to this. NATHAN walks in.

> NATHAN: D'you want a hand? (CHRISTIAN just looks at him) I've got to wait, I'm doing that collection thing, I'll give you a hand.

NATHAN dumps his bag, goes to get a second mop. CHRISTIAN gets back to work, sullen, thinking NATHAN's just weird, volunteering for this. NATHAN joins in, both of them in silence.
   CUT TO – black, sharp fade up to:

4/10 INT. SCHOOL CHANGING ROOM, DAY 9 1305   4/10
NATHAN, CHRISTIAN

The work's abandoned, NATHAN and CHRISTIAN sitting on opposite benches,

CHRISTIAN digging chocolate out of his bag. In the cut, the atmosphere's lightened.

> NATHAN: Donna saw Mr Rogers with his wife in town. Said she's tiny, she's a dwarf, face like this. That's why he's cross all the time, he's got to go to bed with that.

CHRISTIAN laughs. Beat, then:

> CHRISTIAN: She's a twat, that Donna, why d'you hang about with her? You shagging her?

> NATHAN: No way!

CHRISTIAN laughs, chucks NATHAN a bit of chocolate.
    CUT TO – black, sharp fade up to:

4/11 INT. SCHOOL CHANGING ROOM, DAY 9 1308   4/11
NATHAN, CHRISTIAN

NATHAN's now manoeuvred himself so he's sitting next to CHRISTIAN, a good few feet away. NATHAN so controlled, so careful.

> CHRISTIAN: Tracy Anstee. I'd have her.

> NATHAN: Jason said he reckons she's a dyke, she's always with that blonde girl.

> CHRISTIAN: Aww, don't tell me that. Waste.

> NATHAN: I dunno, though. Least she's getting some. Getting more than me.

> CHRISTIAN: And me.

> NATHAN: Doesn't matter where you get it, so long as you do. 'You're only after one thing,' that's them.

> CHRISTIAN: And we are!

> NATHAN: Yeah!

Both laugh. CUT TO – black, sharp fade up to:

4/12 INT. SCHOOL CHANGING ROOM, DAY 9 1311   4/12
NATHAN, CHRISTIAN

NATHAN now closer on the bench, as close as he dares. Both are smoking. CHRISTIAN's in a reverie, not looking at NATHAN. So NATHAN's free to stare at him. Tension.

> CHRISTIAN: We're behind the house, no one's looking. I've got this fucking boner and she's grabbing it, I'm like, yes, I'm going

oaaarh. She's scooping down, she's got me balls an' all. Then
she's like pulling. Gripping dead tight. Then she stops, she's got
to go home, she fucking stops. (Grabs his own crotch, with a
hard-on) Christ, I'm packing it.

He draws on his cigarette. All the time, not looking at NATHAN. Then he sits
back, head back, grabs his crotch again, still hard, groans. Then he lets go, stays
head back, eyes closed. Like it's a signal.

NATHAN's terrified. But the signal's there. Maybe. NATHAN stubs out his fag.
Then he moves slowly, reaches out, carefully takes hold of CHRISTIAN's crotch.
CHRISTIAN gives absolutely no reaction. NATHAN tightens his grip. Shifts closer
for a better grip. Still nothing from CHRISTIAN. NATHAN grips even tighter,
starts a slow to-and-fro movement. A hiss of breath from CHRISTIAN. NATHAN
shifts his other hand to his own crotch, keeps going.

4/12A INT. SCHOOL CHANGING ROOM, DAY 9 1313   4/12A
NATHAN, CHRISTIAN

60 seconds later, NATHAN and CHRISTIAN where they were, but closer, CHRIS-
TIAN unzipped. NATHAN's pounding away, wanking CHRISTIAN off, CHRIST-
IAN still head back, eyes shut, so he doesn't have to see what's happening.
NATHAN's so intent on not breaking the moment that he only grips his own
crotch, nothing more.

CHRISTIAN comes, quickly, little grunts. And then, like a blur,
CHRISTIAN's on his feet, zipping up, grabbing his sports bag, out of the door,
not looking at NATHAN once.

4/13 INT. SCHOOL CORRIDOR/EXT. YARD, DAY 9 1313   4/13
CHRISTIAN, NATHAN

The corridor empty, everyone in the yard at lunchtime. CHRISTIAN walks down
the corridor, fast. NATHAN emerges from the changing room, hand in pocket,
adjusting himself. Without looking back, CHRISTIAN's aware of NATHAN
behind him, and CHRISTIAN breaks into a run.

NATHAN watches him go, slowly breaking into a grin. He pushes through a
nearby set of fire-doors, out into the yard –

4/13A EXT. SCHOOL YARD, DAY 9 1315   4/13A
NATHAN, DONNA

NATHAN walks out of the fire doors, picking up speed, happier and happier. But
his victory's not complete until he's told someone. Then he sees DONNA, way
across the yard. She's sitting all alone, playing on a Gameboy. NATHAN runs,
reaches her, grabs her, whispers about CHRISTIAN. She's shocked, disbelieving,
he whispers again.

And then both NATHAN and DONNA are *exploding*, leaping about, in fits of
laughter, their whoops carrying across the yard. All the other KIDS passing to and
fro, dull, NATHAN and DONNA so happy they're going mental.

4/14 INT. DELANEYS' LIVING ROOM, DAY 9 1325   4/14
STUART, VINCE, HAZEL, BERNARD, ALEXANDER, MRS DELANEY,
CAMERON, HANDSOME MAN

It's a nice house, five bedrooms, tasteful (not too rich, just comfortably well-off). The living room's spacious, two rooms knocked into one, the length of the house. The wake's in full swing – VINCE, HAZEL, BERNARD, etc. MR DELANEY's still upset, but being wonderful, hugging people. MRS DELANEY's at the far end, surrounded by friends. On ALEXANDER, with an audience of MOURNERS.

> ALEXANDER: Course, I was with him the night he died – well, I wasn't with him, or he wouldn't be dead. Or we'd both be dead, oo imagine! I could be dead, this could be me. Mind you, I'd get more of a crowd.

CUT TO – VINCE and STUART helping themselves to the buffet, with CAMERON – 38, ordinary good looks, not apparently gay; mid-introduction:

> CAMERON: Yeah, Stuart and Vince, he used to go on about you. Cameron Roberts, I did Phil's accounts.

> VINCE: Right. Didn't see you at the crematorium.

> CAMERON: No, I'm just paying respects, I didn't know him that well.

> VINCE: Neither did I really.

> CAMERON: Oh, right. (Beat) He talked about you all the time, though.

> VINCE: Yeah. But. He was lovely, we had a laugh and that, but... We were pub-friends, y'know, we just went out drinking.

> CAMERON: (Not hostile) So what d'you do with your real friends?

> STUART: (Laughs) We go out drinking.

On that, STUART walks off, having seen HANDSOME MAN, leaving VINCE stuck, the conversation having taken an unsettling turn. Pause, then CAMERON tries to save it:

> CAMERON: Heard about the service, the pop song. Sounds good. (Looking at STUART, in B/G) I'm glad it was Vince, Phil used to go on about him. Vince this and Vince that. Thought the world of him.

> VINCE: ...I'm Vince.

Beat.

> CAMERON: Oh! Oh – right – *you're* Vince?

> VINCE: Yeah.

> CAMERON: Sorry, right, Stuart and Vince, right. Jesus! It's just

that, Phil said, everyone says Stuart's the better-looking one, so –
you! Right. Sorry, anyway. I'll get me coat.

CAMERON smiles, walks away. On VINCE, thinking about that. And then, for
once in his life, he decides he's chuffed.

CUT TO – MRS DELANEY, with HAZEL, BERNARD, NS MOURNERS.
STUART's found himself on the edge of this gathering, only because HAND-
SOME MAN is also listening. MRS DELANEY's a little dislocated, obviously upset;
all they can do is let her talk.

> MRS DELANEY: Keeps you busy. We've had the building society,
> the bank... The police, of course. (Beat, all awkward) We're
> going back up tomorrow. Collect his things, put the house on the
> market, then it's done. All over.

STUART's mobile rings. All glare at him.

> STUART: – sorry –

He clicks it off. MRS DELANEY has barely noticed, carries on, suddenly on a
different tangent.

> MRS DELANEY: I'd imagine you're the same, Mrs Tyler. When
> your son tells you... about himself. The plans all change. No
> wedding, no grandchildren. (On STUART, listening) Not to be.
> And that's fine. It's the plans you don't make. You don't plan
> your own son's funeral.

4/15 INT. 'THRIVE' OFFICE, DAY 9 1329   4/15
SANDRA

On the computer screen, the words appearing as SANDRA types them in as dicta-
tion, saying:

> SANDRA: You don't plan... your own son's... funeral.

4/15A INT. DELANEYS' HALL,
INTERCUT WITH 'THRIVE' OFFICE DAY 9 1329   4/15A
STUART, HANDSOME MAN/SANDRA

STUART's on his mobile in the hall. Intercut as and when (at SANDRA's end,
STUART's on speaker-phone).

> STUART: Child, sorry, make it child, not son. (We see the correc-
> tion being made) New paragraph –

As STUART talks, his gaze settles on one particular thing. There's a rack of keys
on the wall – house keys, car keys, etc. And another set. STUART reaches out,
turns the fob to face him. A Babylon keyring. Directly above, on one of those
white-boards for scribbled notes, reminders, etc., is written: PHILIP 1507.
STUART talks away, all the while an idea occurring.

> STUART: – you plan for the best of times, full stop. You can plan

their weddings, comma, you can plan for grandchildren, full stop. But some things you never plan, full stop, new paragraph. At the worst of times, Sherwood is there to help, full stop, finished, how's that? Bit slushy.

Reading what's on screen, the truth's slowly dawning on SANDRA, and she picks up the receiver, taking it off speaker-phone.

SANDRA: Stuart, is that really a funeral?

STUART: Slushy's good, it's post-Diana, print it up.

SANDRA: You are, aren't you? You're at a funeral.

STUART: I said so.

SANDRA: You bastard.

SANDRA slams the phone down. STUART barely notices, he's still looking at the keys, the 1507. Then he makes his decision, takes the keys, slips them in his pocket. Just then, HANDSOME MAN's heading out of the living room. STUART smiles as he goes upstairs. Then follows.

4/16 EXT. YARD, DAY 9 1329   4/16
NATHAN, DONNA, CHRISTIAN, MIDGE

NATHAN and DONNA walk along, still excited, the yard full of KIDS.

DONNA: You're like Mozart, you are.

NATHAN: How'm I like Mozart?

DONNA: Like he did everything dead young. I mean the rest of us, what are we doing? Nothing.

NATHAN: Robert Coles, he did that advert for Cheesypops.

DONNA: Apart from him. But you! Doing all sorts! Now!

NATHAN: (Gleeful) And I've only just started!

DONNA: I'm sick of you!

Their laughter interrupted by a flurry of action, shooting past them. CHRISTIAN HOBBS and his mates have got hold of MIDGE's school bag. MIDGE is protesting but won't let go, so they drag him along into one of those school alcoves/alleyways where teachers can't see.
NATHAN and DONNA watch as the MATES tug at the bag, taunting him, like they're trying to push MIDGE into a fight. And they're calling out: poofter, shit-stabber. So far, it's not too rough, only potentially violent. But then CHRISTIAN catches NATHAN's eye, holds the look for a second. Then CHRISTIAN launches forward at MIDGE.

CHRISTIAN: Fucking queer.

He kicks MIDGE on the back of the knees, so MIDGE falls to the ground. CHRISTIAN and his mates all laugh, move on, leaving MIDGE on the floor. NATHAN and DONNA keep walking. Not so happy, now.

4/17 INT. DELANEYS' KITCHEN, DAY 9 1340   4/17
MRS DELANEY, VINCE

A wide, spacious kitchen, MRS DELANEY with VINCE, over a cup of tea. For MRS DELANEY, it's been the longest day of her life. She's upset, exhausted. VINCE is awkward, having waited all day to have this conversation.

VINCE: Mrs Delaney, he didn't take drugs –

MRS DELANEY: I know.

VINCE: It was just that night – I mean, I would say that even if he did, but – take drugs I mean, but... He wasn't like that, he didn't ever –

MRS DELANEY: I know. Thank you Vince, but I know my own son, thank you.

VINCE: Just thought I'd better say.

MRS DELANEY: Thanks.

Silence.

VINCE: Well. I don't want to keep you –

MRS DELANEY: (Upset) – but you didn't see anyone? That night. You didn't see who he was with?

VINCE: There were loads of us, we had some friends up for the weekend. Sort of lost track of him.

MRS DELANEY: Did you...? (Stops) None of my business.

VINCE: What?

MRS DELANEY: That night. Did you... 'cop off'?

Beat. She smiles, which allows VINCE to smile.

MRS DELANEY: Philip always said that. Cop off.

VINCE: I didn't, no.

MRS DELANEY: So...? What's the word, what would Philip have called that? Unlucky. So that makes Philip lucky. Because he certainly took someone back home.

VINCE: It was just some bloke, God knows who it was. He ran away, so – he was prob'ly scared, he must've been –

MRS DELANEY: But tell me – because I can't stop – (Struggles to compose herself, upset) D'you think a woman would have run?

VINCE: ...sorry?

MRS DELANEY: If he'd taken a woman home.

VINCE: How d'you mean?

MRS DELANEY: (Distress building, in tears) If my son had been straight. That's the word, straight, if Philip were straight. I don't know, Vince, you tell me, what...? He'd have found some woman? At the age of thirty-five? Some woman he'd never met? He'd take her home? He'd take heroin with that woman? Would he?

VINCE: (Very quiet) It was a mistake, it's got nothing to do with being gay –

MRS DELANEY: Hasn't it? At thirty-five? *Philip?* He'd find himself at thirty-five taking heroin with a casual *fuck* if he was *straight?*

VINCE: ...he could do.

Silence. MRS DELANEY calmer, drained.

MRS DELANEY: Well. I suppose. What would I know...? (Sudden terror, overwhelmed by the memory) Four days he laid there, and I had to see him – (Suddenly walks out) Thank you, people to see –

Hold on VINCE.

4/17A INT. DELANEYS' HOUSE, UPSTAIRS HALLWAY, DAY 9 1345   4/17A
STUART, VINCE, HANDSOME MAN

(Or any quiet location in the DELANEYS' house). STUART's sitting at the top of the stairs with HANDSOME MAN, very close.

STUART: Just look at today, it's proof, you could drop dead any minute, there's no time to waste. You should try anything. Anyone.

VINCE appears at the bottom of the stairs.

VINCE: Can we go?

STUART: Later.

VINCE is exhausted, looks at STUART, knowing he can't be stopped in mid-cop. He gives up, walks away. But STUART's seen the look, thinks, turns to the HANDSOME MAN.

> STUART: Tell you what. Some other time. (Gives HANDSOME MAN his card) Call me.

He runs after VINCE.

4/18 EXT. DELANEYS' HOUSE, DAY 9 1346   4/18
VINCE, STUART

VINCE and STUART head to the jeep.

> STUART: How's Mrs Delaney, did you say about the drugs?

> VINCE: Naah, we just chatted. (Gets into the jeep, worn out) God. Just take me home.

> STUART: Nope, things to do.

STUART throws him the set of keys.

> VINCE: Whose are these?

STUART just grins, revs up the jeep, speeds off.

4/19 INT. NATHAN'S BEDROOM, DAY 9 1540   4/19
NATHAN, JANICE

Sulky teenage music, full-volume. On dozens of drawings, sketches of a man's face, rather like STUART, and STUART's name dozens of times in that bubble-writing that only teenagers do. Reveal NATHAN, sitting on his bed looking at them.
JANICE walks in (he didn't hear her because of the music). NATHAN instantly leaps up, grabs his drawings.

> JANICE: I did knock –

He shoves his drawings into a drawer – or anywhere that means he can turn his back to her, embarrassed. It's not the first time JANICE has had this reaction; she calmly goes to the CD, turns it off.

> JANICE: I'm going to the cash and carry, they need stuff for school, d'you want to come with me?

> NATHAN: Like I'd rather *die.*

> JANICE: That's a shame. I was going to let you drive.

He looks at her, surprised. She throws him the car keys, he catches them.

4/20 EXT. STREET, DAY 9 1550   4/20
NATHAN, JANICE

A quiet Didsbury street, near NATHAN's house. NATHAN and JANICE are in the
stationary car – ordinary car, nothing posh – NATHAN in the driver's seat, having
a lesson. NATHAN's revving up.

> JANICE: Foot off the clutch. That's it, slowly –

> NATHAN: I *know* –

They drive off down the street, NATHAN driving quite well.

> JANICE: If we get stopped by the police, say I'm diabetic and
> you're taking me home. Take the corner, slowly now. (He does
> so, taking it wide) Yes. Yes, that's dreadful.

> NATHAN: (Laughing) Oy, that's good, that is. Y'know like if
> you're going to sell this in a couple of years' time, you could give
> it to me instead.

> JANICE: Oh I like that, give you a car, for nothing.

> NATHAN: Could do.

> JANICE: I was nineteen before I had a car. I was going out with a
> bloke called Jimmy Moran, I'd drive him home, couldn't get rid
> of him, he'd snog me till three o'clock in the morning.

> NATHAN: (Laughing, embarrassed) Oh shut up!

> JANICE: Great big lips, it was like kissing an arm-band.

> NATHAN: I don't want to know!

> JANICE: He works at the Midland now. Nathan, have you got a
> boyfriend?

Silence, as that sinks in. NATHAN stares ahead, driving, *dying* inside. JANICE
barely leaves a pause, keeps going, all of this unplanned:

> JANICE: I'm not really asking, you don't have to say, but... And I
> don't mind, I really don't mind, but I'm not daft, love. You're
> going out at night, you're not round at Donna's – and I'm not
> having a go, I'm just saying – I'm sorry, love, go on, pull into the
> side – (He keeps driving. More honest:) You're fifteen years old,
> that's what I'm worried about, you're *fifteen*. I don't know where
> you're going, I don't know what you're doing –

> NATHAN: (Anguished) I'm not doing anything, I'm *not* –

> JANICE: All right, I don't mind, I'm just saying, it's not being gay,
> I don't mind about that –

NATHAN: I'm *not*, all right?

JANICE: Okay, look, that's enough, pull in here.

He's about to pull in, but JANICE can't stop herself:

JANICE: So who's Stuart?

That does it. The car is heading towards the kerb – slowly – as NATHAN just flings the door open, gets out of the car while it's still in motion, runs down the street. Behind him, though there's no danger of a crash, JANICE has to grab the wheel and shift across to the driver's seat.

JANICE: Nathan – !

But NATHAN keeps running.

4/21 EXT. DONNA'S HOUSE, DAY 9 1600   4/21
DONNA, NATHAN

DONNA's hanging out of her bedroom window, NATHAN in the back garden.

DONNA: She never did! Oh my God, it's non-stop with you,
you're like a novel!

NATHAN: Can't you get out?

DONNA: I can't, I burnt the ham, what you gonna do? What you
gonna tell her?

NATHAN: I can't.

DONNA: You'll have to, she knows.

NATHAN: I *can't*.

DONNA: You'll have to!

But NATHAN's mind is moving in a different direction, seized by a wild idea, full of passion. At 15, you think nothing can stop you.

NATHAN: I can do what I like. I'm Mozart! I'm fucking Mozart!

He runs away.

4/22 EXT. DONNA'S STREET, DAY 9 1601   4/22
NATHAN

High, wide shot of the street, empty except for NATHAN, who runs, fast as he can, ecstatic, leaving all this behind.

4/23 EXT. PHIL'S HOUSE, DAY 9 1610 4/23
STUART, VINCE

The jeep pulls up, STUART and VINCE get out, head for the house, STUART with the stolen keys.

>VINCE: What if someone sees us?

>STUART: We could be anyone, he's dead, we could be the bailiffs.

He opens the front door.

4/24 INT. PHIL'S HALL, DAY 9 1612 4/24
STUART, VINCE

They walk in, the alarm starts beeping.

>VINCE: Shit!

>STUART: S'all right, it was written down.

He presses 1507 into the keypad, the beeping stops. They walk through, the house giving them the creeps.

4/25 INT. PHIL'S KITCHEN/DINING ROOM, DAY 9 1612 4/25
STUART, VINCE

STUART and VINCE walk in. The whole place is strangely empty (the DELANEYS have been here in the weeks since the death; the furniture's all there, but nothing else, clean surfaces. All the curtains are drawn, and stay closed throughout the scenes in PHIL's house). Both know the body was found in the kitchen, and are aware of the spot, trying not to stare at it, busying themselves by taking off jackets, etc.

>VINCE: People should die more often. If it has this effect on you.

>STUART: Meaning?

>VINCE: Well. It's nice of you. (*Tiny* hint of jealousy) Didn't think you cared about your shags.

>STUART: You do the videos, I'll look for magazines.

>VINCE: She knows he was gay, she's always known.

>STUART: Yeah, but imagine you're dead and your mother goes through your things. Goes through your porn stash – d'you want your mother seeing that? Well, not your mother, a normal mother. (Beat, looks round the room) The poor bastard. (Quieter) I was thinking. I'll get a spare set of keys, for the flat. So you can have them. (Smiles) Come and save me, Vince.

VINCE: (Smiles) Yeah. You can have a set of mine.

STUART: (Brisker) Oh, like anything's going to happen to you.
Right. Porn. And I told you, he was a crap shag, came in two
seconds flat.

STUART heads off. On VINCE.

4/26 INT. PHIL'S LIVING ROOM, DAY 9 1615   4/26
VINCE

VINCE is on the floor in front of the VHS, sorting through PHIL's videos. He slips
in an unlabelled cassette, presses play.
    Sure enough, it's porn, two American men shagging away. VINCE ejects the
cassette, puts it to one side, tries another.

4/27 INT. PHIL'S OFFICE, DAY 9 1625   4/27
STUART

PHIL's got an upstairs office, lined with bookshelves, a flash PC on his desk. On
the computer screen – hard-core porn from the hard drive.
    STUART's grinning away, deleting the pictures (a stack of hard-core porn
magazines at his side). Finds a particular bloke.

STUART: Had him.

4/28 EXT. STUART'S FLAT, DAY 9 1630   4/28
NATHAN, NEIGHBOUR

NATHAN rings the buzzer to STUART's flat for the millionth time. He looks up
at the flats. Nothing. He gives up, walks away. Behind him, a NEIGHBOUR comes
out of the front door. She's 35, smart. NATHAN runs to catch the open door, but
she swings it shut.

NEIGHBOUR: Oh no you don't.

She goes to walk on.

NATHAN: Sorry, d'you know where Stuart Jones is?

NEIGHBOUR: Listen. (She holds out her arms, NATHAN lost)
Peace and quiet. He's not in. Oh blissful day.

And she walks on.

4/29 INT. PHIL'S LIVING ROOM, DAY 9 1635   4/29
VINCE, STUART

VINCE has piled up a stack of 20 porn videos, as STUART walks in with a pile of
maybe thirty magazines.

VINCE: Gay man's legacy, that's what we leave behind. Pile of
trash.

STUART: (Quiet) He had pictures of children. Some of them are babies, it's disgusting.

VINCE: Ha ha.

STUART: He could've done, that would be so brilliant. (He sits, properly serious) Tell you what I did find. (Pause) Don't take this the wrong way.

VINCE: What...?

STUART: He's got... well it's you, he's got photos of you. There's about three dozen, hidden away with this stuff. Just photos of you in the pub, and having a laugh. But dozens of them.

VINCE: He hasn't...

STUART: Course he bloody hasn't! You twat.

VINCE very pissed off: he defends himself, for once.

VINCE: Piss off. As a matter of fact, I'm dead good-looking, I was told.

STUART: Well you are.

VINCE: (thrown by a compliment from STUART) ...oh.

STUART: Let's go.

VINCE starts to assemble the stash, still thrown.

4/30 EXT. CANAL STREET, DAY 9 1650   4/30
NATHAN

NATHAN wanders down Canal Street. It's quiet, late afternoon, men scattered about. NATHAN keeps walking, determined.

4/31 INT. NEW UNION, DAY 9 1655   4/31
NATHAN

NATHAN walks in. It's almost empty, strangely quiet without the night-time music and cabaret, lacking the usual charm. NATHAN's looking for STUART. No sign of him.

4/32 INT. ROMEY'S HOUSE, DAY 9 1700   4/32
ROMEY, STUART, VINCE

ROMEY opens the door, STUART barges in with a stack of porn magazines, VINCE following with videos.

STUART: Present from Phil. Try *Powertool One*, see what you're missing.

4/32A INT. ROMEY'S LIVING ROOM, DAY 9 1710   4/32A
ROMEY, STUART, VINCE, BABY ALFRED

ROMEY, STUART and VINCE, STUART balancing ALFRED on his knee.

> STUART: It was great. Good buffet.

> ROMEY: It's all right, Stuart, you're allowed to be sad. I won't tell anyone.

> STUART: He's still a bastard, though. Dying. We get enough funerals, I don't need reminding, seventeen weeks and I'm thirty. I'm dying in front of everyone.

During this, ROMEY smiles: typical STUART. VINCE, for once, isn't smiling, more and more wound up by the day.

> ROMEY: What about that boy? That student you had on Monday, how old was he?

> STUART: Twenty-one.

> ROMEY: There you are, you're twenty-one. You're as young as who you feel, isn't that the point?

> VINCE: (Distant, edgy) Monday, what happened to me? Fighting off that bloke with the leg, another shit night. Cos we're getting older but there's nothing to stop us, so we don't. We never bloody stop.

> STUART: I'll be there at sixty, walking down Canal Street, knocking back Viagra.

> VINCE: And I'll be chasing after you. Pathetic.

> STUART: I think it's brilliant, I want to die shagging.

> VINCE: Yeah. Phil did that.

4/33 INT. VIA FOSSA, DAY 9 1705   4/33
NATHAN, DONNA, JANICE

NATHAN, looking for STUART, has moved pubs, though even Via Fossa's half-empty. He's up on the balcony, dismally scanning through the few men present, when – he steps back from the balcony. Horrified.

His POV: below, DONNA's led JANICE into the pub, looking for him. NATHAN's freaked out – his mother's in a gay pub, DONNA's betrayed him (though DONNA's glum, forced into this).

Trying to stay out of sight, he watches DONNA lead JANICE across the bar; they're going to make a circuit around Via Fossa. The second they've moved out of sight, NATHAN bolts along the balcony – shoving men out of his way – and runs down the stairs, out of the door.

4/34 EXT. VIA FOSSA, DAY 9 1706   4/34
NATHAN

NATHAN runs hell-for-leather down the street.

4/35 EXT. ALLEYWAY, DAY 9 1710   4/35
NATHAN

NATHAN's in the shadows, getting his breath back. But he's not defeated yet, he's got an idea. He gets out his Babylon keyring, looks at it.

4/36 EXT. BABYLON, DAY 9 1715   4/36
NATHAN, MAN AT DESK

MAN AT DESK is tilling up, and beer barrels are being rolled in as NATHAN walks up.

> MAN AT DESK: We don't open till ten.

> NATHAN: No, I just need to renew my membership.

NATHAN hands over his keyring, the MAN passes it under the scanner.

> MAN AT DESK: Name?

> NATHAN: Bernard Thomas.

> MAN AT DESK: Right, that's two quid – oy!

Because NATHAN's launched himself across the desk to read the computer screen (which is half-turned away). The MAN slams the till shut, grabs the cash, thinking NATHAN's after the money.

> MAN AT DESK: Get off, you little bastard –

But NATHAN's read the address. NATHAN leaps down, runs away.

4/37 EXT. CANAL STREET, DAY 9 1720   4/37
JANICE, DONNA

JANICE and DONNA, sitting on the canal wall, JANICE exhausted.

> JANICE: What about that place?

> DONNA: Lesbians only. (Beat) Not that I've been.

4/38 EXT. HAZEL'S HOUSE, DAY 9 1740   4/38
BERNARD, HAZEL, NATHAN

BERNARD's MG pulls up, HAZEL gets out – shoes in hand – looking at the house, having already seen their visitor.

> HAZEL: Aye aye. One of yours, Bernie?

NATHAN's sitting against the front door, looking at them forlornly.

4/39 INT. EXT. ROMEY'S HOUSE, DAY 9 1745   4/39
STUART, VINCE, BABY ALFRED

STUART and VINCE loading ALFRED into the jeep, VINCE still in a mood when his mobile rings. He recognises HAZEL's number, answers.

>VINCE: Hi, we're just about to – Who did? He's done what...?

VINCE gives STUART such a look, like there's no end to this day.

>STUART: What?

4/40 EXT. HAZEL'S HOUSE, DAY 9 1755   4/40
VINCE, STUART, BABY ALFRED

The jeep pulls up. VINCE steps out, starts unbuckling ALFRED. STUART sits behind the wheel, wanting to drive off. VINCE glares at him. VINCE wins. STUART huffs, gets out.

4/41 INT. HAZEL'S HOUSE, DAY 9 1758   4/41
NATHAN, HAZEL, BERNARD, VINCE, STUART, BABY ALFRED

NATHAN faces HAZEL, BERNARD, VINCE and STUART. HAZEL's holding ALFRED. STUART's defence is to go on the attack.

>STUART: How the fuck did she know my name?

>NATHAN: I dunno, it's Donna, she's always talking, I never said –

>STUART: Nathan, you've made a very big mistake. You've actually imagined that I give a toss. Now go back home to your nice little schoolboy life and stop bothering us –

But NATHAN's brilliant when he panics:

>NATHAN: I can't, cos my mum told my dad and he was furious, he was shouting, he said get out, he called me a poof, he threw me out the house. I can't go back, he'll hit me.

>BERNARD: (Quiet, furious) He won't, cos I'll tell him, I'll have the police on him, I'll tell him myself, where d'you live?

>NATHAN: I'm not saying.

>BERNARD: (To VINCE) What's his surname?

>VINCE: Maloney.

>BERNARD: Right, I'll go through every Maloney in the book till I find him –

NATHAN: It's not my dad –

HAZEL: Don't you defend him, he's not worth the spit, I'll punch him myself.

NATHAN: It's not my dad, it was school, it was these boys at school, they said they'd kill me, I can't go back, they're going to kill me.

Silence.

VINCE: (Told-you-so) Can't believe a word he says.

NATHAN: I can't go back home, I can't. (To STUART) I could stay at yours –

STUART: No.

NATHAN: It's your fault, it's all cos of you, this, you *chose* me. And I'm not going back, I'll go to London, I'll go tonight, I'll live on the streets, I'll be a rent boy and I'll be murdered, I will.

NATHAN thinks he's being so effective. But VINCE, HAZEL and BERNARD look at each other and just start laughing (STUART remains indifferent).

HAZEL: You know you're getting old when the drama queens start looking younger.

NATHAN: (Plaintive) Can't I stay here, then? Just for tonight?

VINCE: He's stupid enough, he could run off.

HAZEL looks at BERNARD.

BERNARD: Christ, does that mean I'm sleeping with you?

HAZEL: You know you want it.

4/42 INT. VINCE'S OLD ROOM, DAY 9 1803   4/42
NATHAN

NATHAN looks round. Apart from BERNARD's stuff, VINCE's old photos are still on the wall. Photos of STUART and VINCE as kids. NATHAN stares at them; at the image of STUART.

4/43 INT. HAZEL'S KITCHEN, DAY 9 1804   4/43
VINCE, STUART, HAZEL, BERNARD

VINCE, STUART, HAZEL and BERNARD gathered hugger-mugger in the kitchen (cigarettes banished to the kitchen because of ALFRED).

STUART: Pack him off home.

"Stuart Alan Jones, looking down on me like the face of God."

"Just remember one thing, Vince. You're fantastic."

"The chicken has landed!"

"You're that nice looking, you'll find a bloke, no time."

"Daniel from last night? Daniel the six foot two barrister with a BMW?"

"Phil's the one I told you about, he's the one met David Beckham."

"Nights with Stuart, they're shit half the time. But I don't care! I love him!"

"So I'm stood there in Battersea Power Station, Turbine B, wearing nothing but me Tommy Hilfiger pants..."

"Do you think a woman would have run?"

"If you fancy a three-some at this time of night, you can't start getting choosy about which particular three."

"Sometimes you see these men. You see them, and you think, that's it."

"Thirty years old! How did that happen?"

"It's all getting a
bit lesbian in here."

"He's here, he's queer,
I'm buying him a beer!"

"Cos they don't tell you,
they don't tell the Golden
Boy. Me, I get it all."

"He's the perfect boyfriend."

"I'm black and a girl. Try that for a week."

"So when did you have Phil, then?"

"My name's Christine Cagney, and I'm an alcoholic."

"Unrequited love. It's fantastic! Cos it never has to change. It never has to grow up. And it never has to die!"

"Shake a leg, Bernie! Let's show 'em!"

"Happy birthday, Vince."

"Oh fuck!
I've got a baby!"

"I'd give him one!"

"Manchester, it's the dregs of humanity,
I wouldn't shag one of them!"

VINCE: You do it, he's your problem.

STUART: Fuck off, Vince. (Heads for the door) I'm going for a piss. (He goes)

HAZEL: We should phone his mother, she'll be frantic. What if he's lying *now*, what if he *is* in danger?

BERNARD: It's cock. That's all it is, cock.

VINCE: Thanks for that, Bernie.

BERNIE: Fifteen, and your mother finds out, it's not (indicates inverted commas) 'gay', it's not 'homosexual', it's cock. Your mother knows you like cock. (Beat) And fair dos. It *is* revolting.

4/44 INT. VINCE'S OLD BEDROOM, DAY 9 1806   4/44
NATHAN, STUART

NATHAN looks round. STUART's in the doorway. Just standing there; looking at him. Then he steps into the room. And in that second, NATHAN knows what *could* happen, the potential for sex electrifying the room. Scared, excited, he looks at STUART, STUART just looks at him. Silence. Then, not knowing what to do, NATHAN indicates a photo.

NATHAN: S'that you? (Silence) How old are you there?

STUART takes a few steps closer (ostensibly to look at the photo, but closer to NATHAN). Silence, as he looks at the photo: STUART, 21 years old.

STUART: Young.

Then silence. They're standing next to each other, looking at the photo, not facing each other. Neither of them moving. NATHAN breathing hard, STUART very calm, fixed. Hold on them, no movement. Heat rising. And then, they just snap, STUART grabs hold of NATHAN, one hand behind his head, pulling him in for a snog, the other hand going to his groin. And NATHAN goes for it, grabbing STUART. Fast, frantic sex, all the more enjoyable for the danger, clothes on, only zips being pulled down. Snogging, grappling with each other. STUART's wanking NATHAN off, in no time at all, NATHAN's coming. He makes a noise, STUART covers his mouth with his own, to shut him up. Quickly, STUART gets NATHAN on to his knees, face-fucks him. With one hand on the back of NATHAN's head, STUART reaches out to balance himself. His palm splays across a photo of him and VINCE. STUART comes, silent. Then they separate. Both start zipping up, straightening their clothing. In doing so, they look at each other, laugh at the sheer adventure of it all. Then STUART hurries out of the room –

4/45 INT. HAZEL'S UPSTAIRS HALL/BATHROOM, DAY 9 1809   4/45
STUART

STUART moves fast, straightening his clothing, shoves open the bathroom door, flushes the toilet, so those downstairs can hear it.

He hurries to the stairs.

4/46 INT. VINCE'S OLD ROOM, DAY 9 1809   4/46
STUART, NATHAN

STUART passes the bedroom, doesn't look back, heads downstairs.
    NATHAN's dazed, grins, looking round the room. He's found the perfect place; he couldn't be happier.

4/47 INT. HAZEL'S LIVING ROOM, DAY 9 1810   4/47
HAZEL, BERNARD, VINCE, STUART, NATHAN, BABY ALFRED

HAZEL, BERNARD and VINCE sitting round. On VINCE, holding ALFRED, as STUART walks back in. STUART just sits down, completely normal. VINCE is immediately aware that something's happened; STUART won't quite meet his eyes, picks up a paper, flicks through it. VINCE tries to stay normal, but he's winding up, tighter and tighter.

> HAZEL: Soon as he's settled, he's sitting down, he's giving us the number, I'll talk to her. (To VINCE) What you doing tonight, love?

> VINCE: Nothing, why?

> BERNARD: You won't shift him tonight, clever little bugger.

> HAZEL: If we can get him home, you're coming with me. I'm not going on my own, his dad might be handy, for all we know.

> VINCE: Take him, it's *his* fault.

> STUART: Oh give it a rest.

As HAZEL talks, NATHAN appears in the doorway, just stands there. All are seated so that HAZEL and BERNARD don't see NATHAN at first, just STUART and VINCE (STUART on edge; NATHAN's broken the unspoken rules, he should've stayed upstairs). And the glances – NATHAN at STUART, STUART looking away, then catching VINCE's eye, then going back to the paper – are all the confirmation that VINCE needs. They've had sex. VINCE's emotions are massive, the jealousy of unrequited love.

> HAZEL: I can't take Bernie, it's their *son* – (To BERNIE) I mean picture it, me standing there, schoolboy on one side, you on the other, what are they going to think? Dirty old man!

> BERNARD: Chance'd be a fine thing.

> HAZEL: And you'd say something like that! All we need!

> VINCE: (At NATHAN) What d'you want?

> NATHAN: Can I have a towel?

HAZEL: Hang on. (Goes to get one)

And as NATHAN holds VINCE's stare, STUART avoiding both of them, the battle lines are well and truly drawn. NATHAN knows that VINCE knows, and enjoys it. In his eyes: power. The power of sex.

NATHAN: (Quiet, at VINCE) Nice room, thanks.

VINCE stays level, voice calm, as close as he can come to an attack.

VINCE: It was a funeral. Cos you didn't even ask, d'you think we're wearing black cos it's the fashion? It was Phil, you met Phil.

NATHAN: Yeah.

VINCE: Well he's dead.

NATHAN: Sorry.

VINCE: Is that it? Sorry?

NATHAN: Didn't really know him. Just had a drink with him.

HAZEL: (Throws him a towel) There you go.

NATHAN: Thanks. (Of the towel, at VINCE) Better clean up.

NATHAN goes.

HAZEL: So's that all right, Vince? If you come with me?

VINCE: Why's it got to be me? (At STUART) It's his problem, it's his fault.

BERNARD: That's asking for trouble. Turning up on the doorstep with Manchester's champion shagger.

VINCE: Oh right. So I can go. I'm harmless.

HAZEL: Anyway, God knows what'll happen, we haven't made the call yet – where you going?

VINCE stands, gives ALFRED to HAZEL, heads for the front door.

VINCE: I've, just, left that stuff in the jeep –

He walks out.

4/48 EXT. HAZEL'S STREET, DAY 9 1815   4/48
VINCE, STUART

VINCE walks out of the house. And he doesn't stop walking, he ignores the jeep, walks down the road, walks away from them all. Go with him, the entire scene on one continuous shot, if possible. Stay on him for a good 20 seconds, HAZEL's house receding away. Then, in B/G, STUART comes out of the house.

> STUART: Vince...? (Sees him) Vince!

VINCE keeps walking, doesn't look back. In B/G, STUART runs to the jeep, starts it up, drives till he's alongside VINCE. The scene stays on the move, VINCE walking, looking straight ahead, STUART cruising at his side.

> STUART: What are you doing? (No reply) Oy, I'm talking to you, where d'you think you're going? (No reply) I'll give you a lift. Come on, I'll take you home. (No reply) We'll go for a drink, yeah? We'll go to mine, we'll go out, whatever you want. Get in the car. (No reply) Right, I'm going, just fuck off then, I'm going. (No reply) Oh stop it. *Please*, just get in the car.

And then VINCE starts to run. STUART just lets the jeep roll to a stop, and we lose him in B/G, staying on VINCE as he runs faster and faster. For all his problems, the movement exhilarates him, air in his lungs, energy.

Faster and faster, leaving them all behind, like for once in his life he's *doing* something.

He's escaping.

EPISODE FIVE

5/1 INT. STUART'S FLAT, DAY 10 0759   5/1
STUART, GORGEOUS MAN 1

The alarm clicks from 0759 to 0800, and goes off. On STUART, left-hand side of the bed, facing left. He begins to stir.

5/2 INT. DAZZ'S FLAT, DAY 10 0800   5/2
NATHAN, DAZZ

Tight shot: we should think we're in the same bedroom, same-colour duvet. On NATHAN, right-hand side of the bed, facing right, as someone at his side begins to stir, hearing the alarm.

5/3 INT. STUART'S FLAT, DAY 10 0800   5/3
STUART, GORGEOUS MAN 1

STUART reaches out, slams the alarm off. He sinks back into the bed for a second, hungover, then turns, pulls the duvet off the man at his side –

5/4 INT. DAZZ'S FLAT, DAY 10 0800   5/4

NATHAN, DAZZ

The duvet's pulled off NATHAN, widen to reveal DAZZ (19, a hard sort of camp, a Village boy).

> DAZZ: Right, shift your arse, I've got to sign on.

DAZZ leaps out of bed, runs out. NATHAN sits up; we see the tiny bedroom, decorated on the cheap with some camp touches, and a tip (beer cans, clothes). He's a campaigner, Outrage posters, etc. NATHAN's below a huge, wall-sized poster which says 'Smash the Fascist Heterosexual Orthodoxy'.

5/5 INT. STUART'S BEDROOM, DAY 10 0801   5/5
STUART, GORGEOUS MAN 1

STUART pulls on his Calvins, a naked, half-asleep GORGEOUS MAN in bed.

> STUART: Come on, move, I've got work. Oy! I said, out!

STUART runs out.

5/6 INT. STUART'S FLAT, DAY 10 0801   5/6
STUART, GORGEOUS MAN 2

STUART runs out. Passing naked GORGEOUS MAN #2, who's got coffee.

> STUART: And you!

5/7 EXT. DAZZ'S FLAT, DAY 10 0810   5/7
NATHAN, DAZZ

DAZZ and NATHAN emerge on to the walkway.

> DAZZ: That was all right, last night, wasn't it? Bit of a laugh, am I
> gonna see you again, or what?

NATHAN tries to summon all of STUART's arrogance.

> NATHAN: You can see me now.

> DAZZ: (Laughs in his face) Oh fuck off.

DAZZ saunters off, NATHAN, humiliated, goes the other way. See the full setting,
a council block in Hulme.

5/8 EXT. STUART'S FLATS, DAY 10 0815   5/8
STUART, MARIE, THOMAS, BEN, GORGEOUS MAN 1, GORGEOUS MAN 2

STUART emerging with GORGEOUS MEN 1 and 2, when:

> THOMAS: Uncle Stuart –

THOMAS (8) and BEN (7) run towards him. STUART stoops down, picks them
up, hugs them, genuinely pleased to see them; he's great with kids.

> STUART: Call the police, mad children on the loose!

Across the road, MARIE's standing by her car. She's STUART's sister, 32 – gener-
ally a bit harassed, but right now, smiling.

> MARIE: I lost the bet, they do recognise you. Thomas, go on, say
> your piece.

> THOMAS: Mum says your phone's broken, cos you never phone
> back.

> STUART: Tell your mother she's not clever and she's not funny.

The GORGEOUS MEN are now heading off down the street, GORGEOUS MAN
1 calling out, 'Thanks then, see you'.

> THOMAS: Who's that?

> MARIE: Those nice men just popped round to fix your uncle's
> plumbing.

5/9 INT. HAZEL'S KITCHEN, DAY 10 0831   5/9
HAZEL, BERNARD, NATHAN

BERNARD's in his dressing gown, fag on, rolling crackers. HAZEL's livid,
holding a school shirt on a hanger, looks at BERNARD: 'Here we go', as they hear

the front door slam. HAZEL's ready as NATHAN runs in.

> NATHAN: S'that my shirt, is it ironed? Is there any hot water? I met this bloke in the Paradise Factory, thought he was nice, but I woke up this morning –

> HAZEL: You could have been *dead*.

Silence.

> HAZEL (cont.): Your mother's on the way, d'you want me to tell her? She's hanging on to this by the skin of her teeth, if I tell her this, she'll have you back home, even if she has to call the police. D'you want me to tell her? Do you?

> NATHAN: ...no.

> HAZEL: Anything else to say?

> NATHAN: Sorry.

> HAZEL: You're in this house on a favour, sunshine. Don't piss me off.

HAZEL shoves the shirt at him, NATHAN goes, head down.

5/10 EXT. HAZEL'S HOUSE, DAY 10 0840   5/10
JANICE, HAZEL, NATHAN, BERNARD

The door opens on JANICE – smiling but tired, hiding the fact she's been living in hell the past fortnight. HAZEL's all smiles in the doorway, with NATHAN, who's now in school uniform.

> JANICE: Sorry I'm late.

> HAZEL: Here he is, scrubbed and pressed, see you tonight.

NATHAN goes to the car, head down, sullen in front of his mother. As JANICE follows, BERNARD appears at HAZEL's side, mutters.

> BERNARD: Dunno why you put up with it.

JANICE stops, heads back. She's so ashamed, *hates* doing this.

> JANICE: Oh, that's for the shopping – (Gives HAZEL £25)And a bit extra, if he needs pens, he likes Ball Pentels, but don't buy him more than two at a time, he's always losing them.

JANICE goes, BERNARD gives HAZEL a look – oh *that's* why – HAZEL holding her head up, not looking at him, defiant.

5/11 EXT. VELODROME, DAY 10 0850   5/11
STUART, MARIE, THOMAS, BEN

STUART's jeep parked next to MARIE's car, STUART distributing McMuffins to THOMAS and BEN in the back of the car. MARIE's standing outside, so the boys don't hear. Dialogue kept light, throwaway.

> STUART: Tonight, it's not much warning –

> MARIE: I know, I did ask Louise, but – (Indicates the BOYS, moves away) Ever since their dad went, they think I'm going to disappear too. If you come and babysit, they'll be so excited they'll hardly notice I've gone.

> STUART: So what's his name?

> MARIE: Malcolm. Don't laugh. He's in the same office, he's an idiot, really, he's got these teeth. But he asked me out, that's good enough for me.

> THOMAS: (Calls out) Uncle Stuart!

> STUART: Don't say uncle, it makes me sound old.

> THOMAS: Stuart, can you drive a tractor?

> STUART: Yes I can. (To MARIE) Listen to him. First-generation Mancunian. (Beat) It's just work, I'm up to my eyes, can't you ask Mum?

> MARIE: Oh, and tell her I've got a date.

> STUART: Good point.

Beat.

> MARIE: D'you ever go on dates? Proper sit-down-to-dinner dates?

> STUART: I did once. Shagged the waiter.

Both laugh. Beat, then;

> MARIE: The boys would love to see you. And you need to keep them sweet – when you're an old man, they'll be the ones looking after you, you're never going to have kids of your own.

Touching a nerve, which makes STUART respond;

> STUART: Okay, I'll do it, fine. Course I will.

5/12 EXT. SCHOOL, DAY 10 0855   5/12
NATHAN, JANICE, DONNA

NATHAN's still sullen as JANICE pulls up outside school.

> JANICE: Right, I'll pick you up, usual time.

> NATHAN: Don't give me a lift, it's embarrassing.

> JANICE: If you'd rather not be embarrassed, then you know what to do. (Silence) Come home tonight, love, just come home for your tea, your sister would love to see you. And there won't be any trouble – (NATHAN just goes, she calls after him) I'll pick you up tonight. I'm not giving up, Nathan, *I'm* not walking out –

He gets out of the car, fast, walks towards DONNA. DONNA shoots JANICE a look – sorry for her – then walks off with NATHAN. On JANICE, clutching the wheel, despairing, exhausted; she's done nothing wrong, *nothing*.

5/13 INT. HARLO'S, DAY 10 1030   5/13
VINCE

VINCE on his mobile, while carrying and filling a shopping basket.

> VINCE: They've got an offer on coffee, two for one, might as well stock up. And you get double the points on your card.

5/14 INT. HAZEL'S KITCHEN, INTERCUT WITH HARLO'S, DAY 10 1030   5/14
HAZEL, BERNARD/VINCE, CAMERON

HAZEL on the phone, BERNARD still rolling crackers.

> HAZEL: Oh, get some Weetabix.

> VINCE: Thought your breakfast was twenty Bensons.

> HAZEL: It's for Little Lord Fauntleroy.

> VINCE: I'm not shopping for him! What else does he want, Angel Delight, party rings? Nappies?

> HAZEL: And get me the big box of Surf, I've got double the laundry, it's all bedsheets, I'd forgotten how much teenage boys masturbate.

> VINCE: *Mum!*

> HAZEL: Stiff as a board!

> BERNARD: (Hooting with laughter) Hazel, don't wash 'em, I'll have 'em!

HAZEL: Bernie said don't wash 'em, he'll have 'em!

During this, CAMERON walks up behind VINCE.

VINCE: It's like an 0898 number. I'll bring it round this afternoon, and we're having words about this Nathan business, it's a fortnight now, it's ridiculous. (Hangs up, annoyed, pushes past CAMERON) 'Scuse me, sir. (Goes to NS ASSISTANT) Alison, put that with staff discount, and put my name on it, ta.

He turns from NS ASSISTANT, walks past CAMERON again.

CAMERON: You're busy, I'll just go.

VINCE turns back, recognises him. He finds CAMERON's natural confidence attractive from the start.

VINCE: Oh my God, sorry, yeah –

CAMERON: Cameron Roberts, we met at Phil's funeral.

VINCE: Yeah, course we did, sorry. Vince.

CAMERON: I know.

Beat.

VINCE: Well. Bit of a coincidence.

CAMERON: Not really, Phil said you worked here, so. I came looking. Just thought you might fancy dinner tonight.

VINCE: (Steps forward, signalling alarm, sotto) Sorry, sort of – not at work, y'know?

CAMERON: Is that yes or no?

VINCE: I dunno, I might be doing all sorts –

CAMERON: All right, no pressure, here's my card. Think about it.

VINCE: Yeah, right. Nice card. I'd give you mine, but I haven't got one, no point, really, what would it say? Vince Tyler, shelf stacker –

CAMERON: (Indicates VINCE's badge) Assistant manager. Don't put yourself down. (Walks away, smiling) Call me.

On VINCE, in a sweat, but still chuffed, watching CAMERON go.

5/15 INT. THRIVE, DAY 10 1100   5/15
SANDRA, STUART, MARTIN BROOKS

SANDRA's leading STUART through the open area, indicating, at a distance, MARTIN BROOKS – 45, perspiring, bald.

> SANDRA: Martin Brooks, he's staying overnight, they're fussing about the five-year budget. Burton wants you to wine and dine him, talk him round, get a signature by tomorrow morning.

> STUART: Why's it got to be me?

> SANDRA: Now he's dull as ditchwater, wife and three kids, one at Oxford, blah blah blah, so no shock tactics, just behave. Nice meal, couple of brandies, and get him to sign.

They reach MARTIN.

> STUART: Martin.

> MARTIN: Stuart, heard a lot about you.

> STUART: All of it lies. Now, Sandra can book us a restaurant, or she could check the Bridgewater Hall if you want to take in a concert –

STUART's mobile rings. He grabs the phone, knowing from the screen it's VINCE (but no CU on the display).

> STUART (CONT.): Excuse me – (On the phone) So we're talking now?

5/16 INT. VINCE'S OFFICE, DAY 10 1102   5/16
VINCE

VINCE's office is white-walled, small, austere, charts and rotas on the wall.

> VINCE: Oh shut your face, complete emergency – I've been asked out. On a date.

5/17 EXT. ROUNDABOUT, DAY 10 1300   5/17
STUART, VINCE

STUART and VINCE sit in the jeep, with a sandwich and takeaway coffee, location not clear at first. STUART's looking at CAMERON's business card.

> VINCE: D'you remember? We were standing by the buffet, he was taller than you. Australian.

> STUART: Oh yeah, the blind Australian. Was he nice?

> VINCE: Well. Like he used to be nice, when he was young, but he must be, what? At least thirty-six.

As VINCE goes on, fiddling with his sandwich, all insecurity, he doesn't notice STUART dial CAMERON's number on his mobile.

> VINCE (cont.): He just said dinner. Lots of people have dinner, who doesn't have dinner? He's an accountant, he's probably going to sell me a pension. Phil's dead, so he's got a gap in his books.

> STUART: Mr Roberts? I've got Mr Tyler for you, putting you through.

VINCE mortified, mouthing, 'No!' as STUART offers him the phone. STUART just smiles, VINCE has to take the phone.

> VINCE: Hi, it's Vince, yeah. No, he's a trainee, bit useless. (STUART keeps mouthing 'go on!') I'm sort of busy, that's all, how about I call you next week...? (CAMERON hugely persuasive) No... Thing is, I can't, I'm really sort of... All right then. Okay. (Hangs up. Beat) I'm having dinner. Eight o'clock tonight.

> STUART: Yes! (Stands up in the jeep, calls out) He's got a date!

Revealing that the jeep's parked on the middle of a roundabout.

> VINCE: I've got a pension. You bastard.

5/18 EXT. DIDSBURY STREET, DAY 10 1430   5/18
NATHAN, DONNA

A cross-country run, going through the streets of Didsbury, back to the school. A few lardy boys and girls lumber past; the stragglers, and far behind the stragglers, NATHAN and DONNA, in PE kit, walk along, having a cigarette.

> DONNA: They're all talking, Amanda Boyce for starters.

> NATHAN: What's she say?

> DONNA: She said how come Nathan Maloney doesn't walk to school any more? And Chinese Susan chips in, she said, he's never home, like there's a divorce or something.

> NATHAN: What did you say?

> DONNA: I said nothing, I said I dunno.

> NATHAN: (Quiet, gleeful) That's brilliant.

> DONNA: It's not brilliant! Listen, school hears about this, you'll have Education-Welfare down your back. Happened to Billy Valentine, they put him in care, he disappeared, he went to Cardiff. And he had real problems.

> NATHAN: I've got real problems!

DONNA: Oh like what? Like your mother's been going through your things, big deal.

NATHAN: She knew everything, she'd been spying.

DONNA: So? She's your mother, it's her job!

NATHAN: She thinks if I move back home, I'll go back to normal. Like I'm sick, and I'll get better.

DONNA: She never said that –

NATHAN: Donna, you don't know her. You don't know anything, cos you're straight, right, you're part of the system, right? You're part of the fascist heterosexual orthodoxy.

NATHAN jogs ahead, DONNA's just wry, amused.

DONNA: I'm black and I'm a girl, try that for a week.

DONNA follows.

5/19 EXT. THRIVE, DAY 10 1600   5/19
STUART, MARTIN

STUART walks with MARTIN to the jeep, STUART bored, on automatic pilot.

STUART: The concert's at eight, I'll pick you up ten to –

MARTIN: I did think, uh... I mean, the concert, but... (Deep breath) I thought we'd have a touch more fun. You know. If we went to... your sort of place.

STUART: My sort of place...?

MARTIN: Your sort of place.

STUART: Jesus Christ, is there no one straight left in the world? (Slaps him on the back, delighted) Martin! Twist my arm!

5/20 INT. HAZEL'S HOUSE, DAY 10 1610   5/20
NATHAN, HAZEL, JANICE, VINCE

NATHAN's sullen, getting school books out of his bag, JANICE and HAZEL sitting, like they go through a security check at the end of every day, while VINCE tries to ignore it – pissed off with NATHAN – putting shopping away.

JANICE: And that history project, when's it due?

NATHAN: Monday.

JANICE: Right, I'll have a look Sunday night – (To HAZEL) is that all right?

HAZEL: Fine, come for tea.

NATHAN: (Stomps out) It's like having two mothers.

JANICE: And whose fault is that – ?

Beat, NATHAN gone, JANICE on the edge, HAZEL kind.

HAZEL: Give it time, we'll wear him down. I've banned *EastEnders*, he's livid –

VINCE cuts across, bad mood, stronger than usual (in unpacking the shopping, he hasn't noticed how on edge JANICE is).

VINCE: It's very simple, Janice. You go upstairs, you pack his bags, shove him in the car and take him home! Who's in charge, you or him?

Stopped in his tracks by JANICE, suddenly in tears, HAZEL looking daggers.

JANICE: He says London. Every time I try, he says London. And he *could*. Plenty boys his age just take off – (Breaks off, upset)

HAZEL: He likes it here too much. While he's here, he's safe.

JANICE: I just don't know *why*. What have I done wrong?

HAZEL: He's fifteen, that's all. First time in his life, he gets to be centre-stage. Happens all over, Janice, some boys don't come out of the closet, they explode.

VINCE: What about his dad, can't he do anything?

JANICE: He won't talk about it. (Pause. Quiet;) Won't talk at all. Not one word. (Pause. Then all the anger breaks out) I can't tell *anyone*. If I even tell his *school*. They'd tell social services, they'd have to. And there's Helen, she's ten years old, what happens to her? She gets interviewed? She gets her name, on a register, at ten years old?

HAZEL: They won't, love, all they'd do is visit –

JANICE: Oh well *you'd* know, wouldn't you?

Nasty silence.

JANICE (cont.): I'm sorry, I didn't mean to… (Bright, artificial smile) Got it wrong, didn't I? Somewhere along the line, I got it all wrong. (to VINCE) He'll be all right though, won't he? I mean, if he's out on Canal Street… Keep an eye on him, could you?
VINCE: Course I will.

JANICE: (Still flustered) Thanks, I'd better... Thank you.

JANICE goes.

> HAZEL: Oh well done, Vincent, reduce a grown woman to tears.
> Like no one's talked to her till you come blundering in, what's
> the matter with you?

> VINCE: (Feeble) I've got a date.

5/21 INT. VINCE'S BATHROOM, DAY 10 1930   5/21
VINCE

VINCE in the mirror, brushing his teeth, looking at himself, despairing.
    CUT TO – VINCE, plucking nostril hairs with tweezers.
    CUT TO – VINCE, using a cotton bud to get gunk out of the corner of his eyes.
    CUT TO – VINCE, doing his hair, all gelled flat.
    CUT TO – VINCE, doing his hair, gelled all spiky.
    CUT TO – VINCE, showering his hair.
    CUT TO – VINCE, doing his hair. As normal.

5/22 INT. VINCE'S BEDROOM, DAY 10 1940   5/22
VINCE

VINCE, in a full-length mirror, trying on a shirt. He tries to get a good look at
his arse, doesn't like what he sees.
    CUT TO – VINCE, in a different shirt.
    CUT TO – VINCE, in yet another different shirt.
    CUT TO – VINCE, in a suit.
    CUT TO – VINCE, in the original outfit, unhappy, trying out the line:

> VINCE: No, I don't want a pension. Cameron, just stop right
> there. No pension. No.

5/23 EXT. RESTAURANT, NIGHT 10 1959   5/23
VINCE

VINCE, approaching the restaurant, on his mobile.

> VINCE: It's all your fault. If I end up with life insurance and
> endowment policies and stocks and shares and things, you're
> paying for it, all right? Where are you, anyway?

5/24 EXT. CANAL STREET, INTERCUT
WITH EXT. RESTAURANT, NIGHT 10 1959   5/24
STUART, MARTIN/VINCE

STUART on his mobile, MARTIN at his side.

> STUART: We're going to Via Fossa, I've got a new friend, his
> name's Martin. So you won't be missed.

VINCE: Thanks a lot, oh my God, I'm here, I'm going in.

STUART: Good luck! Keep your phone on. And Vince –
(Quieter; he means it) Just remember one thing. You're fantastic.

5/25 INT. RESTAURANT, NIGHT 10 2000   5/25
VINCE, CAMERON

VINCE steps inside, sees, across a distance, CAMERON, already at a
table. CAMERON waves. VINCE waves back, mutters into his mobile.

VINCE: I'm a fantastic twat.

He clicks the phone off. Deep breath, and he heads over to CAMERON.

5/26 INT. RESTAURANT, NIGHT 10 2015   5/26
VINCE, CAMERON

VINCE and CAMERON sit with their menus. CAMERON's right into eye-contact,
intimacy, honest and direct. Which for VINCE, actually works; he's still got first-
date nerves – which makes CAMERON like him all the more – but VINCE is
smiling, happy. Someone's listening to him for once.

CAMERON: What about the Rembrandt, is that still going?

VINCE: Yeah, I go there. And Via Fossa, and the Union. And
Manto's, and Metz, and Napoleon's. New York New York. And
Cruz, and Babylon, and Paradise. And Poptastic. Just every now
and then.

CAMERON: I think that makes you officially a scene queen.

VINCE: I'm not. (Beat) I just go out a lot. (Beat) How come you
don't?

CAMERON: Vince. What is there, on that street, that's going to
surprise me?

VINCE: Yeah, but. If you don't go down there, how are you going
to meet someone?

CAMERON: (Right at him) Hello?

VINCE: Right, yeah, you having a starter? I'm not, I never have
starters. Yes I will, I'm starving, I'm having a starter, blimey, look
at the starters, hundreds of them, where's that wine?

5/27 INT. VIA FOSSA, NIGHT 10 2030   5/27
STUART, MARTIN, NATHAN, DONNA, DAZZ

STUART with MARTIN.

STUART: Seen anyone you like?

MARTIN: (Terrified, knocks back his drink) Ooh, um. There is one.

STUART: Which one? I might know him. (MARTIN just looks at him) Oh. Right.

MARTIN: Sorry. I don't suppose – I mean, you wouldn't, not in a million years, but – (a desperate hope) I'll sign the contract. If you're prepared to… I mean it, I will, I'll sign. *If.*

STUART: That's my boyfriend on the phone. He's seeing his accountant tonight.

MARTIN: …sorry. I'll sign it anyway. Sorry.

STUART sees NATHAN enter the pub, a distance away, DONNA at his side.

STUART: Tell you what, how about him? Tall blonde one. He's up for anything, I'll put in a good word.

MARTIN: How old is he?

STUART: Fifteen.

MARTIN: Ooh, no, I don't think so, fifteen, that's a bit revolting, isn't it?

STUART: Absolutely.

CUT TO – NATHAN and DONNA, as DAZZ descends on them, NATHAN instantly mortified.

DAZZ: Nathan, look, I can see you now! Bet you can't remember my name, you dirty shagger – you hanging round for a bit?

NATHAN: No, we're going –

DONNA: We're not, we just got here!

NATHAN: We're going, all right?

DAZZ: Nathan love, calm down. This might come as a shock, but I'm not in love with you, you're quite safe. Back in a minute, I'll have a dry Martini. (To DONNA) It's Daniel, by the way, Dazz.

DAZZ goes.

DONNA: Daniel from last night? Daniel the six-foot-two barrister with a BMW?

NATHAN: No, that's a different Daniel.

DONNA laughs out loud.

5/28 INT. RESTAURANT, NIGHT 10 2033   5/28
VINCE

VINCE has been left alone. Which has sent him to his mobile, and contact with STUART slams VINCE back to his standard insecure self.

> VINCE: It's a nightmare! Says he's thirty-six, the liar, I'm sitting here with an old man, it's like the auditions for *Cocoon 3*. And even then he's not interested, I'm doing my best, he's eyeing up the waiters –

5/28A INT. VIA FOSSA, INTERCUT WITH
RESTAURANT, NIGHT 10 2034   5/28
STUART, MARTIN, NATHAN/VINCE, CAMERON

STUART on his mobile, MARTIN at his side.

> STUART: Sod the waiters, tell him that story about the broken leg, that always works –

NATHAN passes STUART, on his way to the cigarette machine.

> NATHAN: Is that Vince? Say hello from me!

> STUART: Some twat says hello.

> VINCE: Is that Nathan? Stuart, listen, don't let him wander off, Mum said he stayed out last night, and his mother's in pieces, she had a right go at me, do us a favour, keep an eye on him –

> STUART: Never mind him, think about yourself for once.

Hangs up, just as CAMERON returns to the table. VINCE keeps his mobile in hand – thinking of NATHAN with STUART, and his promise to JANICE.

> CAMERON: We could go somewhere afterwards, I don't know, is Cruz open? You're the expert –

> VINCE: Yeah, listen, I've got to make this call, there's this boy, and no one's looking after him, it's a bit of a crisis, you don't mind...?

VINCE presses send, STUART gets the call.

> VINCE: Stuart, seriously, it's your fault he's left home, he could wander off anywhere –
> STUART: Hold on, call waiting – (Clicks) Yeah?

5/29 INT. MARIE'S HOUSE, INTERCUT WITH
VIA FOSSA, NIGHT 10 2034   5/29
MARIE/STUART, MARTIN

5/29 – 5/34 played *top speed*, not a single pause. But no split-screen.

MARIE's kitchen, in an ordinary Barratt-home type house. MARIE's all dressed up with nowhere to go, the only one on a land-line.

> MARIE: Thank you, Stuart, thank you so much. I've had Ben crying his eyes out, that's all he needs, another man to abandon him –
>
> STUART: I did phone, Marie, I left a message, it's an emergency, I've got to work –
>
> MARIE: You're in a bar, I can hear it! How many dates d'you think I get? A mother with two kids?
>
> STUART: Hold on, call waiting – (Clicks) Yes?

5/30 INT. THRIVE, INTERCUT WITH VIA FOSSA, NIGHT 10 2035   5/30
SANDRA/STUART, MARTIN

SANDRA at her desk – in her coat, like she's been called back in.

> SANDRA: Stuart, are you with Martin Brooks? Cos his mobile's switched off, his wife's on the phone, she's had the roof fall in or something –
>
> STUART: Martin, it's your wife –
>
> MARTIN: I'm not here!
>
> STUART: He's not here, hold on, call waiting –

5/31 INT. RESTAURANT, NIGHT 10 2036   5/31
VINCE, CAMERON

> VINCE: (To CAMERON, an apology) Call waiting, he's a busy man –
>
> CAMERON: Look, no offence, but d'you think you could put it down for a minute?
>
> VINCE: Yeah, sure, sorry – (Hangs up)
>
> CAMERON: Right, cos if you want to go clubbing, I can –

VINCE's mobile rings.

> VINCE: I'm sorry, it's this boy, I promised his mother –
> (Answers the phone) Hello?

5/32 INT. MARIE'S HOUSE, INTERCUT WITH RESTAURANT, NIGHT 10 2037
5/32

MARIE/VINCE, CAMERON

> MARIE: Vince, he's kept me waiting long enough, put him on the phone!

> VINCE: I'm not with him!

> MARIE: You're always with him! I'm supposed to be on a date and he's ruined it –

> VINCE: Marie, I'm not, honestly – hold on, call waiting – (Clicks) Yes?

5/33 INT. THRIVE, INTERCUT WITH RESTAURANT, NIGHT 10 2038
5/33

SANDRA/VINCE, CAMERON

> SANDRA: Vince, put him on, I know full well he's taken Martin Brooks to some godforsaken dive –

> VINCE: I'm not with Stuart!

> SANDRA: His wife's going mental –

> VINCE: Whose wife?

> SANDRA: Martin Brooks!

> VINCE: Who the hell is Martin Brooks? Hold on, call waiting – (Clicks) What?

5/34 INT. VIA FOSSA, INTERCUT WITH RESTAURANT (5/31), INTERCUT WITH MARIE'S HOUSE (5/32), INTERCUT WITH THRIVE (5/33) NIGHT 10 2039
5/34

STUART, MARTIN/VINCE, CAMERON/MARIE/SANDRA

> STUART: You hung up on me!

> VINCE: Are you with Martin Brooks?

> STUART: How d'you know Martin Brooks?

> VINCE: I've got Sandra, chasing Martin Brooks.

> STUART: I don't know any Martin Brooks, I've never heard of Martin Brooks.

> VINCE: Hold on – (Clicks) He's not with Martin Brooks.

> MARIE: Who the hell is Martin Brooks?

VINCE: Sorry, wrong one, hold on – (Clicks) Sandra, no Martin Brooks –

SANDRA: He *is* with Martin Brooks! And his roof's fallen in!

VINCE: Whose roof's fallen in?

SANDRA: Martin Brooks!

VINCE: Hold on – (Clicks) Marie, is your date with Martin Brooks?

MARIE: Who the *fuck* is *Martin Brooks?*

VINCE: I dunno, but he's got a wife and a dodgy roof –

MARIE: I'm supposed to be with Malcolm!

VINCE: Who the fuck is Malcolm?

CAMERON: Wait a minute, I know Martin Brooks, let me have a word –

VINCE is so surprised, he lets CAMERON take the phone. And he's even more surprised when CAMERON stands, walks out –

5/35 EXT. RESTAURANT, NIGHT 10 2040   5/35
CAMERON, VINCE

CAMERON strides out, slings the mobile phone, as far as he can, into the canal. VINCE arrives two steps behind him.

VINCE: Oy! That's my phone –

CAMERON just grabs him. Big, strong snog. Then he lets him go.

CAMERON: Call me.

CAMERON walks off. On VINCE, stunned, feeble;

VINCE: What with...?

5/36 INT. VIA FOSSA, NIGHT 10 2055   5/36
STUART, MARTIN, VINCE, DAZZ, DONNA, NATHAN

STUART with MARTIN. VINCE walks up between them, slams his pint down.

VINCE: Bastard accountants.

STUART: Sweetheart, I've missed you.

STUART kisses VINCE on the lips, just two, three seconds, lets go. Beat.

VINCE: I'm stocking up on this aftershave.

CUT TO – DAZZ and DONNA, laughing – DONNA loves DAZZ, thinks he's funny and marvellous – as NATHAN returns with drinks.

DAZZ: Oy, Donna's been saying, you've had him?

Their POV, STUART introducing VINCE to MARTIN.

DAZZ (cont.) Well that's the last you'll see of him – if he had you, he's a chicken hawk. They chase after you, buy you dinner, all that. Once they've shagged you, won't look at you.

NATHAN: Yeah, well I've had him twice.

DONNA: He's never bought you dinner.

DAZZ: D'you like him?

NATHAN: He's all right.

DONNA: Oh, like, Nathan's not completely in love.

DAZZ: Word of advice, Nathan. He can swan about, but there's one thing he's short of. He's not young. And he knows it. Your age, you can make him beg.

On NATHAN, taking this to heart.

5/37 INT. VIA FOSSA, NIGHT 10 2300   5/37
VINCE, STUART, GARETH, NATHAN, DONNA, DAZZ, MIDDLE-AGED MAN

VINCE in B/G, STUART leading MARTIN over to a MIDDLE-AGED MAN.

STUART: It's no good looking, go and talk – (to MIDDLE-AGED MAN) What's your name?

MIDDLE-AGED MAN says 'Adrian'.

STUART (cont.) Adrian, Martin, Martin, Adrian, off you go.

STUART leaves them together, walks back to VINCE, as VINCE slams down another empty (he's has a few, a bit wired, manic, and returns to the subject for the hundredth time).

VINCE: Waste of time, he didn't even like me.

STUART: He must've liked you!

VINCE: No shag! He's gay, we go on a date, where's the shag? I don't give a toss, see that bloke over there? He's been looking, I'm going over –

STUART: He asked you out, he kissed you.

VINCE: And then he went home! It's unnatural!

STUART: Vince, is it so hard to believe that someone fancies you?

VINCE: I don't care, I'm shagging, I am –

VINCE, drunk, heads over to the bloke (GARETH, 31, nice but not beautiful).
STUART watches as VINCE barges into a conversation with GARETH. He looks across to see MARTIN with the MIDDLE-AGED MAN.
Then NATHAN, DONNA and DAZZ in fits of laughter. One of those moments where STUART feels completely out of it – and a bit to blame for what VINCE is like.
A resigned smile, he walks away.

5/38 INT. VINCE'S FLAT, NIGHT 10 2359   5/38
VINCE, GARETH

VINCE now standing in the middle of his flat, snogging GARETH, both going like the clappers, pulling off each other's shirts (though not getting naked). But GARETH's a shocking shag, a man who's learnt to snog off porn films, mouth wide open, tongue hanging out. VINCE pulls back.

VINCE: Sorry, d'you mind shutting your mouth a bit?

GARETH: Yeah, sure.

Back to snogging, GARETH's mouth still wide open. VINCE pulls back.

VINCE: It's just a bit more sexy. If you keep your mouth shut a bit.

GARETH: Yeah, sure.

Back to snogging, GARETH's mouth still open. Then GARETH pulls back.

GARETH: Oh my God, you've got *Genesis of the Daleks.*

VINCE: …yeah.

GARETH: Can we watch it?

VINCE: Um, we can watch it after, yeah.

GARETH: Can we watch it now?

5/39 INT. VINCE'S FLAT, NIGHT 10 0025   5/39
VINCE, GARETH

GARETH sitting transfixed by the TV, Daleks on screen, VINCE sitting back, a distance away, *so* pissed off.

GARETH: Cos right, this was the first time Davros ever appeared, he's manipulating the war between the Kaleds and the Thals so his own creations can survive –

VINCE: I know.

GARETH: Cos those are the first Daleks ever, they weren't even called Daleks, they were called the Mark Three Travel Machine –

VINCE: I know, it's my tape.

GARETH: Three more episodes, *molto bene, molto!*

GARETH gleeful, VINCE just gives up.

5/39A EXT. THRIVE, DAY 11 0900   5/39A
STUART, MARTIN

Daylight. STUART and MARTIN, with coffee, in the jeep. STUART's quiet, reflective (the fact that he let down MARIE niggling at him).

MARTIN: He was all right, he was nice. Apart from the spitting. Suppose you got lucky. (no reply) Good clubs, though, must be marvellous. Doing that all the time.

STUART: Do it all the time, and it stops being marvellous.

MARTIN: Still, it's a Saturday, should be good tonight –

STUART: What time's your train?

MARTIN: I'll cancel, I'll tell Anne I've got to work –

STUART: Martin, go home. Go home to your wife, and your kids. Just go. (starts the engine)

MARTIN: (crestfallen) Well maybe the next time I come up –

STUART: No.

Poor MARTIN left with no choice as the jeep pulls out of shot.

5/40 INT. VINCE'S BATHROOM, DAY 11 0901   5/40
VINCE

VINCE, in his dressing gown, shoves water in his face, looks at himself in the mirror, bleary. What a night.

5/41 INT. VINCE'S FLAT, DAY 11 0902   5/41
VINCE, GARETH

VINCE comes out of the bathroom, GARETH just leaving. (They probably did have sex at four in the morning. Brief and awful.)

GARETH: You've got *The Seeds of Doom*, that's a classic, I'll come round and watch it sometime, is that all right?

VINCE: Yeah.

GARETH: Bye then – beware the Mentiads!

GARETH goes. On VINCE, deep in thought. Then he goes to his jacket from last night, roots in the pocket, pulls out CAMERON's business card. VINCE just looks at it.

5/42 EXT. ROMEY'S HOUSE, DAY 11 1500   5/42
LISA, STUART, ALFRED

LISA opens the door to STUART, who's carrying ALFRED.

STUART: I took him to Alderley Edge, he loved it.

LISA: Vince not with you?

STUART: Why should he be?

LISA: I was talking to Alfred.

5/43 INT. ROMEY'S HALL/LIVING ROOM, DAY 11 1500   5/43
STUART, LISA, NATHAN, ROMEY, SIOBHAN, SUZIE, ALFRED

STUART carries ALFRED to the living room, LISA following, smiling.

LISA: We've had a great afternoon, we've been entertaining another one of your babies.

STUART enters the living room, to find NATHAN in full flow with ROMEY, SIOBHAN and SUZIE.

NATHAN: Cos when Helen was five, I was ten, she used to ride piggy back but she'd grab my hair – (sees STUART) Hiya.

STUART: What are you doing here?

NATHAN: I was passing by – I'm just saying, weekends, I could look after Alfred, y'know, babysitting. Cos you're working all week, you must be worn out. At your age.

LISA: We like Nathan, Nathan can stay.

5/44 INT. ROMEY'S CONSERVATORY, DAY 11 1510   5/44
STUART, ROMEY, LISA, LANCE, ALFRED

STUART suffering, with ALFRED, as ROMEY and LISA take the piss, loving it (really making each other laugh, a couple).

ROMEY: Can't get rid of him!

LISA: It's great, it's like having a houseboy, he can do the garden.

ROMEY: It's the Stuart Jones Foundation for Fallen Boys. Bob-a-job week.

STUART: Can I help it if he's obsessed?

LISA: Yeah, obsessed at fifteen, what does that make you? A Hornby train set? A Playstation?

LISA and ROMEY laughing – not at the joke particularly, but at STUART's discomfort – as LANCE walks in (30, smiling, friendly, Ghanaian).

LANCE: Sorry, am I interrupting? This must be Stuart! Heard all about you, mate.

STUART: I've heard nothing about you. Mate.

LANCE: Lance, nice to meet you.

ROMEY: I have told you, Lance works at the university, we did that seminar on ethics. If you listened.

LISA: (Light, happy, no giveaway signs) He's moved in, he's got the room at the back, he's our token straight.

LANCE: (Of ALFRED) Oh look at Alfie, isn't he hot in that? D'you mind? (Takes ALFRED off STUART) Come here, big fella.

STUART: Moved in since when?

LANCE: It's not for long, my visa expires in five months, I had to move flats last week, couldn't get a five-month lease, so Romey helped me out. I'm another one of her lost causes.

STUART: Christ, you can't turn your back on this house.

LISA: And yet you still do.

LANCE: (To ALFRED) Who can fly? Who can fly, then? (Lifts him up) You can fly! Yes you can! Aaand again!

Etc., with ALFRED, covering: STUART just looking, and he catches LISA's eye. Her cool smile; she knows exactly what he's thinking, feeling supplanted by a man in the house, with ALFRED 24 hours a day.

5/45 INT. VINCE'S OFFICE, DAY 11 1600   5/45
VINCE, ROSALIE

On CAMERON's card, being tapped away on VINCE's desk.
    Reveal VINCE at his desk, as ROSALIE knocks, comes in. Now she's past the initial contact stage, she's growing in confidence with VINCE.

ROSALIE: Knock knock. It's Eileen's last day, we're going out for a drink, d'you fancy coming?

VINCE: Um. No, sort of busy.

ROSALIE: Anything interesting?

VINCE: No, just – this friend, I might not go.

ROSALIE: Is it a date?

VINCE: Um. Might be.

ROSALIE: (Faint smile) Good for you. Have a nice time. (Beat) If you don't go, we're in the Feathers at seven.

ROSALIE goes. VINCE looks at CAMERON's card, suddenly picks up the phone, dials the number. On edge, so ready to slam the phone down, but:

VINCE: Hello, it's me. Vince. Hiya.

5/46 EXT. MARIE'S HOUSE, DAY 11 1700   5/46
STUART, MARIE

MARIE opens the front door. STUART's standing there, with flowers. She slams the door in his face.

5/47 INT. MARIE'S KITCHEN, DAY 11 1703   5/47
STUART, MARIE

STUART puts the flowers down on the kitchen table. Both clipped with each other, distant in the way only a brother and sister can be.

STUART: I did phone, I left a message.

MARIE: Is that what you do on Saturdays? Go round and apologise for the week? (Beat) The childminder's a bit stupid with messages.

STUART: Get an answerphone.

MARIE: I had one. Robert took it.

STUART: (Gets out his wallet) Get yourself a new one.

MARIE: The car needs a service, the clutch is going.

STUART puts away his wallet, gets out his cheque book. An old routine.

STUART: How much?

MARIE: Two hundred. (Beat; she loves stringing this out) And Tom's nagging for software, he wants a graphics package or something.

STUART: Call it five hundred, yeah?

MARIE: Fine. (She watches him writing, then:) Oh, and Mum and Dad are getting divorced.

Beat.

STUART: Yeah yeah, funny joke.

MARIE: And you've seen them, have you? You've driven all of ten miles to go and see them? Cos they don't tell you, they don't tell the Golden Boy. Me, I get it all.

STUART: What have they said?

MARIE: You could write them a cheque. Cos that makes everything all right, doesn't it? (Snatches the cheque) If you don't believe me, go and see them. I'll draw you a map.

5/48 EXT. CANAL STREET, NIGHT 11 2200   5/48
VINCE, CAMERON

VINCE with CAMERON, CAMERON heading towards Via Fossa.

VINCE: Honestly, we could go down Castlefield –

CAMERON: You like it here, you said. It's your date, we're doing what you like.

CAMERON leads the way in.

5/49 INT. VIA FOSSA, NIGHT 11 2205   5/49
VINCE, CAMERON, HAZEL, BERNARD, STUART

VINCE and CAMERON stand with drinks, VINCE on edge, his home ground.
    During the opening dialogue, VINCE is alarmed to see HAZEL – in full party mode, laughing, BERNARD nearby – crossing towards them. She sees VINCE, is about to call out, then sees CAMERON. She glides past, with just a big, sly wink for VINCE, not intruding.

CAMERON: And the funny thing is, the telly's different, even the language is different, you expect all that, but I arrived in this country, d'you know the first thing I noticed? The moon's upside down.

VINCE: …yeah?

CAMERON: It is, though, no one ever told me. Cos you think about it, you've travelled all the way round, the moon's upside down, it's weird. (VINCE watching HAZEL go) Oh well, I thought it was interesting. Used to be a good chat-up line, I must've worn it out – she was at the funeral, that woman.

VINCE: What woman?

Suddenly STUART flings himself in, more pissed than we've ever seen him.

STUART: Where the fuck have you been?

VINCE: Hiya – Stuart, Cameron, you've met –

STUART: That's right, we met by the buffet. (Which makes him laugh) I liked that buffet, it was fucking excellent.

VINCE: You're pissed.

STUART: So get me a drink.

5/50 INT. VIA FOSSA, NIGHT 11 2208   5/50
VINCE, STUART, CAMERON

VINCE at the bar. Though he's more intent at looking across at STUART with CAMERON, STUART moving in slightly. A move VINCE has seen before; it both alarms and fascinates him.

CUT TO – STUART with CAMERON. It's not what STUART says, but his manner; the full come-on, the smile, the eye-contact. (And in copping-off mode, he's a fraction less drunk, more focused.) CAMERON's very contained, maybe interested; we can't tell his reaction, until VINCE returns.

CAMERON: What does an Account Director do?

STUART: I direct accounts. Some of it's shit, but some of the clients are good, Manchester indie labels, stuff like that. I could do it in my sleep, I dunno, I might move, I'm looking round.

CAMERON: What for?

STUART: Anything. There's always something better, just waiting to come along. D'you know that feeling?

VINCE arrives, with drinks.

VINCE: Here you go.

CAMERON: Took your time, I missed you –

And in saying that, CAMERON takes hold of VINCE, snogs him.

STUART: Don't mind me.

STUART wanders off, CAMERON lets go of VINCE, who's flustered.

VINCE: Where's he going?

CAMERON: Up his own arse.

5/51 INT. VINCE'S FLAT, NIGHT 11 2359   5/51
VINCE, CAMERON

VINCE leads CAMERON in, VINCE so on edge he's giving off sparks.

    VINCE: There it is, not much, d'you want a drink?

    CAMERON: You having one?

    VINCE: I'll just have one, I can't stay up, I'll have to chuck you
    out, I'm working first thing.

    CAMERON: Gin and tonic?

    VINCE: Yup, gin and tonic!

VINCE grabs the gin off the table, goes out to the kitchen (tonic and ice in the
fridge), makes himself busy, calling through.

    VINCE: Sorry 'bout Stuart, haven't seen him that pissed in ages.

CAMERON stands in the kitchen doorway.

    CAMERON: Some friend. He was making a pass at me.

    VINCE: No, he's always like that.

    CAMERON: Vince, I've been round the block. He was making a
    pass.

    VINCE: No, really, he wouldn't fancy you.

    CAMERON: Oh, thanks.

    VINCE: No, I mean, it's just types, y'know? He wouldn't.

    CAMERON: He did.

    VINCE: ...d'you think?

    CAMERON: Definitely.

CAMERON goes back into the flat. Stay on VINCE. In amongst the pictures on
his kitchen wall, there's a photo of STUART. He looks at it, as the fact sinks in, a
seismic movement in his head: STUART fancied CAMERON.

    CAMERON OOV: It's nice, nice place. *Doctor Who.* We used to get
    that, scared me as a kid. That one with the shop window
    dummies. (VINCE carries the drinks through) And that one with
    the maggots, that was good. How many tapes have you got? Are
    you one of those anorak blokes?

VINCE hands CAMERON his drink. And that movement, contact, explodes. VINCE grabs CAMERON, CAMERON grabs VINCE, both try to put their drinks down, never mind if they fall over, as they go for it, grappling.

They lurch one way. They lurch the other way. Eating each other. They start fumbling with shirt buttons, frantic. They knock things flying – except props on hire – covering as much of the surface area of the flat as possible.
Then they knock over a huge stack of videotapes.

> CAMERON: Your tapes –

> VINCE: Sod the tapes –

They continue grappling, unbuttoning, heading towards the bedroom. VINCE looks back.

> VINCE: Which tapes – ?

But CAMERON grabs him, snogs him. They all-but-fall backwards into the bedroom, shirts finally coming off, trousers the next to be attacked, as VINCE reaches out and – Slams the door on us.

EPISODE SIX

6/1 INT. DANCE CLASS/GYM, DAY 12 1630   6/1
MARGARET, STUART

Music: Mousse T vs Hot'N'Juicy, 'Horny 98'. But, for once, a merciful lack of gay men; it's an aerobics class full of middle-aged Cheshire women. Big hair and leotards. We're travelling down the ranks to find the woman at the back – MARGARET, in her 50s, determined, keeping perfect time. Closer on her, into a mid-shot as STUART appears behind, at her shoulder.

> STUART: Excuse me, madam, we've had complaints about excessive perspiration, could you please leave?

> MARGARET: (Keeps going throughout) Cheeky sod.

> STUART: Orange juice?

> MARGARET: With a vodka.

6/2 INT. GYM CAFÉ, DAY 12 1650   6/2
STUART, MARGARET, FANTASTIC MAN

A café with gym activities going on in B/G behind windows. STUART at the table with two orange juices as MARGARET sits down. They've a good relationship, but brittle; MARGARET could be a difficult woman to get on with. And STUART's different in her company; distant, more reserved.

> MARGARET: I suppose Marie's told you, she could never keep quiet. (Of his shirt) Is that new?

> STUART: No, it's ages old.

> MARGARET: You see? I'd have bought you that. I buy you things and you don't wear them.

> STUART: So what's he been saying?

> MARGARET: Oh, he's the expert, now. Apparently, you can get a form from the town hall, no lawyers, no expense, you can get divorced for forty-five pounds.

> STUART: Don't you need a reason?

> MARGARET: How much did it cost?

> STUART: Don't know, eighty.

> MARGARET: Eight*een*?

> STUART: Eightee.

MARGARET: On a shirt.

STUART: He must've said why.

MARGARET: I stopped listening a long time back.

As MARGARET talks, STUART sees a FANTASTIC MAN in gym gear approach a table of friends behind MARGARET. FANTASTIC MAN sees STUART, smiles, is about to go over – he's an ex-shag. STUART makes the smallest, well-practised flick of the eyes, perhaps a tiny flick of the hand – 'back off'. FANTASTIC MAN looks at MARGARET, understands, retreats.

MARGARET (cont.): And he's always got something to nag about, every single day. It's like Marie, Robert taking off like that, oh, it's food and drink to him. Nothing he loves more than a bit of trouble.

STUART: So what have *you* said?

MARGARET: I'm looking at flats. Nice little place in Hale, I've kept myself in trim, I'll have a fine old time. You can show me round, you can be my guide. Singles bars, you must know them all.

6/3 INT. HARLO'S, DAY 12 1720   6/3
VINCE, ROSALIE, CAMERON, SANDRA

A customer complaints/information desk, VINCE just picking out club card leaflets as ROSALIE comes up.

ROSALIE: Come on, you haven't said a word, how's it going? That date of yours, the new girlfriend.

VINCE: (Thrown) Um, not so bad –

ROSALIE: So you're still seeing her? How long's that been now, what's her name?

VINCE: (Suddenly the boss) Rosalie, I'm with a customer.

ROSALIE: Oh sorry.

He shoots her a get-back-to-work look, and ROSALIE goes, crushed, as VINCE turns to his customer. CAMERON. VINCE hands over the leaflets, talks like they're strangers, the dialogue loaded with sex.

VINCE: There's all sorts of benefits with the club card, sir, save up the points and you can get air miles, weekend breaks –

CAMERON: Are any of the benefits in-store?

VINCE: What would you have in mind, sir?

CAMERON: Well, Mr, uh – (Looks at the name badge) Tyler, I

just thought there might be the chance to shag one of the staff.

VINCE enjoying it, but careful of NS ASSISTANTS passing by.

> VINCE: I'll have to check the small print, but I'm sure that's possible. Exactly what sort of shag does sir have in mind?

> CAMERON: Oh, I thought the full fuck.

> VINCE: Very good, sir, and that's a special offer this week. Bonus points. I can have it delivered to your car in ten minutes –

Interrupted by SANDRA walking in, shoving a mobile phone at VINCE.

> SANDRA: This goes well beyond my job description. And he didn't pay for it; if he says he did, he's lying, it's all on insurance.

And she walks off. The phone rings.

> VINCE: (To CAMERON) Hold on a minute – (On the phone) Hiya –

6/4 INT. STUART'S JEEP, INTERCUT WITH HARLO'S, DAY 12 1721   6/4
STUART/VINCE, CAMERON

STUART driving top-speed, back to his old self and then some, wild, manic.

> STUART: We're going out! It's student night at Paradise, it's about time I had an educated shag –

> VINCE: I can't, I'm busy –

> STUART: Bring him with you – (Beeps at a car) Fuck off! (On the phone) Vince, you've got to – my parents are going mad, they're off their fucking heads!

6/5 EXT. CAR PARK, NIGHT 12 0115   6/5
STUART, VINCE, CAMERON, ALEXANDER

STUART slams on to the bonnet of the jeep. VINCE and CAMERON help him up, and into the passenger seat, STUART off his head, slurring.

> STUART: He was dancing like a twat, d'you see him? He looks nice, then he dances like a twat.

STUART keeps on muttering 'like a twat', etc., and giggling under:

> VINCE: I'll put him to bed, you drive home, I'll be round in twenty minutes. And it's bonus points, remember?

> CAMERON: I should've gone for that two-for-one on Nescafé.

A voice rings out:

ALEXANDER: Vince, help me, oh Jesus Christ help me!

ALEXANDER's running across the car park, four packed holdalls and a hatbox bouncing around him. He's genuinely frantic, scared.

ALEXANDER (cont.): They're going to kill me, they've got knives and everything, they wouldn't stop following, they're going to kill me.

VINCE: Who?

ALEXANDER: No one, you fucker, it's just a good entrance. (During this, he starts slinging his stuff in the jeep) Look, it's me I'm back I'm home! Rodrigo went mad, chucked me out, chased me round Balham with a gun.

VINCE: What about your job?

ALEXANDER: Binned it, they put me on the Saturday night shift, and me a homosexual, can I stay at yours?

VINCE: Yeah, but I was staying at Cameron's – uh, this is Cameron, Cameron, Alexander –

CAMERON: We've sort of met before, actually, I was at Philip Delaney's funeral –

ALEXANDER: Oo, Australian, very nice. Down Under, didgeridoos, mammals with pouches – loads of material, fab.

STUART: Can we go?

CAMERON: (To VINCE) It's all right, you sort out this lot, I'll see you tomorrow.

CAMERON gives VINCE a kiss (not a big snog). During this:

ALEXANDER: Oo, don't mind me.

ALEXANDER gets into the back of the jeep, saying 'y'all right, chocolate?' to STUART, who mutters away. Stay on VINCE and CAMERON.

VINCE: You don't mind, though?

CAMERON: (Genuinely amused) Your friends are mad, and you're mad too. (Kiss) See you tomorrow.

CAMERON walks to his car, VINCE gets in the driver's seat of the jeep.

ALEXANDER: I turn my back for a second! Vincent Tyler, is that or is that not a boyfriend?

Hard on the line, CUT TO –

6/6 INT. STUART'S FLAT, NIGHT 12 0145 6/6
VINCE, ALEXANDER, STUART

VINCE and ALEXANDER tip STUART into bed, pull the duvet over, dialogue immediately continuous from 6/5.

> VINCE: It's not boyfriend-boyfriend. We're just having a laugh.

> ALEXANDER: He's a boyfriend, you liar, boyfriend capital B.

> VINCE: He's not, he's just a bloke, that's all.

Hard on the line, CUT TO –

6/7 INT. VINCE'S BEDROOM, NIGHT 12 0230 6/7
VINCE, ALEXANDER

VINCE and ALEXANDER tucked up in bed, both in T-shirts. Quieter late-night chat, old friends, dialogue immediately continuous from 6/6.

> ALEXANDER: Looked like a boyfriend to me.

> VINCE: Oh give it a rest.

> ALEXANDER: All right then, tell me. When you have a wank, d'you think about him?

> VINCE: What's that got to do with it?

> ALEXANDER: Do you think about Cameron?

> VINCE: ...no.

> ALEXANDER: Congratulations. He's your boyfriend.

> VINCE: (Sighs) Suppose.

> ALEXANDER: Oh sound happy, for God's sake. Good shag?

> VINCE: Magnificent shag.

> ALEXANDER: There you are then.

> VINCE: I dunno, it's like... He's a bit non-scene.

> ALEXANDER: Ooh.

> VINCE: I mean, he comes out with me, he goes to Canal Street, but... He's sort of outside it, d'you know what I mean? Sometimes he looks at me like I've been brought up by a pack of wolves. (Switches off the bedside lamp) Anyway. Early days.

Silence in the dark, then:

> ALEXANDER: I was brought up by a family of ducks. (Beat) Oh, the social workers would chase after us, swim! mother would say, swim for your life! They caught me at the age of six, lured me into a trap with a slice of Mighty White.

> VINCE: (Laughing) Oh God, you're going to talk all night.

> ALEXANDER: To this day, I can't have a piece of bread without dipping it in water.

> VINCE: (Turns away, to sleep) Good night.

> ALEXANDER: Wak wak.

Both of them laugh. Then it dies away. Silence. Then both start giggling like kids.

6/8 EXT. THE JONES' HOUSE, DAY 13 1600   6/8
STUART, MARIE

The Jones' house is in Cheshire, maybe Cheadle, the sort of place you retire to; nice, well-kept, only two bedrooms. *Not too rich.* STUART and MARIE getting out of the jeep.

> MARIE: And *talk* to him, right? I've talked myself to death, it's your turn, go and talk, and I don't mean chat, I mean talk, proper talk.

As they approach the front door, MARIE gets her keys out.

> STUART: How come you've got keys?

> MARIE: They're getting old, of course I've got keys.

MARIE lets them in.

6/9 INT. JONES' HOUSE, DAY 13 1600   6/9
STUART, MARIE, MARGARET, CLIVE

MARIE and STUART walk in. Down the hall, MARGARET's in the kitchen. Dialogue on the hoof as they walk down the hall, into the kitchen, kisses exchanged. Much of this played on STUART, unusually quiet.

> MARGARET: Careful, that's the carpet.

> MARIE: He paid for it, he can do what he likes with it.

> MARGARET: Boys not with you?

> MARIE: No, I thought we'd have peace and quiet.

> MARGARET: Who are they with?

MARIE: No one, I left them playing on the edge of a cliff.

MARGARET: (To STUART) He's in the garden. And don't
mention the car, that noise in the boot set him off.

STUART crosses the kitchen, to look out of the window. For a small house, it's got
a long garden – not too pretty, much of it turned over to vegetables, cloches, etc.
At the far end, CLIVE JONES is working away, back turned to the house. Dialogue
under this:

MARIE: (Laughing) Did he go to bed?

MARGARET: (Laughing) Nervous stomach, threw up his tea, in
bed before *Watchdog*.

On STUART.

6/10 EXT. HAZEL'S HOUSE, DAY 13 1602   6/10
VINCE, CAMERON, HAZEL, BERNARD, NATHAN, IRENE

VINCE and CAMERON getting out of CAMERON's car.

VINCE: Oh, good timing.

In the middle of the lane, a big Pied Piper truck is parked, sounds its horn.
Immediately, someone steps out of every house in the row, carrying stacks of
Christmas cracker boxes. HAZEL and BERNARD step out of HAZEL's.

VINCE: Blimey, how many have you done?

HAZEL: It's Bernie, he's saving up for a carburettor.

VINCE and CAMERON have to follow HAZEL and BERNARD to the van, queuing
up with neighbours. At the van, a thin 16-year-old BOY counts boxes, ticks a list,
pays out fivers, and a HENCHMAN shoves the boxes in the van.

VINCE: Right, so, Mum, this is Cameron –

CAMERON: We've sort of met before, actually -

VINCE: And this is Bernie, he's the lodger –

BERNARD: It's not a carburettor, it's a crank shaft.

Behind them, NATHAN, in school uniform, appears with more boxes.

VINCE: And, this is Nathan, lodger number two.

NATHAN: I'm not a lodger, I'm a refugee.

HAZEL: (To the BOY) Don't cross me off, Beefy, there's more to
come –

Now HAZEL turns to CAMERON, properly, on her guard, strong; one of the few times we realise she's VINCE's mother, not just a friend.

> HAZEL (cont.): So. Accountant, he says.

> CAMERON: (Enjoys the interrogation) Yeah, that's right.

> HAZEL: This is all cash in hand, so don't you go sniffing about.

> CAMERON: Won't say a word.

> HAZEL: Own house?

> CAMERON: Yes.

> HAZEL: Own car?

> CAMERON: Yes.

> VINCE: He's got his own teeth as well.

> HAZEL: Don't be too sure, they've made Poligrip all but invisible, in't that right, Bernard?

> BERNARD: Cheeky tart.

> HAZEL: All right then, Cameron. You'll do. (Calls to a neighbour) Irene, our Vince has got himself a fella.

IRENE (67, tiny, carrying a single box) says 'Very nice too'.

> HAZEL: Is it buggery, means I'm getting old. Come on, those boxes won't shift by magic.

HAZEL strides back to the house. CAMERON's amused, likes her. (In B/G, NATHAN's getting his boxes ticked off.)

> CAMERON: Is she like that with all your boyfriends?

> NATHAN: What boyfriends? You're the first.

VINCE shoots NATHAN a look, leads CAMERON towards the house.

6/11 EXT. JONES' GARDEN, DAY 13 1604　　　　6/11
CLIVE, STUART, MARGARET, MARIE

CLIVE JONES is 61, a weathered face. He invented the word taciturn. He's in gardening clothes, digging away, no acknowledgement as STUART walks up. Pause, then:

> STUART: It's looking good.

> CLIVE: Should do.

Silence, CLIVE keeps digging.

> STUART: How's things?

CLIVE just nods, okay. Pause, then:

> CLIVE: Busy?

> STUART: Yeah.

> CLIVE: Good.

Pause.

> CLIVE: There's a fork over there. Unless that suit's too expensive
> for digging.

STUART smiles, takes off his jacket – finds somewhere to hang it – and sets about joining in with CLIVE.
CUT TO – the kitchen window. MARGARET and MARIE busying themselves, chatting, but watching the garden in that eye-on-the-menfolk way.

6/12 EXT. JONES' GARDEN, DAY 14 1620   6/12
STUART, CLIVE

STUART and CLIVE now hard at work, lifting a heavy wooden pallet, struggling, then dumping it down. Both knackered, getting their breath back. They look at each other, laughing a little at the state they're in. Pause, CLIVE losing the smile, but the physical exertion's broken the ice a bit.

> CLIVE: Suppose you've heard.

> STUART: Yeah.

Pause.

> CLIVE: It's that endowment policy, matured last month. Might as
> well use it. Thought we could get divorced. Either that, or we
> could go to France. (Pause) Your mother's made the booking.
> Paris, next month.

Beat.

> STUART: Right. (Pause; more angry) Is that it? Is that all it was?
> This week's game?

> CLIVE: (Of MARGARET in the kitchen) Keeps her busy.

> STUART: What about Marie? She's been worried sick.
> She's got the boys to look after and – (Breaks off) Fine. Fine.
> Why am I surprised? You just – you just enjoy yourself, okay, enjoy
> yourself and waste our time, *fine.*

STUART strides off towards the house. CLIVE watches him go, his expression unreadable.

6/13 INT. JEEP, DAY 14 1655   6/13
STUART, MARIE

STUART driving top-speed, MARIE in the passenger seat.

> STUART: They're turning into lunatics! Sitting in that house like they're just… bored! Christ, if ever there was an argument against settling down!

> MARIE: What are you telling me for? Every week, I have to listen to that!

6/14 EXT. MARIE'S HOUSE, DAY 14 1700   6/14
STUART, MARIE

MARIE getting out of the jeep. STUART stays behind the wheel, his most defensive position.

> MARIE: The boys'll be home soon.

> STUART: Things to do.

> MARIE: See you, then.

She's about to go, but stops, has to say it.

> MARIE (cont.): You could tell them, Stuart, they're not going to drop dead of a heart attack. And if they do, we get the house.

> STUART: Even if I was shagging a different woman every night, it's none of their business.

> MARIE: But I've *seen* you. You're so bloody proud, how come they don't fit in to that?

> STUART: You can't talk to those two about *anything*! How long did you take to tell them that Robert was leaving? He was halfway down the M6!

> MARIE: But I told them in the end, what else was I going to do? (Right at him) Lie, for the rest of my life?

> STUART: Fuck off, Marie.

> MARIE: Fuck off yourself.

This said with affection, as she leans in, gives him a kiss on the cheek. As he smiles, then revs up, speeds off, on MARIE, watching him go.

6/15 EXT. CITY STREET, DAY 14 1710
VINCE, CAMERON, NATHAN, ALEXANDER

A pedestrian street in the city centre, like Market Street. VINCE and CAMERON walk along with shopping bags, heading for a bench, where ALEXANDER and NATHAN are sitting, also with bags.

> VINCE: I did warn you, call round my mother's, you get a list of shopping. (Arrives at the bench, to NATHAN) Hiya, d'you get the felt pens?

> NATHAN: Yeah, I got a pack of ten in Smith's.

> ALEXANDER: What's she need felt pens for? Tattoo parlour?

> VINCE: She's got this new scheme, selling detergent door-to-door or something.

> CAMERON: So why does she need felt pens?

> VINCE: In Hazel World, it all makes sense. Last Christmas, this bloke promised her tinsel, ten pence a truckload, it all went wrong and she ended up with half a ton of coffee –

For the second half of the speech above, we're on ALEXANDER. Looking across the crowd, suddenly alert. He talks across VINCE, his voice low, contained. All his usual humour gone.

> ALEXANDER: Oh would you look at that.

All look, only VINCE knowing immediately who he means. An ordinary couple, mid 50s, perfectly harmless, are walking across the street, some distance away, at a right angle to the boys. ALEXANDER calls out, cold.

> ALEXANDER: Hello!

The couple keep walking.

> ALEXANDER: Hello? *Hello?* I said hello!

They keep walking, not the slightest turn of the head. They're not even ignoring him; it's like there's nothing. CAMERON and NATHAN mystified, VINCE only sad. ALEXANDER louder, harder.

> ALEXANDER: I said hello! Oy, I said hello! Look at me, *I said hello!*

They just walk on, ALEXANDER staring after them. Then, all waiting for ALEXANDER to break the silence, which he does by turning to VINCE, back to normal, bright. Too bright.

> ALEXANDER: That's right, cos Hazel had half a ton of coffee in the shed, six months it sat there, by August it was solid, Bernie

had to chip it out – (Suddenly stands, explodes, vicious) Fuck
'em, just *fuck* 'em!

ALEXANDER storms away, the opposite direction to the couple. Long, long
pause. Then VINCE to NATHAN, quiet.

VINCE: His mum and dad.

6/16 INT. VIA FOSSA, NIGHT 14 2100   6/16
VINCE, CAMERON, ALEXANDER, HAZEL, BERNARD, NATHAN, DONNA,
DAZZ

VINCE, CAMERON, HAZEL, BERNARD, NATHAN, DONNA, DAZZ and
OTHERS gathered, ALEXANDER centre-stage, happy. Intercut with NATHAN,
watching, admiring as the extended family sorts out ALEXANDER's problem. All
played fast, dialogue zinging across.

ALEXANDER: Right, what have we got?

HAZEL: Stan's got a room but it smells of meat, Pablo's got a bed
but we think his mother might have died in it, and there's the
promise of a camp bed from Kitty –

ALEXANDER: Are we talking zed bed, sun lounger or just a bed
that's very camp?

HAZEL: Knowing Kitty, I'd go for the last one.

BERNARD: Calvin's in later, he's got a room.

VINCE: Nice room, it's above the Longsight chippy.

ALEXANDER: I'd smell of grease!

HAZEL: No change there, then.

BERNARD: (Suddenly excited) Jackie Cathcart!

HAZEL: Jackie Cathcart!

ALEXANDER: Jackie Cathcart!

VINCE: Oh brilliant room, it's en-suite!

HAZEL: And Billy's not back till Christmas, problem solved!

ALEXANDER: Bring me the head of Jackie Cathcart! Oh thank
God, a bed, my children can sleep in the warmth, I'm saved,
sweet Lord, I'm saved!

ALEXANDER more theatrical than ever at the end, so everyone's laughing, even
one or two clapping. Close on NATHAN, now. Eyes wide, shining; he thinks this
world is the best you could find.

6/17 INT. VIA FOSSA, NIGHT 14 2130   6/17
STUART, VINCE, CAMERON, NATHAN, DONNA, DAZZ, HAZEL, BERNARD, ALEXANDER, JANICE

NATHAN, DONNA, DAZZ, BERNARD, ALEXANDER and OTHERS in B/G (no HAZEL, she's off on a mission). VINCE and CAMERON have moved to a different table, because STUART's arrived. STUART's withdrawn, private, VINCE focused on him, excluding CAMERON.

> STUART: And Marie, like she's all concern – d'you remember when she was seventeen? 'I *know* about you.'

> VINCE: 'I've seen your magazines, I'm gonna tell Mum and Dad.'

> STUART: I had to fucking pay her! Who needs it? Drink?

STUART goes to get the drinks.

> CAMERON: So what's the problem?

> VINCE: …long story.

CUT TO – NATHAN, DONNA and DAZZ, with BERNARD, ALEXANDER and OTHERS nearby, STUART in B/G getting served at the bar. NATHAN's horrified as HAZEL leads JANICE in.

> NATHAN: Oh what's she *like*?

> HAZEL: Here we go, what you having, Janice?

> JANICE: I'll get them –

> HAZEL: No, first one's on me, it's a welcome.

As HAZEL takes the order, gin and tonic, on DONNA and DAZZ, muttering:

> DAZZ: Who's that then?

> DONNA: His mother.

> DAZZ: (Snorts with laughter) Kidding!

Cut back to main dialogue:

> HAZEL: There's an idea – Nathan, you get them in, I've seen that pocket money, it's twice what I earn.

> NATHAN: What d'you think you're doing?

> JANICE: I've come out for a drink, that's allowed, isn't it?

> HAZEL: I've been telling your mum, best day of my life, my son came out, I found all this. It's not just for you, Nathan.

NATHAN: You're shaming me –

JANICE: I'm with Hazel, I'm not bothering you –

NATHAN: You're following me round, it's shaming – (To DONNA and DAZZ) We're going –

DAZZ: Drinks for a quid in Velvet.

DONNA: (To DAZZ) Oh shut up, don't – (NATHAN and DAZZ leave, she follows) She's made the effort, she's got a new skirt –

DAZZ: Listen to her, Jiminy Cricket.

DONNA: (Just blanks DAZZ) Nathan, one drink!

But during this exchange, NATHAN's looking round. He looks at ALEXANDER – oblivious to all this, laughing away – then back at JANICE. One of those moments when he's so fifteen, proud of his problems.

NATHAN: Fuck 'em. Just *fuck* 'em.

He turns, goes, DAZZ following. DONNA looks back at JANICE, follows.
CUT TO – POV of NATHAN and his gang walking out. Reverse, revealing this to be STUART, who's seen the exchange. He then looks across – some distance away – at HAZEL and JANICE, JANICE upset but marvellous, strong, never giving up. Dialogue carries across to STUART.

HAZEL: Give it time. Vince used to be embarrassed, every time I showed up. Still is, some nights, but that's Bacardi for you.

JANICE: It's not as if there's any choice, I can't give up on him. We'll wear him down.

STUART looks to NATHAN. His POV: NATHAN disappearing out of the door. On CU STUART, deep in thought, MIX TO:

6/18 EXT. SCHOOL, DAY 15 1535   6/18
NATHAN, DONNA, CHRISTIAN, STUART

NATHAN and DONNA walking out of school at the end of the day, kids all around. We see, but NATHAN doesn't, CHRISTIAN HOBBS running up behind him. CHRISTIAN slams a football into the back of NATHAN's head.

NATHAN: Piss off, Christian.

CHRISTIAN: D'you hear that, boys? He told me to piss off, Nathan Maloney can swear!

In saying this, CHRISTIAN's overtaken NATHAN and DONNA so he's now in front, stands on the road, facing NATHAN, CHRISTIAN's mates circling round. CHRISTIAN's holding the ball, threatening to throw it, fake throws, just pulling it back in time, but making NATHAN flinch.

CHRISTIAN: Come on then, tell us the rest, everyone says you've left home, what's happened? Trouble at home? Your mother been shagging about?

NATHAN: Shut it.

DONNA: Christian Hobbs, you're just so *wrong*.

Next speech, we're just on CHRISTIAN – no giveaway reaction shot from NATHAN – as, focus on CHRISTIAN F/G, in B/G a big black blur slowly prowls up behind CHRISTIAN.

CHRISTIAN: Cos I've shafted her, she was begging. We've all had her, she'd screw a dog, your mother. Aww, did Nathan run away? Poor little boy, cos his father can't get it up, what's the matter, Nathan, what happened? She ask you to give her one?

Headlights flare, horn blasts, sudden throw of focus to reveal the blur as STUART's jeep, an inch behind CHRISTIAN, who jumps out of his skin.

STUART: Oy, you. Open your mouth one more time and I'll shove my cock in it.

NATHAN and DONNA – and some of CHRISTIAN's mates – laugh. CHRISTIAN wants to say something back, but is wary of opening his mouth, so he just sneers weakly and joins his mates, slinking away. Once he's a distance away, CHRISTIAN can call out 'twat!', but it's feeble.

NATHAN: That's my lift, see ya.

And he's so happy as he leaves DONNA, runs to the jeep. The second NATHAN's in, STUART drives off, dialogue on the move.

STUART: I'm taking you home.

NATHAN: Brilliant, Hazel's doing pizza, she's cooking it herself, she got this recipe –

STUART: I said *home*.

6/19 EXT. MALONEYS' HOUSE, DAY 15 1545   6/19
STUART, NATHAN, ROY, JANICE, HELEN

The jeep pulls up. NATHAN's sullen, just sits there.

STUART: Go on. Give them a chance.

NATHAN: I'm still going back to Hazel's.

STUART: Nathan, your mother and father *know*. You don't know how lucky you are. Go and argue, go and shout, go and – go and watch telly with them, I don't care. Just get in there.

NATHAN: If I do… (Grins) Can I have another shag?

STUART: Cheeky sod.

Beat, both smiling. (And under this, we barely register the low purr of a car engine, maybe an out-of-focus smudge behind them, a car pulling up.)

STUART: Good luck.

NATHAN holds his stare, then angles his head, asking for a kiss. Such an expert. STUART leans over. It's a goodbye kiss, nothing more, but it lasts – more at NATHAN's instigation – maybe three, four seconds, then – *WHAM!*
The entire jeep is jolted forward a foot, STUART and NATHAN all but jerked out of their seats. Behind them, the car engine's wild, now, reversing.

STUART: What the fuck – ?

WHAM! The car rams the jeep again, shoving it forward. As it reverses to attack again, STUART jumps out, runs towards it, furious.

STUART: What the fuck d'you think you're doing – ?

The car door's flung open – NB, this needn't be JANICE's car, they can have another – and we see ROY MALONEY for the first time. Ordinarily, he's a quiet, besuited deputy bank manager, early 40s. But right now, he's berserk, gets out, looking at STUART with murder in his eyes. Which STUART recognises. For the first time in his life, STUART backs off.

STUART: Oh shit.

NATHAN's getting out of the jeep.

NATHAN: It's my dad –

ROY can barely speak – not just angry, close to tears.

ROY: Nathan, get inside the house. (At STUART, voice building) He's fifteen years old. He's fifteen. That boy is *fifteen!*

STUART: (Loves the danger) So? That jeep's only six months, and you've still gone and buggered it!

ROY: You little bastard –

ROY takes a swing at him – clumsy, he's never been in a fight in his life, but STUART retreats, pulls out his mobile, holds it up like a shield, thumb on 9.

STUART: I'm warning you. Nine. Nine. One more nine, and I'll have the police –

ROY: Phone 'em! Bring 'em here! And I'll tell them what you've done to a fifteen year old boy!

STUART: ...good point.

JANICE runs out of the house.

JANICE: Roy, what the hell are you doing?

ROY: What I should've done a long time back – that's him, is it? Stuart? Stuart Jones?

ROY takes another swing, STUART backing off.

JANICE: Roy, for God's sake, don't be so stupid!

ROY: Janice, take him inside! Take him inside, right now!

STUART: Take him upstairs and lock him in the closet!

ROY: You bastard, you little bloody bastard –

And ROY might be about to actually kill STUART, but HELEN comes running out of the house.

HELEN: What's happened to the car, Mum, have you seen the car?

JANICE: Don't, love, get back inside –

NATHAN: Helen, don't, get in the house –

HELEN's distracted ROY, he's now despairing.

ROY: Go back inside, will you just – *please* – get back inside the bloody house – ?

HELEN: (A bit scared) What's he done, what's Nathan done?

JANICE scoops up HELEN, and it's the second's distraction STUART needs, he belts past ROY to the jeep, leaps in, starts the engine, drives away.

ROY: Bastard!

On STUART, as he drives halfway down the street. Then suddenly, he brakes. STUART looks back. ROY's now with NATHAN outside the house, we can hear him shouting:

ROY: Get in there! Get in that house and Christ, are you going to pay for this –

Decision made, STUART reverses all the way back, like a wild thing. ROY's in such a state, he doesn't realise why STUART's come back, and he grabs the bumper, which has fallen off his car, to use as a weapon.

ROY: Come back for more? D'you want more? Cos I'll give you
more, I'll give you plenty, you little bastard –

But on this rant, a look between STUART and NATHAN, who's frozen. STUART
opens the passenger door. NATHAN runs, jumps in.

STUART: Roy, sweetheart. Less of the little.

ROY swings the bumper, misses, as the jeep drives off. ROY's shattered, looks to
the house, the family home. JANICE is back in the doorway, horrified, staring at
him like he's a stranger.
    On ROY. An ordinary man, standing in the middle of an ordinary street. And
he just cries his heart out.

6/20 INT. VIA FOSSA, NIGHT 15 2000   6/20
STUART, NATHAN, VINCE, CAMERON, HAZEL, BERNARD, ALEXANDER

Opening on a burst of laughter, STUART and NATHAN surrounded by VINCE,
CAMERON, HAZEL, BERNARD and ALEXANDER. STUART and NATHAN are
like two people who've survived a war together.

NATHAN: And he's like going, nine, nine, one more nine! And
my dad's like red, he's got this face like he's exploding –

STUART: I thought, if he bursts a blood vessel on this suit, he's a
dead man –

NATHAN: Nine, nine, one more nine!

Much of the laughter has been mixed with shock, and HAZEL can see the serious
side, stands.

HAZEL: (To NATHAN) Well I'm going to phone your mother,
someone's got to.

VINCE is smiling, but eyes flicking from NATHAN to STUART. Such good friends.

VINCE: Nathan Maloney, you're a lucky bastard. First of all you
invent a violent father, then you actually get one.

CAMERON: How's that lucky?

VINCE: Long story.

NATHAN: Fifteen, he kept saying! Fifteen years old!

During NATHAN's line, STUART's mobile rings, he answers.

STUART: What?

6/21 INT. ROMEY'S HOUSE INTERCUT WITH
VIA FOSSA, NIGHT 15 2001   6/20
ROMEY, LANCE/STUART

ROMEY on the phone, a little on edge.

> ROMEY: At last! If you returned just one of my calls –

> STUART: Look, you wouldn't believe the day I've had – I've been attacked!

> ROMEY: Yeah, can you come round? This evening? It's quite important –

During this, LANCE comes into shot, puts an arm round ROMEY, in support.

> STUART: The jeep's a write-off – I can't, I'm seeing Alfred tomorrow, I won't forget – and it's all because of that Nathan –

> NATHAN: Nine! Nine!

> STUART: I'm pressing charges, I'm suing for assault –

> ROMEY: Stuart! I'm getting married.

6/22 INT/EXT. ROMEY'S HOUSE, NIGHT 15 2030   6/22
ROMEY, STUART, VINCE, CAMERON

ROMEY opens the door, STUART barges through.

> STUART: You're doing *what*?

CUT TO – VINCE and CAMERON getting out of CAMERON's car. VINCE sheepish, CAMERON losing his patience with all this.

> CAMERON: I'll phone the restaurant, see if we can get a table for later.

> VINCE: Better cancel.

6/23 INT. ROMEY'S FRONT ROOM, NIGHT 15 2035   6/23
STUART, VINCE, CAMERON, ROMEY, LISA, SIOBHAN, LANCE, SUZIE, ALFRED

STUART contained, impassive, holding ALFRED, as ROMEY explains, LANCE at her side, VINCE at STUART's, LISA, SIOBHAN and SUZIE also listening. CAMERON's standing in the doorway, pissed off.

> LANCE: My visa's running out. If I get married, if we can convince the Home Office it's a proper relationship, I can stay! It's that simple. And Romey offered, I didn't ask her.

> ROMEY: It's a certificate, it doesn't mean anything.

STUART: I didn't say it did, why's everyone having a go at me?

LISA: Oh just look at you!

LANCE: Of course you're worried, Stu. I mean, there's Alfred.

VINCE: What about him?

LANCE: Well, obviously, I'll have to live here full-time – I've checked up on it, the Home Office can investigate whenever they want, so I'll be here, permanently, I've got no choice. But you're his father –

STUART: Who said I wasn't?

LANCE: You could be here just as much as me. (Beat) If you made the effort.

Beat, STUART looking at LANCE, who might not be as nice as he seems; in that second, the battle lines are drawn.

6/24 INT. ROMEY'S KITCHEN/CONSERVATORY, NIGHT 15 2050   6/24
CAMERON, LISA

CAMERON's helping himself to some bread and cheese, as LISA comes in.

CAMERON: Sorry, d'you mind? Starving.

LISA: Help yourself. What was it again?

CAMERON: Cameron.

LISA nods, doesn't offer her name; she's tense, for her own, hidden reasons.

CAMERON: Guess you've known them ages. Stuart and Vince.

LISA: Far too long.

CAMERON: Is it always like this? Vince running after him.

LISA: It's the greatest love story never told. Cameron, long after you're gone, he'll still have Vince. Stuart's little acolyte, poor sod. If it's any consolation, Vince can wait all he likes, that shag's never going to happen.

Silence. CAMERON looking right at her. The sound of big, heavy things falling into place in LISA's head.

LISA: Shit. You're with *Vince*.

CAMERON: ...yeah.

LISA: Shit. It's just – half the time he turns up with some shag, and – I mean Stuart, there's always some bloke, I thought you were – Shit.

CAMERON: (Cool, quiet) Easy mistake. Stuart and Vince.

LISA: (Light, bluffing) I mean he loves him, they love each other, they're friends, I love my friends, don't you? That's all it is. Friendship.

CAMERON: It's not as if I didn't know.

Beat.

LISA: There's some Cambazola at the back of the fridge, help yourself. Have it all.

LISA goes, sharpish. Probably to laugh her head off. On CAMERON.

6/25 INT. ROMEY'S FRONT ROOM, NIGHT 15 2052   6/25
ROMEY, LANCE, STUART, VINCE, SIOBHAN, LISA, SUZIE, ALFRED

ROMEY, LANCE, STUART with ALFRED, VINCE, SIOBHAN, SUZIE, LISA just returning. SIOBHAN's opening a bottle of champagne.

SIOBHAN: So what if it's not a proper wedding? Any excuse for a drink!

ROMEY: Try telling my mother, she's going to kill me.

SIOBHAN: Don't have too much, Suzie. One drink and she never stops talking.

Improvise chat, laughter, as we lose the crowd, moving in close on STUART, who's still holding ALFRED, impassive, looking straight ahead. VINCE squeezes his arm, in support, STUART doesn't react.
    Lose VINCE, into CU STUART, the party noise distant now, not touching him.

6/25A EXT. STUART'S FLAT, NIGHT 15 2130   6/25A
STUART, CLIVE, ALFRED

STUART, weary, gets out of a taxi, with ALFRED and a bag of ALFRED's overnight things. He's heading for the door when a parked car beeps at him. He looks round, CLIVE getting out. STUART thrown, CLIVE uneasy (a result of his trying to be approachable).

CLIVE: I've been to see Frank, he's back in hospital. Thought I'd just… Anyway. You've got your hands full.

STUART: Alfred. He's Romey's, my friend Romey, she's having a party. I said I'd take him. All that cigarette smoke and stuff.

CLIVE: She's left her baby with you?

STUART: Yeah, how is he? Frank?

CLIVE: He's all right. Are we standing here, or…?

STUART: Sorry, yeah.

They head for the flat.

6/25B INT. STUART'S FLAT, NIGHT 15 2140   6/25B
STUART, CLIVE, ALFRED

ALFRED settled, STUART and CLIVE tentative with each other.

CLIVE: Must cost a bit, this place.

STUART: I can afford it.

CLIVE: Overdrawn?

STUART: No.

Pause. Then CLIVE smiles.

CLIVE: Suppose you think we're mad.

STUART: Completely.

CLIVE: It wasn't a joke. The divorce, I did think about it. I'm only fifty-five, I could do anything.

STUART: You'd fall apart without each other.

CLIVE: No, I don't think we would. You know what she's like, your mother. It's not easy. (Light, casual) Marie's been on the phone, having a go. That's the thing about your sister, she says what she thinks.

STUART: And then says it all again.

A smile between them. Pause, then:

CLIVE: She leaves her baby with you?

STUART: She's a friend.

CLIVE: How d'you know her?

STUART: (Shrugs) Way back.

CLIVE: Must be a very good friend.

STUART: (smiles) She's not *that* sort of friend.

CLIVE: (Right at him, quiet) Stuart, I didn't think that for a second.

Silence. That's the closest CLIVE has come, in all these years, to referring to his son's sexuality. And both these men are scared. Hold the pause, then CLIVE's struggling.

CLIVE: Because... (Trails off, lost, then:) Your mother and me, no wonder we end up like this. Sometimes I look at her and think, we've said everything there is to say. (Beat) Sometimes I think we haven't said anything at all.

Silence, both staring at each other.

CLIVE: If ever. If ever there's anything...

STUART: ...like what?

If CLIVE said it now, perhaps STUART could. Everything hinges on this moment. And then, the moment fails.

CLIVE: I'm keeping you, I'd better be going.

CLIVE's next line OOV, on STUART; his regret.

CLIVE (cont.): I'll only have your mother nagging, she's got this thing about me driving at night. Like I'm eighty years old.

6/25C EXT. HAZEL'S HOUSE, NIGHT 15 2230   6/25C
HAZEL, STUART, ALFRED

HAZEL opens the door, STUART shoves ALFRED, in his carry-cot, and ALFRED's overnight bag into her arms.

HAZEL: Pick him up first thing, mind, I'm in the small claims court at ten.

STUART just dashes off into the night.

6/26 INT. BABYLON, NIGHT 15 0130   6/26
STUART, VINCE, CAMERON

STUART – grinning, happy – centre of the dance floor, with VINCE. They're dancing like crazy. CUT TO – CAMERON, on one of the balconies. Watching them. CUT TO – STUART and VINCE. STUART takes an E, swallows, then puts a second E on his tongue, offers it to VINCE. VINCE is like 'get off', but laughing, and then STUART darts forward, shoves it from his tongue into VINCE's mouth. VINCE makes like he hates it. But keeps laughing, dancing. On CAMERON.

6/27 INT. VINCE'S BEDROOM, NIGHT 15 0230   6/27
VINCE, CAMERON

VINCE and CAMERON having sex – not fucking – CAMERON on top. We're just on faces as they snog. Then CAMERON lifts himself up, looks down.

> CAMERON: Who d'you think of?

> VINCE: (Off his head, giggling)…you what?

> CAMERON: When you close your eyes.

VINCE just laughs, reaches up to snog CAMERON, but CAMERON pulls back, gets out of bed. VINCE is so out of it, he just sinks down to sleep, smiling to himself.

6/28 INT. BAR, NIGHT 16, 2000   6/28
CAMERON, STUART

CAMERON sits alone, waiting, tense. Tapping a beer-mat. No warning, STUART slides into the seat opposite. Smiling, natural.

> STUART: I know, it's been bothering me, what are we going to do?

> CAMERON: About what?

> STUART: Vince's birthday.

> CAMERON: Depends if I'm still here.

6/29 INT. BAR, NIGHT 16 2010   6/29
CAMERON, STUART

CAMERON and STUART now in a secluded corner. Tension, CAMERON direct, STUART at his most guarded, ice-cold.

> CAMERON: What is it, a family? All those people gathered round, your own little make-believe family. If you think that's a family then you're fucked. (Closer, more intense) It's sex. You live your life by sex. Your terms, your conditions, sex. That's all Vince is waiting for, cos that's all you give. And don't tell me you didn't know. (Less angry) Look, I can just go, I don't think he'd even notice. But he's worth the chance. He deserves the chance, doesn't he?

> STUART: So what am I supposed to do?

> CAMERON: Leave him alone.

> STUART: He's my friend, he's –

> CAMERON: (Angry) Just leave him alone. If you're any sort of friend. Cos there's no such thing as Vince, he doesn't exist on his own, you don't let him. Just Stuart and Vince. All the time. (Beat; more honest) And I like him. So maybe I'm stupid. But I really like him.

Then CAMERON – hating appearing vulnerable in front of STUART - abruptly stands, goes.

On STUART, impassive. Bring in V/O:

> STUART V/O: I've known him since he was fourteen. That's almost sixteen years. He's going to be thirty, thirty years old, and there he is. Still at my side. Stuart and Vince.

6/30 INT. HAZEL'S HOUSE, NIGHT 16 2300   6/30
STUART, HAZEL

CU STUART, location unclear at first, speech continuous from 6/29.

> STUART: And he deserves it. He's never asked for anything, and he deserves it all. I'll do it.

Now revealing HAZEL, listening, though STUART's facing dead ahead, almost to camera, all contained energy.

> HAZEL: I'll chip in, I've been saving.

> STUART: I'm paying for everything. It's his birthday, he's going to be thirty. I'm not standing back now. My flat. My money. My gift. Just you wait. He's going to have the biggest fucking party you've ever seen in your life.

EPISODE SEVEN

7/1 INT. OUTSIDE STUART'S FLAT, NIGHT 17 2115   7/1
VINCE, CAMERON, STUART

The lift gate opens, VINCE and CAMERON get out.

> VINCE: Oh my God! Oh my *God*! Oh-my-God. I'm rubbish at this, how do I look?

> CAMERON: You look fine. (Knocks at the door) I don't see why they couldn't use my place.

> VINCE: His flat's huge.

> CAMERON: Yeah, doesn't mean my house is small.

> VINCE: Oh my God! Is that any good? Oh my God!

STUART half-opens the door so he's filling the frame, blocking the view inside, like he's irritated. VINCE can't quite meet his eye.

> STUART: What d'you want?

> CAMERON: We're just passing by, thought we'd pick up those CDs.

> STUART: You can't stay long, I'm busy.

He opens the door, they walk in, VINCE first.

7/2 INT. STUART'S FLAT, NIGHT 17 2116   7/2
VINCE, STUART, CAMERON, HAZEL, BERNARD, NATHAN, DONNA, ROMEY, LISA, SIOBHAN, SUZIE, LANCE, SANDRA, ALEXANDER, DANE, DAZZ

And the flat is full: HAZEL, BERNARD, NATHAN, DONNA, ROMEY, LISA, SIOBHAN, SUZIE, LANCE, SANDRA, ALEXANDER, DANE and as many NS GUESTS as possible (70% men). The flat's decorated with VINCE; big Warhol prints of his face, even life-size cut-outs of him.

> ALL: *Surprise!*

> VINCE: Oh my God!

Huge noise, clapping, cheering, and people run to VINCE, DANE first, with big girly arm-waving, others piling in. On STUART and CAMERON, standing back, STUART not fooled. Both edgy.

> STUART: How long's he known?

> CAMERON: Ages.

STUART: Did you tell him?

CAMERON: No. He's not stupid.

CUT TO – VINCE, as HAZEL hugs him. BERNARD's there, carrying a translucent plastic gallon-bucket, liquid sloshing inside.

HAZEL: I'm never going to live this down, I told the Christmas Club I'm forty-one. Should've drowned you when you were a kitten.

BERNARD: Congratulations, love. (Kisses him, then holds up his bucket) Look, they've reached a diagnosis! They think it's migrainis neuralgia, they need a twenty-four hour sample by Monday so they can test me –

HAZEL: It's piss. It's a bucket of his piss.

Their attention taken by ALEXANDER, at the far end where there's a hired-in disco rig – turntables surrounded by chaser lights, etc. He's on the mike.

ALEXANDER: Bit of hush, you lot, bit of hush – (Cries of 'get on with it') Thank you. My name's Christine Cagney, and I'm an alcoholic. Now it's disco trash all night, here's a rave from the grave, a revived forty-five. But enough of Hazel.

HAZEL: Oy, you cheeky sod, I'll have you!

ALEXANDER: That'll be a first!

Music starts, loud (and it should be HiNRG versions of disco classics all night, no house, nothing modern). People start dancing; instantly, the feeling it's going to be a wild party. HAZEL and DANE lead the way.

DANE: Shake it, girl!

HAZEL: Watch me!

ALEXANDER joins them, mad disco bunnies. VINCE is watching, chuffed, STUART and CAMERON next to him.

VINCE: (To STUART) Thanks.

STUART: (Cool) Thirty. You cunt.

Then STUART grins, holds out his arms for a great big hug. VINCE goes into the hug, but once STUART's got him, he holds VINCE tight, joyous, swings him round, both laughing.

STUART: Thirty years old! How did that happen? How did that happen?

STUART's like this all night, deliberately closer to VINCE than usual, not just intimate but *sexual.* And right now, he catches CAMERON's eye over VINCE's shoulder, enjoying it. Then he pulls VINCE over to the dancing, both start leaping about, people still coming up to VINCE, saying hello. On CAMERON, excluded.

CUT TO – DAZZ arriving, going up to NATHAN and DONNA.

> DAZZ: Look at this, I know *millions* of people, hiya. (Gives NATHAN a kiss) I've been to the council, I'm seeing some woman on Tuesday.

> NATHAN: (To DONNA, excited) We're getting a flat off the council!

> DONNA: How come? Tell me nothing!

> NATHAN: Soon as I'm sixteen, me and Dazz, sharing – tell 'em you're gay and they give you a flat!

> DAZZ: Tell 'em your dad's a queerbasher, you get a penthouse – Donna, did no one say it's a party? Shame, you could have dressed up.

> NATHAN: Come and see the bedroom, that's where we did it, first time!

NATHAN and DAZZ run off, leaving DONNA – who *has* dressed up, and looks lovely – all alone. She fiddles with her clothes, like they're to blame.

7/3 INT. STUART'S FLAT, NIGHT 17 2140   7/3
VINCE, STUART, CAMERON, HAZEL, BERNARD, NATHAN, DONNA, ROMEY, LISA, SIOBHAN, SUZIE, LANCE, SANDRA, ALEXANDER, DANE, DAZZ

VINCE, in a sweat, after dancing, and CAMERON with SANDRA, in the kitchen, where the drinks are (though CAMERON's on orange juice).

> VINCE: And, this is Cameron, my boyfriend, you've sort of met –

> SANDRA: You've got a boyfriend, Stuart never said, hello.

> CAMERON: Nice to meet you.

> VINCE: I bet you organised all this.

> SANDRA: I didn't, no, Stuart did, he did it all himself –

ROMEY passes through, to SANDRA.

> ROMEY: The caterer's ready, he wants you to sign the invoice, and the disco man said you've got to sign the insurance form before he goes, is that all right?

> SANDRA: Yeah. (Romey goes. Awkward) Well. Stuart did pay. 'Scuse me.

SANDRA goes.

>VINCE: Must've cost a fortune.

>CAMERON: He earns a fortune.

CUT TO – NATHAN, DONNA and DAZZ at a table piled high with presents.

>NATHAN: Donna's getting all worried cos her present's going off, she bought him cheese!

>DAZZ: What d'you mean, she bought him cheese?

>NATHAN: She bought him cheese!

>DONNA: It's a Brie, it's nice, it's French.

But NATHAN and DAZZ are giggling away like only gay teenage boys can.

>NATHAN: It smells all cheesy! Like a knob!

>DAZZ: Like smegma!

Which completely cracks them up.

>DONNA: I'm getting a drink.

>DAZZ: Vodka and Red Bull, thanks.

>NATHAN: Smegma!

DONNA walks away with dignity, NATHAN and DAZZ hooting behind her.

7/4 INT. STUART'S BEDROOM, NIGHT 17 2200   7/4
VINCE, STUART, CAMERON, HAZEL, BERNARD, NATHAN, DONNA, ROMEY, LISA, SIOBHAN, SUZIE, LANCE, SANDRA, ALEXANDER, DANE, DAZZ, ALFRED

VINCE, STUART and ROMEY look down at ALFRED, in his carry-cot.

>VINCE: How's he going to sleep, with all this noise?

>ROMEY: He's used to it, Siobhan plays whale songs all night. Look at him. No idea.

LANCE comes in.

>LANCE: Thought we could do the photos.

>STUART: If that's all right with Vince. It's his party.

>ROMEY: It's just for this marriage thing, we're getting our photos taken wherever we go, like we've known each other for ages. Just

in case the Home Office asks for proof. You don't mind, do you?

VINCE: Course not.

LANCE and ROMEY go. Beat, as VINCE and STUART just look at each other, smile, old friends. Quiet, more reflective.

VINCE: (Of ALFRED) Look at him. Nought years old. (Beat) D'you remember in school? We used to talk about being *twenty*. We did that experiment in biology, put a raisin in water and it goes back to being a grape. I've been sitting in the bath all day, doesn't work.

STUART: All those plans we made. We were going to get a flat and live together.

VINCE: Yeah.

STUART: Still could. You could move in here. We could get a house, I'll pay.

VINCE: Don't know what Cameron would say.

STUART: He's bought you a car. For your birthday.

VINCE: He hasn't, he bought me that boxed set of *Trial of a Time Lord*. Which I've already got.

STUART moves in on VINCE, closer than ever, looking him right in the eye, VINCE unnerved. This is deliberate on STUART's part, calculated; but at the same time, perhaps it's the only way he knows how to be intimate with someone he loves.

STUART: It's parked round the corner, he's bringing it round when we do the presents. It's only a Mini, four hundred quid. But it's a *car*.

VINCE: (Disconcerted) …that's a bit heavy.

STUART: (Right in VINCE's face) You know what I'd do. (A whisper) Run. Run like the wind.

Silence, STUART staring, VINCE unnerved. Then STUART kisses VINCE on the lips. Just for a second. VINCE has never had such a come-on from STUART, can't handle it.

VINCE: …party, they'll be, uh…

VINCE walks out. STUART looks out through the bedroom partition, seeing CAMERON standing centre of the party, watching him. STUART's known he's been there all along, gives him a great big wave, like he doesn't give a toss how much he pisses CAMERON off.

7/5 INT. STUART'S FLAT, NIGHT 17 2204   7/5
VINCE, STUART, CAMERON, HAZEL, BERNARD, NATHAN, DONNA, ROMEY,
LISA, SIOBHAN, SUZIE, LANCE, SANDRA, ALEXANDER, DANE, DAZZ

HAZEL's mixing a cocktail, with NATHAN, DONNA and DAZZ.

> HAZEL: Harvey Wallbanger, best drink on God's earth. Just a sip,
> mind, then you're back on the pop.

DAZZ sees VINCE leaving the bedroom, going up to CAMERON.

> DAZZ: What's he do, that Cameron bloke?

> HAZEL: He's an accountant. I knew the Tylers would marry into
> money one day. (But NATHAN & DAZZ are snorting with laugh-
> ter) What?

> DAZZ: Shagging an accountant!

> HAZEL: Oy, d'you mind?

> DONNA: He's nice.

> DAZZ: Nice! Imagine shagging someone 'nice'!

> NATHAN: He's not a proper boyfriend, cos you know Vince.
> Shuts his eyes and thinks of Stuart!

> DAZZ: *Sad* man! (The record's just changed) Oo fab, Nathan,
> we're dancing to this –

> NATHAN: Hazel, save us a cocktail –

NATHAN and DAZZ slam down their glasses, run off. HAZEL watches them with
a weather eye, DONNA's embarrassed.

> DONNA: Sorry 'bout them.

> HAZEL: Pass me that ladle.

> DONNA: (Does so) It's him, Dazz. Nathan thinks he's so impres-
> sive.

HAZEL takes NATHAN and DAZZ's glasses, puts them right in front of her.

> HAZEL: Drinks coming up. (Reaches under the counter) They're
> taking the piss, they can have some of Bernie's.

She brings out BERNARD's bucket, gets ready with the ladle. DONNA's shocked,
loves it. Her chance to giggle.
> CUT TO – SIOBHAN taking photos of ROMEY and LANCE.

> SIOBHAN: Big kiss! (They snog for the camera) Everyone in!

Vince, come on, Stuart! Lisa, Suzie! Craig, and you.

CAMERON: Cameron.

SIOBHAN: In a group, Romey and Lance at the front.

VINCE, CAMERON, STUART, LISA and SUZIE step into the photo. STUART puts his arm round VINCE, blocking CAMERON, SIOBHAN saying 'Smile! Hold it! And again!', etc., all obeying, throughout this. LISA's smiling, ever-so-quietly provoking the situation.

LISA: Romey, have you told them? (To STUART) They've set a date for the wedding.

ROMEY: Yeah, the twenty-fifth.

VINCE: Blimey, another party, I've never been so busy.

ROMEY: (Awkward) Thing is. We're keeping it small, it's sort of private.

LISA: You're not invited.

SIOBHAN: That's it, thanks, end of the film.

They step out of their photo-grouping.

LANCE: (Cheery, blunt) I mean, no offence, but if you lot come to the registry office and someone from the Home Office turns up, it's all going to look a bit *gay*, isn't it? Last thing we need – Siobhan, load another film, we'll go and change.

ROMEY: We brought a change of clothes, so it looks like we've been to more than one party.

VINCE: Yeah, but everyone in the background's wearing the same things.

LANCE: Well, it is Manchester.

ROMEY and LANCE head off, on LISA, STUART, SUZIE, VINCE and CAMERON (that comment alone confirming that no one likes LANCE).

LISA: Lance was looking at the birth certificate this morning, nice blank space where the father's name goes. That makes adoption so much easier.

VINCE: Didn't you put your name down?

LISA: He didn't want to. Too much responsibility. Like you said, Stuart, no harm in leaving it blank, what could possibly go wrong?

STUART: Fuck off.

LISA: Ooh, nice comeback.

SANDRA calls across.

SANDRA: Vince, someone for you, at the door.

7/6 INT. STUART'S DOORWAY/HALL, NIGHT 17 2210   7/6
VINCE, JANICE

JANICE is standing in the hall, nervous, embarrassed, clutching a present. She looks round, smiles, as VINCE comes to the door.

VINCE: Janice, don't stand there, come in –

JANICE: No, um – I would've called round in the day, but. Didn't want to spoil the surprise.

VINCE: Come and have a drink.

JANICE: Suppose Nathan's in there.

VINCE: Yeah, he's all right, Mum's looking after him, he won't mind –

JANICE: He doesn't want me turning up. (Gives him the present) That's to say thanks. For looking after him. (Beat) Not long till his birthday. Sixteen, he'll be able to live anywhere. How'm I going to find him then? (Beat, artificially bright) His dad's moved out. I asked him to. It's not permanent, we'll just – we'll see what happens – I'd better go, have a nice time.

She hurries away, before she becomes more upset. VINCE watches her go, so sorry for her. He turns, walks back in.

7/7 INT. STUART'S FLAT, NIGHT 17 2212   7/7
VINCE, STUART, CAMERON, HAZEL, BERNARD, NATHAN, DONNA, ROMEY, LISA, SIOBHAN, SUZIE, LANCE, SANDRA, ALEXANDER, DANE, DAZZ

VINCE walks in, stops, looks across the room. VINCE'S POV: NATHAN, dancing with DAZZ, having a great time. Then he looks across at STUART, who's on his own, just surveying the party.
    CUT TO – ALEXANDER, back at the mike, stopping the music.

ALEXANDER: Right, shut your noise! Bit of hush, Vince, sit down, it's time for presents. And if anyone's got him a Jeff Stryker cock and balls, you're getting booted out, that's so unoriginal.

7/8 INT. STUART'S FLAT, NIGHT 17 2235　　　　　7/8
VINCE, STUART, CAMERON, HAZEL, BERNARD, NATHAN, DONNA, ROMEY, LISA, SIOBHAN, SUZIE, LANCE, SANDRA, ALEXANDER, DANE, DAZZ

All now sitting around, VINCE at the centre, loads of presents already unwrapped at his feet. He's just unwrapped an unboxed VHS.

> ALEXANDER: You'll never guess, it's every episode of *Saved by the Bell* with Zack taking his shirt off, I've been four years taping that.

> LISA: What's *Saved by the Bell?*

> ALEXANDER: (Despairs, to DANE) Lesbians!

> HAZEL: Get a move on, Vince, I want to dance.

VINCE picks up a small, gift-wrapped box.

> CAMERON: That's from me.

> VINCE: You've given me a present.

> CAMERON: That was to throw you off the scent.

All this as VINCE tears off the paper, tips up the cardboard box. As he already knows, a set of car keys falls out. And VINCE knows he's rehearsed the 'Oh my God' in front of CAMERON so many times.

> VINCE: Oh my God.

Which is enough to tell CAMERON. He looks at STUART. Who's smiling away. Covering this:

> DANE: No! You're kidding me!

> ALEXANDER: Cameron, you bastard, I've never been so upstaged.

> CAMERON: It's parked outside.

> ALEXANDER: Last one down's sleeping with Dane!

> DANE: Oh don't *all* rush.

GUESTS head for the door. Lots of noise. On STUART as the exodus starts. He just sits there, distant, as though it's nothing to do with him, people passing background and foreground, leaving.

7/9 EXT. STUART'S FLAT, NIGHT 17 2242　　　　　7/9
VINCE, CAMERON, HAZEL, BERNARD, DONNA, ROMEY, LISA, SIOBHAN, SUZIE, LANCE, SANDRA, ALEXANDER, DANE, DAZZ

Guests – including ALEXANDER, DANE, HAZEL, BERNARD, ROMEY, LANCE,

LISA, SIOBHAN, SUZIE, SANDRA, DONNA and DAZZ – gathering round as VINCE comes out with CAMERON. Parked outside is a battered old bright-red Mini.

> VINCE: That's why you haven't been drinking.

> CAMERON: It's only second hand, but it'll get you about.

As VINCE goes to the car, on DAZZ, with DONNA and HAZEL (DAZZ holding a glass of orangey liquid).

> DAZZ: It's a Mini! A clapped-out old Mini, that's pathetic!

> HAZEL: (Takes his glass) I'll get you some more of that drink.
> (Mutters to BERNARD) Bernie, give us your bucket.

CUT TO: VINCE in the driver's seat, starting the engine and winding down the window for ALEXANDER to peer in. ALEXANDER *sotto*.

> ALEXANDER: Oo Vince, serious present, it's like being *married*.

> VINCE: (Mutters, more to himself) Run like the wind.

He starts the engine, the car drives off. Claps and cheers from all.

7/10 INT. STUART'S FLAT, NIGHT 17 2244   7/10
STUART, NATHAN, ALFRED

On STUART, set against the night, against the glass of the window at the far end of the flat. He's looking down at the Mini as it potters round on a lap of honour, beeping, the cheering just audible. STUART rests his forehead against the glass, above the drop, right on the edge. Knowing what's to come. And dreading it.
    There's a snuffle from ALFRED. STUART looks across the bedroom, then ALFRED's quiet again. On STUART. Thinking of LANCE and ALFRED. He rubs his face; for the first time, he looks tired, troubled, defences down.
    He looks up. At the far end of the flat, a great distance away, he sees he's not alone. NATHAN's still there, watching him, solemn. And for a moment, STUART's disconcerted, caught for a second with his guard down. He smiles, as though shrugging it off. NATHAN doesn't smile, just looks at him.
    STUART smiles as though shrugging it off, and walks away.

7/11 INT. OUTSIDE STUART'S FLAT, NIGHT 17 2255   7/11
VINCE, CAMERON, HAZEL, BERNARD, DONNA, ROMEY, LISA, SIOBHAN, SUZIE, LANCE, SANDRA, ALEXANDER, DANE, DAZZ

Tight shot of the lift door clanging open, GUESTS pouring out, VINCE and CAMERON leading the way, VINCE smiling but niggly.

> VINCE: I love it, I'm just saying, I'm going to pay half, you can't
> spend all that –

7/12 INT. STUART'S FLAT, NIGHT 17 2256   **7/12**
VINCE, STUART, CAMERON, HAZEL, BERNARD, NATHAN, DONNA, ROMEY,
LISA, SIOBHAN, SUZIE, LANCE, SANDRA, ALEXANDER, DANE, DAZZ, K9

VINCE and CAMERON lead the way in.

> VINCE: You take the keys cos I'll only get pissed – (This time, he
> means it:) Oh my God!

Because there, in the middle of the room, is K9. A real, genuine, fully functional
K9, beetling about on its own. VINCE is *gobsmacked*. He looks round, knowing
who's responsible, sees STUART, standing there nonchalantly with a radio-
control unit.

> VINCE: Where d'you get it? Did you hire it or what?

> STUART: Happy birthday.

> VINCE: But you got the party and everything –

> STUART: Okay, I'll take it back. Watch this.

He presses a control, K9 spins round on the spot. GUESTS still piling in through
the door, laughing, enjoying the joke.

> VINCE: That is completely, completely fantastic! God, I'm so
> sad!

He runs to STUART, hugs him, takes the control unit, starts playing with it. On
CAMERON. He throws the car keys up in the air, catches them. More than pissed
off; giving up.

7/13 INT. STUART'S FLAT, NIGHT 17 2310   **7/13**
VINCE, STUART, CAMERON, HAZEL, BERNARD, NATHAN, DONNA, ROMEY,
LISA, SIOBHAN, SUZIE, LANCE, SANDRA, ALEXANDER, DANE, DAZZ

Time-lapse, establish the party back in full swing, dancing.
CUT TO – SIOBHAN sitting with SANDRA. SANDRA's well on the way to
getting pissed, SIOBHAN's trying to cop off. During the dialogue, K9 comes into
shot carrying drinks on its back, SIOBHAN and SANDRA put down their glasses
and pick up full ones, K9 reverses out. They don't even look at it.

> SANDRA: I take his dry cleaning. I fix his jeep. I buy his
> condoms. In bulk.

> SIOBHAN: Don't you see, Stuart's not attracted to women, we're
> the great unknown. So he reduces us, we're secretaries and
> mothers and bit-part-players, it keeps him in control, cos other-
> wise... (Right in close) We scare him to death.

> SANDRA: That's so true! That's spot on, that is! Siobhan, you've
> opened my eyes.

SIOBHAN: Anything else I can open?

SANDRA: Hey! Cheeky!

They both fall about laughing, SIOBHAN using the laughter to shift closer.
CUT TO – STUART pouring himself a drink as CAMERON comes up. Hold the silence, keep the action going as both get drinks, CAMERON thumping things down, ignoring STUART, all testosterone. STUART's just calm, smiling. Which eventually provokes CAMERON:

CAMERON: (Controlled anger) You're never going to fuck him. So why d'you keep him *waiting*? He's not thirty, he's twelve, you're keeping him at twelve.

STUART just keeps smiling, his most enigmatic.

7/14 EXT. STUART'S FLAT, NIGHT 17 2312   7/14
ROSALIE

A taxi pulls away, a woman carrying a present and a bottle goes to the front door. As she reaches the buzzer and presses it, we see that it's ROSALIE.

ROSALIE: Hello…?

7/15 INT. STUART'S FLAT, NIGHT 17 2312   7/15
VINCE, STUART, CAMERON, HAZEL, BERNARD, NATHAN, DONNA, ROMEY, LISA, SIOBHAN, SUZIE, LANCE, SANDRA, ALEXANDER, DANE, DAZZ

BERNARD's talking to some BLOKES as he grabs the intercom handset.

BERNARD: Come on up and get your cock out.

7/16 EXT. STUART'S FLAT, NIGHT 17 2312   7/16
ROSALIE

ROSALIE laughs, embarrassed. The door buzzes, she pushes it open.

7/17 INT. STUART'S FLAT, NIGHT 17 2313   7/17
VINCE, STUART, CAMERON, HAZEL, BERNARD, NATHAN, DONNA, ROMEY, LISA, SIOBHAN, SUZIE, LANCE, SANDRA, ALEXANDER, DANE, DAZZ

DANE's now at the mike.

DANE: Gather round, bit of hush. Baby crying in chalet three. Vince, you ready for this? Ladies and gentlemen, Miss Alexander Savage!

ALEXANDER appears in a fabulous frock – the dress HAZEL's been wearing all night. Whoops and cheers, as the music starts: Spice Girls, 'The Lady Is A Vamp', a big, brassy number. On VINCE, laughing away as HAZEL appears at VINCE's side, in ALEX's clothes/BERNARD's jacket/whatever.

HAZEL: Looks better on him.

VINCE: You're more of a gay man than I am.

7/18 INT. ENTRANCE HALL, NIGHT 17 2314　　　　7/18
ROSALIE

The lift's arrived, ROSALIE steps in, heaves the gate shut. Shot looking down the lift-shaft as the lift ascends.

7/19 INT. STUART'S FLAT, NIGHT 17 2315　　　　7/19
VINCE, STUART, CAMERON, HAZEL, BERNARD, NATHAN, DONNA, ROMEY, LISA, SIOBHAN, SUZIE, LANCE, SANDRA, ALEXANDER, DANE, DAZZ

ALEXANDER mimes to the track, outrageous, all loving it.
　　On VINCE, laughing.

7/20 INT. OUTSIDE STUART'S FLAT, NIGHT 17 2316　　　　7/20
ROSALIE

ROSALIE heaves the lift gate open. The door to the flat's open, Spice Girls blaring out. ROSALIE heads in (behind her, the lift goes down).

7/21 INT. STUART'S FLAT, NIGHT 17 2316　　　　7/21
VINCE, STUART, CAMERON, HAZEL, BERNARD, NATHAN, DONNA, ROMEY, LISA, SIOBHAN, SUZIE, LANCE, SANDRA, ALEXANDER, DANE, DAZZ, ROSALIE

Follow ROSALIE in, the crowd watching ALEXANDER at the far end. But she glances at a couple snogging by the door. She looks again; they're both men; nothing wrong with that. She walks further in.
　　The track reaches its climax, ALEXANDER being brilliant. ROSALIE just stands back, smiling, nervous as the room bursts into cheers and applause.
　　VINCE sees her. ROSALIE smiles. VINCE jumps up, hurries towards her, horrified, smiling too much.

> ROSALIE: Happy birthday.
>
> VINCE: Thanks, yeah, didn't know you were coming – (She gives him the present) Thanks, it's, it's a bit wild, they're all drunk. Don't know half of them.
>
> ROSALIE: Happy birthday. (Kisses him on the cheek, clumsy) I'm late, he said, your mate Stuart, he said don't come till late.
>
> VINCE: I'm *hungry*. Are you hungry? We could go for a curry, I've had enough of this, we could go –
>
> STUART: Here she is!

STUART appears, grinning viciously, the perfect host.

> STUART: Rosalie, have you met Cameron? Come and say hello.

Fast, STUART leads ROSALIE across the room, VINCE following, helpless.

STUART: Cameron! This is Cameron, he's Vince's boyfriend, they've been going out for ages, Cameron says Vince shags like a rabbit, he's bought him a car, he's the perfect boyfriend.

CAMERON: ...hello.

ROSALIE: Hi.

SIOBHAN, SUZIE and SANDRA go past, coats on, leaving, calling out:

SANDRA: I'm off, Siobhan's taking me clubbing!

STUART: Sandra, you're married!

SANDRA: We're only dancing!

STUART: What's the club?

SIOBHAN: (A glint in her eye) Sapphic Delight.

They go. During all this, ROSALIE's bewildered, realising it's all true, can't look at VINCE, who's dying. STUART turns to them with a smile.

STUART: Christ, even the dykes are on the pull, watch yourself, Rosey, they're a twisted lot. Put your coat in the bedroom, Vince, get her a drink –

ROSALIE scurries to the bedroom, head down, still clutching her bottle. VINCE looks at STUART with anger, *astonishment*, follows ROSALIE. CAMERON turns to STUART, incredulous.

CAMERON: Is that the girl from work?

STUART just laughs.

7/22 INT. STUART'S BEDROOM, NIGHT 17 2318   7/22
VINCE, STUART, CAMERON, HAZEL, BERNARD, NATHAN, DONNA, ROMEY, LISA, LANCE, ALEXANDER, DANE, DAZZ, ROSALIE, ALFRED

ROSALIE's head is spinning, she's trying to be normal, smiling, struggling out of her coat, all fingers and thumbs. VINCE just stands there, dismayed.

ROSALIE: This bloody coat. Oh blimey, there's a baby, whose is that? Bless him. It's a bit big, this place, it's huge, you'd have the heating on full-time, taxi couldn't find it, drove round for ages.

VINCE: He is my boyfriend. He's... He's nice, he's...

Having got rid of her coat, she suddenly picks it up again.

ROSALIE: Actually, I'll head off home, I've had this head all day, it's a bit loud, I'll be clobbered, best if I go, happy birthday, then.

She walks past him, out, fast as she can, still clutching her bottle.

7/23 INT. STUART'S FLAT, NIGHT 17 2319   7/23
VINCE, STUART, CAMERON, HAZEL, BERNARD, NATHAN, DONNA, ROMEY,
LISA, LANCE, ALEXANDER, DANE, DAZZ, ROSALIE

ROSALIE walks out, fast, VINCE following, half-running. CAMERON steps
forward, VINCE charges past, mutters, urgent:

>   VINCE: Fuck off.

7/24 INT. OUTSIDE STUART'S FLAT, NIGHT 17 2319   7/24
VINCE, ROSALIE

ROSALIE goes to the lift, presses the button, VINCE behind her.

>   VINCE: I didn't know he'd invited you, he's a bastard, look I'm
>   sorry. I should have said.

>   ROSALIE: (Completely lost) There's John, John down the depot,
>   he's gay, he's lovely, everyone likes John, everyone *knows*. What's
>   so different about you?

Beat. VINCE despairs of ever explaining this.

>   VINCE: That's all he is. Gay. That's all anyone talks about, he's
>   Gay John, he could win the lottery, he could – he could die, they
>   wouldn't say John's dead, they'd say that gay bloke down the
>   depot's dead.

>   ROSALIE: (Sharper, now) Least he doesn't lie.

>   VINCE: I didn't lie – I mean, I did, but I didn't – It's like – I
>   dunno, it's like – it's like, if I was in a wheelchair. The last thing
>   you want is everyone talking about the wheelchair.

The lift's arrived, she heaves it open, gets in.

>   ROSALIE: Oh, so it's a handicap now?

>   VINCE: That's not what I mean –

She can't look at him, swings it shut, the lift descends. VINCE won't let her go,
runs for the stairs.

7/25 INT. STAIRWELL, NIGHT 17 2321   7/25
VINCE

VINCE bombs down the stairs.

7/26 INT. LIFT, NIGHT 17 2321 7/26
ROSALIE

On ROSALIE. And now it's sinking in: the invite, the set-up, the *trap*. She's close to tears, the sheer humiliation.

7/27 INT. STAIRWELL, NIGHT 17 2322 7/27
VINCE

VINCE keeps running.

7/28 INT. ENTRANCE HALL, NIGHT 17 2322 7/28
VINCE, ROSALIE

ROSALIE's now right on the edge as she heaves the door open, heads for the exit as VINCE runs from the stairs, out of breath.

> VINCE: It's the middle of the night, I'll phone you a taxi –

And she turns to him. *Rages* at him.

> ROSALIE: You said *girlfriend!* All those times you said girlfriend. D'you sit with your mates? You and the boys, d'you sit and laugh at me? Cos I'm such a big joke, that girl at work, she fancies me, she's so funny cos she's so stupid.

> VINCE: I'm really sorry, I should've told you –

> ROSALIE: You're just a liar, Vince. You're a liar and – (Gives the word such venom) and you're a *poof*. You're a dirty little poof.

She pushes through the door, walks off into the night. On VINCE, heaving for breath, watching her go.

7/29 INT. STUART'S FLAT, NIGHT 17 2330 7/29
VINCE, STUART, CAMERON, HAZEL, BERNARD, NATHAN, DONNA, ROMEY, LISA, LANCE, ALEXANDER, DANE, DAZZ

VINCE is with CAMERON, both shoving his presents into two cardboard boxes, fast, wanting to get out. STUART's just standing there, watching. All low-level; VINCE doesn't want anyone else to know there's a problem.

> CAMERON: (Angry, at STUART) What the fuck was that for? She's only a kid –

> VINCE: Just leave it, leave it, we're going, let's just go –

> CAMERON: What's he going to do at work? Christ, but you're a bastard.

> VINCE: That's it, we're going.

VINCE picks up his box, looks at STUART. And the worst thing is, VINCE isn't angry, he's profoundly sad; this isn't any old argument, it's like the entire friendship has just been junked. Sixteen years. A waste of time. STUART just keeps smiling. VINCE turns away, goes. CAMERON's got the second box, so his arms are full.

> CAMERON: What about the robot?

K9's on the table. VINCE just keeps heading for the door.

> VINCE: I don't want it.

VINCE walks out, CAMERON following. STUART watches them go.
Then he turns to face the party, GUESTS dancing about. Through the bedroom partition, he can see ROMEY and LANCE, with ALFRED. Then, across the other side, STUART sees that NATHAN's looking at him. Like he's been following the whole thing. STUART ignores him, walks to the centre of the room, a still point in amongst the dancers. He stands there. Then he starts dancing, hard, thrashing, like nothing but the party matters.

7/30 INT. STUART'S FLAT, DAY 18 1400   7/30
STUART

The next day. Wide shot of the flat. It's a tip. Signs of stirring in the bedroom.

7/31 INT. STUART'S BEDROOM, DAY 18 1400   7/31
STUART

STUART sits up, half asleep. Hangover. A Vince/Warhol print looming over him.

7/32 INT. STUART'S FLAT, DAY 18 1410   7/32
STUART

STUART's in his dressing gown, picking through the debris on top of the table, finding bits of food, wolfing down old chicken wings, anything. He lifts some wrapping paper. Someone bought VINCE an R18 porn tape.

7/33 INT. STUART'S FLAT, DAY 18 1412   7/33
STUART

STUART sits on the settee, the tape in the machine. He presses the remote. Then his hands move down, under his dressing gown. He settles back, starts to have a wank.

7/34 INT. STUART'S FLAT, DAY 18 1417   7/34
STUART

Closer on STUART in the same position, still watching the TV, pounding away, faster and faster.
He comes. No big orgasm, just an ordinary wank. He's got spunk on his hand, looks around, wishing he'd brought a tissue and too lazy to go and get one. He looks at his hand. He eats some of the spunk, just curious, then wishes he hadn't, makes a face.

7/35 INT. STUART'S BATHROOM, DAY 18 1430   7/35
STUART

STUART's in the shower. He's more intent on getting rid of the hangover, just holding his head under the hot water.

7/36 INT. STUART'S FLAT, DAY 18 1440   7/36
STUART, HAZEL

STUART walks out of the bathroom, naked, towelling his hair. He realises – no big reaction – that HAZEL's there, at the far end. She's got a cardboard box, is sorting through the rubbish, putting things in the box.

> HAZEL: I've seen better.

He makes no effort to cover himself, just stands there.

> HAZEL: He left half his presents behind, gave me the keys.
> (pause, she keeps searching) Gather I missed all the drama. Too
> busy dancing. Title of my autobiography, that is.

> STUART: There's a tape in the video, belongs to him.

Hold on them both as HAZEL keeps searching.

7/37 INT. STUART'S BEDROOM, DAY 18 1445   7/37
STUART, HAZEL

STUART gets into some clothes, HAZEL visible through the partition, walking up and down like she owns the place. STUART glances at her, lacking the façade of last night; he's wary of her, of what she's going to say.

7/38 INT. STUART'S FLAT, DAY 18 1448   7/38
STUART, HAZEL

HAZEL's in the kitchen area, making minimal efforts to tidy up. As STUART emerges from the bedroom, she plonks down a mug of coffee.

> HAZEL: There you go.

> STUART: Ta.

> HAZEL: Right, I'll be off.

Beat between them, each wondering if the other's going to talk about VINCE. But neither of them does, HAZEL walks away to pick up the box. Only when she's some distance away does she broach the subject, casual.

> HAZEL: He's been defending you all morning. Saying it was just
> a joke.

> STUART: Typical, he could never stay cross for long.

HAZEL: Nathan. Nathan's been defending you. And that made
Vince say a thing or two, like you shagging Nathan upstairs in our
house, me in the kitchen.

STUART: All right Hazel, you can fuck off.

Pause, as she puts her coat on. Then, as she talks – still casual, never sentimental
– we realise that she's known STUART for years and years. And understands him.

HAZEL: Vince comes home, he says, there's this new boy at
school, this Irish boy. I had weeks of it, Stuart this, Stuart that.
Then weeks he didn't mention you at all. Like the two of you had
a secret. You tipped up soon enough, that Bank Holiday, both of
you drunk. Fourteen and drunk. Soon as I saw you, I thought
clever little bastard.

STUART: That's right, everyone have a go at me.

HAZEL: I said *clever*.

Which makes him look at her properly. Hold the look, long pause, STUART realising she's sussed him. Which allows him to be more honest, more real than he
ever was last night.

HAZEL: That's one hell of a push you gave him. (Beat) Can't do
things on the quiet, can you? Has to be a spectacle. Couldn't you
just tell him to sod off?

STUART: Like he'd listen. (Pause) Hazel, he'd follow me round
forever.

HAZEL: Yeah.

Pause.

STUART: Cameron's all right. He's good for him.

HAZEL: Cameron won't last.

STUART: Might do.

HAZEL: He won't. Still. Leaves room for the next Cameron.
(Brisk) I'm off, I'm late. One more thing, don't suppose you've
seen a bucket of piss?

Both laugh. She picks up her box.

STUART: ...have you said anything?

HAZEL: None of my business. He's trying to make sense of it,
poor sod. But if you want it to make sense, you've got to see
Vince as important. And he's never going to manage that, is he?

She goes up to him, and the fact that she's holding the box means there's no danger of any hugging nonsense, she just gives him a kiss on the head.

> HAZEL: See you, kid. Look after yourself.

> STUART: Always have done.

She walks away, calls out, not looking back.

> HAZEL: Keys are on the table, he doesn't want them back.

She goes.

7/39 INT. STUART'S FLAT, DAY 18 1510   7/39
STUART

STUART's sitting on the table with the radio-control, making K9 go round and round in circles.

7/40 INT. STUART'S FLAT, DAY 18 1520   7/40
STUART

STUART's just mooching about, idly going through the debris. But he's actually at the table where HAZEL left VINCE's keys. He picks them up; it's taken him this long to pick them up.
    He crosses the flat, then realises he doesn't know what to do with them, slams them down, walks away.

7/41 INT. STUART'S FLAT, DAY 18 1530   7/41
STUART

STUART's at the computer, on the gaymanchester IRC, when the phone rings, he picks it up.

> STUART: What? What do *you* want? Fuck off. (Beat, more interested) What for...?

7/42 EXT. STUART'S FLAT, DAY 18 1534   7/42
STUART

STUART's in the jeep, revs the engine, sunglasses on, cigarette, music loud; the public persona back in place as he roars off.

7/43 EXT. PARK, DAY 18 1555   7/43
STUART, LISA, ALFRED

STUART and LISA walk along with ALFRED in his buggy. A quiet, peaceful Sunday, families out for a walk with their kids. STUART and LISA look like the straightest couple in the world. Underneath that image, both edgy, cautious; two old enemies, out for a stroll.

> LISA: Don't pretend you're not bothered. The moment she marries him, your child will have a new father.

STUART: I'm much more interested in why it bothers you.

Pause. LISA hates being vulnerable in front of him. But needs must.

LISA: He's moved in permanently. Just in case the Home Office
checks up. He's got his things in our bedroom – *her* bedroom.
Just in case.

STUART: (Delighted) He's sleeping with her! Oh my God,
they're having sex!

LISA: Stuart. I have very good reason to believe she's a lesbian.

STUART: Have they? Have they shagged?

LISA: (Ignores him) She's put his name on the deeds to the
house. Just in case. It's her house, she can do what she wants.
(Beat, more edgy) I've been living there for six years. Paying half
the mortgage. With nothing in writing.

STUART: (Enjoys her discomfort) And you the solicitor.

LISA: If Romey and I split up, I'd get nothing.

STUART: Aah, and I thought this was a love story, it's just a mortgage.

LISA: I'm simplifying for my audience. (Beat, quieter) She's only
doing the right thing, she always does the right thing, she's
saving a man from being deported. She's so bloody correct.
(Back to work) So, it's down to us. To stop her.

They keep walking, STUART *so* fascinated, but keeping his cool.

7/44 EXT. PARK, LAKESIDE, DAY 18 1601   7/44
STUART, LISA, ALFRED

STUART and LISA sit on a bench, STUART throwing bread to the ducks for
ALFRED's amusement. LISA's just taken out a stack of handwritten letters.

LISA: First six months we went out, she wrote to me all the time.
She thinks letters are romantic, it's the sort of thing she does.
Still writes to me now, like it's some sort of record. The thoughts
of Romey Sullivan.

STUART: (Grins) Lesbian letters. Can I read them?

LISA: I doubt it, it's joined-up handwriting. But they'll make the
Home Office see things in a very different light. (Gets out an
official letter) Here's the address, it's a Mrs Lake, she's in charge
of Lance's visa application –

STUART: Hold on, why've *I* got to send them?

LISA: These could only have come from inside the house.

STUART: You send them!

LISA: You're in and out of that house all the time. And, of course, you're a malicious bastard.

STUART: We could send them anonymously.

LISA: They've still come from inside the house, someone's got to take the blame. And Romey's going to be furious, she'll never forgive you. But she's got a very good solicitor to remind her that she can't deny the father access.

STUART: So it all becomes my fault – ?

LISA: (More direct) I look after that kid every day, every night he's screaming the place down, you owe me.

Silence, LISA holding the stare, STUART deep in thought.

7/45 EXT. PARK, PLAYGROUND, DAY 18 1610　　　　　7/45
STUART, LISA, ALFRED

They've now got ALFRED, in his buggy, on a roundabout, spin it round slowly (or can he be on a swing? Something like that). Hold the silence, then:

STUART: I'll think about it.

LISA holds out the letters. He takes them.

7/46 EXT. PARK, NEAR PLAYGROUND, DAY 18 1615　　　7/46
STUART, LISA, ALFRED

LISA and STUART kneeling by ALFRED, buckling him in, LISA ready to take him home.

LISA: I don't want Vince to know about this.

STUART: S'all right. I don't see so much of him these days.

A beat between them, STUART just a fraction vulnerable, LISA aware of this, sympathetic, even though she doesn't know all the circumstances.

LISA: Give me an answer by Tuesday, phone me at the office. (Stops, her last appeal) She's got no reason to ever get divorced, he's got a meal ticket for life. He's not going away.

STUART gives ALFRED a kiss.

STUART: See ya, big fella.

LISA wheels ALFRED away. When she's a few yards away, STUART can't resist calling out, scoring a point.

> STUART: Lisa, by the way. Sending letters isn't romantic.
> Keeping them is.

She looks back; she might actually be sad for him.

> LISA: How would *you* know?

She walks off, STUART left alone, with the letters. Again, he's the still point; families, ordinary life, all around him.

7/47 INT. STUART'S FLAT, DAY 18 1635   7/47
STUART, SEVEN WOMEN

STUART's now sitting with a whisky and a cigarette, reading LISA's letters.
   Reveal, behind and around him, an army of seven WOMEN, in cleaner's uniforms, cleaning the flat, hoovering, polishing, washing up. STUART just sits there like they don't exist, focused on the letters. He winces.

> STUART: Too much information.

But he picks up the next letter anyway.

7/48 INT. STUART'S FLAT, DAY 18 1730   7/48
STUART, NATHAN

The flat's now sparkling clean – which makes it seem more empty – just one Vince/Warhol print left. STUART's fast asleep on the settee, as unattractive as a man can be. The buzzer goes, he jerks awake.

> STUART: Leave me alone!

He stomps over to the intercom.

> STUART: What?

> NATHAN OOV: It's me, I was just passing –

> STUART: Nathan, fuck off.

> NATHAN OOV: (Gabbles) They've been round all day, Vince
> and Cameron, they're calling you all sorts, I just thought – I
> mean – are you all right?

Pause. All day long, no one's asked STUART that.

> NATHAN OOV: Stuart?

> STUART: Fuck off.

He hangs up, walks away. Halfway across the flat, he sees LISA's letters. An idea. A great big fucking idea.

He runs back to the intercom.

    STUART: Nathan – ? Nathan! *Nathan!*

Beat (NATHAN OOV running back to the intercom).

    NATHAN OOV: Yeah?

    STUART: Come on up.

STUART presses the door release. Pause, as he thinks it through. Suddenly his idea gets better, he runs to the front door, out –

7/49 INT. OUTSIDE STUART'S FLAT, DAY 18 1731   7/49
STUART

STUART runs to the lift, pulls the lift gate half open. The noise of the lift stopping, halfway up. STUART runs back into the flat.

7/50 INT. STUART'S FLAT, DAY 18 1731   7/50
STUART

STUART races across the flat, into the bedroom.

7/51 INT. STUART'S BEDROOM, DAY 18 1732   7/51
STUART

STUART starts pulling off his clothes, frantic, like a mad thing, until he's down to his Calvins, a shirt thrown over, unbuttoned. He runs out.

7/52 INT. STUART'S FLAT, DAY 18 1732   7/52
STUART

STUART runs across the flat, heading out.

7/53 INT. OUTSIDE STUART'S FLAT, DAY 18 1732   7/53
STUART

STUART runs up to the lift, closes the gate again. The sound of the lift resuming its journey. He runs back into the flat.

7/54 INT. STUART'S FLAT, DAY 18 1733   7/54
STUART, NATHAN

STUART leaves the door open behind him, *belts* across the flat, jumps on to the settee, flicks on the TV, Mr Nonchalant again. NATHAN arrives in B/G, walks in, cautious.

    NATHAN: It's dodgy, that lift, I got stuck. Hiya. (No reply)
    Cameron thinks you're mad, like really mad, I said, you don't
    even know him. And Vince said you'd be laughing, I told him, I
    said that's not fair, he's not like that –

STUART: Nathan, you're a little boy. Don't fucking think you know me.

Pause. STUART exhales, then, quieter:

STUART: Maybe you should go. It's not Vince, it's... lots of things.

NATHAN: Like what?

Beat. Then STUART goes to the table, picks up LISA's letters, looks at NATHAN, sad, troubled.

7/55 INT. STUART'S FLAT, DAY 18 1745   7/55
STUART, NATHAN

STUART sits with NATHAN – he's manipulating him, but STUART's not a liar, as such. He's drawing on what he really feels, holding the letters, having explained.

STUART: I send them, she's going to hate me. Alfred's going to grow up in that house, his mother hating me. My own kid. (More exposed) Only had him in the first place cos I thought it would be a laugh. One big laugh, yeah.

NATHAN: So what you gonna do?

STUART just shrugs. Pause, NATHAN deep in thought (at 15, it's such a compliment to be told an adult's problem). Perhaps STUART's waiting for him to make the necessary conclusion; perhaps he regrets his own vulnerability, so he leaps into action, jumps over the back of the settee.

STUART: Come on!

7/56 INT. STUART'S FLAT, DAY 18 1800   7/56
STUART, NATHAN

From somewhere, STUART's got a full-sized ping-pong table (had it for years, never used it). It's now in the middle of the room, both playing, having a laugh, leaping about, slightly sending it up, either one going 'yesss!' when they win a point, ad-lib.

7/57 INT. STUART'S FLAT, DAY 18 1810   7/57
STUART, NATHAN

A completely different mood now, intense, both competitive, a long rally, the ball going to and fro, each determined to win. Men.
    Then NATHAN wins. No big, funny 'yesss!' but a real, hard-earnt –
    NATHAN: *Yes.*

Pause, both lifting out of the tension, STUART genuinely pissed off. And quietly, as if from nowhere:

NATHAN: What if someone else sent the letters?

STUART: Like who?

Beat.

NATHAN: Dunno.

Pause. Almost there, but NATHAN hasn't quite made it yet. STUART wanders through to the bedroom.

7/57A INT. BEDROOM, DAY 18 1811   7/57A
STUART, NATHAN

STUART finds something to do, though he's gone to the bedroom just to lead NATHAN in there. And sure enough, after a few seconds, NATHAN follows.

NATHAN: It's like I could draw this room. That night, I just lay there. All night, just looking. I could draw every single bit of it.

STUART sits on the bed.

STUART: It was a laugh, that night, yeah.

NATHAN: Was it?

STUART: I've had worse. (Smiles) And you won't have better.

NATHAN laughs. And then, tentative, he wanders over, sits on the bed, close but not too close to STUART. Pause, then:

NATHAN: D'you love Alfred?

STUART: Sometimes you talk like such a kid.

NATHAN: D'you love him, though?

STUART: Isn't it obvious?

NATHAN: It's not, no.

Pause. NATHAN shifts a little closer.

NATHAN (cont.): That night. Lying here. I really thought I loved you.

And STUART smiles, ruffles the top of NATHAN's head, gives him a little kiss on the forehead. Like old friends. But now they're even closer together.

NATHAN: Like girls in school going on about Jamie Theakston. Teenage crush, that's all. (Quieter) It's just cos, that first time I met you. On the street. You just looked at me. And you *knew.*

STUART's quiet, actually connecting with NATHAN.

>STUART: I moved to Manchester. First day at school, and there was Vince. He knew.

Pause.

>NATHAN: (Kind) He'll come back.

>STUART: He's not coming back.

NATHAN reaches out, some clumsy imitation of STUART's ruffling-hair gesture. Sympathy from a kid. Which STUART appreciates, he smiles. Which makes NATHAN smile. STUART takes a deep breath, like 'aren't-we-twats', stands, breaking the moment – perhaps changing his mind, not going through with the seduction.

But he's no sooner standing, and about to step past NATHAN, than NATHAN takes hold of his arm; he doesn't have to pull, it just happens, he brings STUART down and they're both necking.

STUART moves on top of him, and they're really necking, going for it. And never mind his plans, STUART needs to hear this:

>STUART: Wasn't a crush. You loved me, didn't you?

>NATHAN: …yeah.

>STUART: Past tense?

NATHAN's scared, won't answer that, grabs STUART instead. More snogging, then:

>NATHAN: I could do it. The letters, I could send them. I've been in that house, I could've taken them. I'll do it, I will.

More snogging, then STUART breaks off, pulls off NATHAN's T-shirt, gets back to snogging, then:

>STUART: Still comes back to me, Romey's going to think I asked you.

>NATHAN: I'll say you didn't, I'll take the blame.

>STUART: She's going to ask why.

>NATHAN: I dunno, cos I didn't want you to lose Alfred. Cos even if you wanted me to do it, you'd never ask –

NATHAN stops STUART, looks right at him. A long, hard, accurate look, slowly understanding STUART, and what's happening here.

>NATHAN (cont.): (Colder) Yeah, that's right. You wouldn't ask. You'd get me to do it, but not by asking.

STUART moves back in, hands moving down to NATHAN's crotch, the move from snogging to sex, but again NATHAN stops him. Suddenly in charge. Hold the look between them, STUART realising he's been sussed.

> NATHAN: (Suddenly happy) Look at you. All you had to do was ask!

Then NATHAN just smiles, so happy, stands, grabbing his T-shirt, walks out.

7/58 INT. STUART'S FLAT, DAY 18 1840   7/58
STUART, NATHAN

NATHAN walks through, shoving his T-shirt on, STUART follows him out of the bedroom. Roles completely reversed; NATHAN's happy, grinning, STUART glowering, hating this loss of face, but still needing NATHAN.

> NATHAN: Cos you're just mad, you are, you never *say*! D'you want me to take the letters? Ask me, go on! Ask me!

> STUART: I'm not bothered, okay?

> NATHAN: D'you love him, though? D'you love Alfred? Cos you don't say it, you can't, can you, look at you, you can't! (Suddenly) D'you love *Vince*?

> STUART: All right, Nathan, fuck off.

> NATHAN: You can't say it! That's brilliant! (Picks up the letters) Go on, ask me. Just ask me.

> STUART: I'll sort it out, I don't need you.

> NATHAN: I'll do it. I'm gonna get killed for this, but I'm still gonna do it. Not for a shag. I'll do it cos I'm stupid and I sort of love you. Said it! You should try it!

> STUART: Put them down.

> NATHAN: Too late! Cos I'm in love.

NATHAN grabs his jacket, heads for the door, stops, looks back. STUART has just turned away, pissed off, like it's over. But in the huge vault of this flat, he looks like Citizen Kane in Xanadu. And NATHAN loves him *so* much, feels sorry for him. NATHAN's quiet, now, his most adult.

> NATHAN: I used to be so jealous. You and Vince spent every Sunday hanging round this place, I'd have given anything. (Beat) And d'you know what Vince would do, if he was here? Lance is going to be *deported*. He'd stop you, Vince would stop you. (Sad smile) No Vince. You've just got me.

Pause. Then NATHAN goes.

7/59 INT. OUTSIDE STUART'S FLAT, DAY 18 1843   7/59
STUART, NATHAN

The lift's whirring and clanking, on its way up. NATHAN realises STUART's in the doorway. STUART's quiet, needing one more favour:

> STUART: You're right. About Vince. If he hears about this, he'll come running round.

> NATHAN: (Enjoys it) So..?

> STUART: So don't tell him.

> NATHAN: You asking?

> STUART: (Hates this) Yeah.

> NATHAN: Okay. (Smiles) You could say thanks.

STUART just shrugs, won't be told what to do by a kid. NATHAN delighted.

> NATHAN: Can't say it! (With affection) Stuart Jones, you're such a twat.

NATHAN gets in the lift, closes the door, descends.
STUART watches him go. Waits a few seconds. Then he darts over to the lift, pulls the gate half-open. The sound of the lift shuddering to a halt. STUART waits a few seconds more, then hears a banging from way down the lift-shaft. Then more banging, and a distant voice, echoing:

> NATHAN OOV: Hello...? Hello! (Beat) Um, can anyone hear me..?

STUART's silently laughing fit to burst, goes back to his flat, shuts the door.

> NATHAN OOV: Hello...?

7/60 INT. STUART'S FLAT, NIGHT 18 2200   7/60
STUART

Night's come round again. STUART's got the disco rig playing, full volume, a light track, pure pop. He's dancing on his own – not wild, just dancing.
On his face. He's fixed on the music, not happy, not sad. Just in his own private world.

EPISODE EIGHT

8/1 EXT. CAR SHOWROOM, DAY 19 0930
STUART, ROMEY, ALFRED

8/1

STUART walks along with ROMEY and ALFRED, just reaching the showroom forecourt, cars parked outside, others inside behind floor-to-ceiling windows.

> ROMEY: D'you think I *look* lesbian? I mean, the Home Office deals with fake weddings all the time, maybe they can just tell.

> STUART: What time are they coming?

> ROMEY: Half three, Lance is climbing the wall.

> STUART: It's probably just routine. (Picks up ALFRED) Thanks for the lift. You look after your mother, big fella.

8/2 INT. CAR SHOWROOM, DAY 19 0931
STUART, ROMEY, ROGER, ALFRED

8/2

ROGER CLEMENTS has got one of those desks in the middle of the showroom. He's 40, red-faced; a salesman. He's looking out through the windows, sees STUART give ALFRED a kiss, then an affectionate (guilty) kiss for ROMEY, saying goodbye. They look like the perfect family. ROGER stands, slaps on his salesman's grin, goes to work.

8/3 EXT. CAR SHOWROOM, DAY 19 0940
STUART, ROGER

8/3

ROGER's with STUART, holding paperwork, next to a brand-new Sport jeep.

> ROGER: You might want to check out the Sahara, it's that bit more robust, I'm thinking, family man –

> STUART: I like this one.

> ROGER: Just *think* Sahara, it's a tad more expensive but I've got to be honest about the Sport – (More confidential, grinning) We get a lot of gay guys buying this one. And fair enough, they're cutting edge, those boys, but a man like yourself, I'm thinking image –

> STUART: I like this one.

> ROGER: Good choice! (Even closer, a man-to-man joke) Thing about those lads, money to burn. Then they die young, so we get the resale value. (Heading back inside) Take it for a spin, sign this when you get back.

As he walks away, STUART just looks at him. *Looks* at him.

8/4 INT. CAR SHOWROOM, DAY 19 0945   8/4
STUART, ROGER

ROGER's back at his desk. He hears an engine, looks up. STUART's driven the
jeep back on to the forecourt, facing ROGER. STUART sits there, engine running.
Impassive. ROGER gives a cheery wave, holds up the papers. STUART looks at
ROGER. ROGER looks at STUART. STUART guns the engine. Staring at ROGER.
It's like the entire jeep tenses up. A second before it happens, the smile slips from
ROGER's face. And STUART drives the jeep through the window. A million pieces
of glass go flying as the jeep explodes into the showroom, brakes. ROGER – in no
danger of being hurt – staggers back, shocked, tumbles on to the floor, lies there
looking up at STUART, aghast.

      STUART: Where do I sign?

8/5 INT. HARLO'S, DAY 19 1000   8/5
VINCE, ROSALIE, MARCIE, JILL

VINCE in the aisles, with a clipboard, ticking stuff off. Far down the aisle,
ROSALIE is with JILL, loading food from a trolley on to the shelves. VINCE
glances at her, wary. She doesn't look at him at all. MARCIE's strolling up behind
VINCE. When MARCIE's in a good mood, she *bristles.*

      MARCIE: I'm back! Have you missed me?

      VINCE: And how was Scotland?

      MARCIE: Scottish. So what's the news, Mr Tyler, sir?

      VINCE: Refrigeration's going to close, ten jobs gone –

      MARCIE: Not shop news, I don't want shop news, I want news!
      (Walks on) Jill! Rosalie! Steady the buffers, she's back!

VINCE watches her heading for them. Oh shit.

8/6 INT. HARLO'S, DAY 19 1003   8/6
VINCE, ROSALIE, MARCIE, JILL

Minutes later, VINCE now head down, circling round the aisle where ROSALIE,
MARCIE and JILL are gathered.
    He turns the corner, sees them. Their chat is low, muttered, secret (and
they're still stacking shelves). ROSALIE says something. MARCIE and JILL turn
round, dart a look at VINCE – not smiling – turn back to each other.
    VINCE walks away, as though busy. Then, behind him, OOV, he can hear
ROSALIE, MARCIE and JILL burst into laughter, mocking and shrill. On VINCE,
walking. That old, familiar dread. The laughter carries into:

8/7 INT. SCHOOL CLASSROOM, DAY 19 1100   8/7
NATHAN, DONNA, CHRISTIAN, MR LYTHAM

An English lesson. NATHAN sits with NS BOYS, DONNA a distance away with NS
GIRLS, CHRISTIAN HOBBS at the back with his MATES. The teacher's MR

LYTHAM. He's 44; if MR LYTHAM was in a meeting, he'd insist on being the chairman. He's got a moustache. And a blazer.

> MR LYTHAM: Wilfred Owen was shot dead on November the fourth 1918, just seven days before the Armistice –   -

> CHRISTIAN: Thing is, sir, he was queer, Wilfred Owen, it says in the front. You can't teach us about poofs, you're not allowed –

> MR LYTHAM: Thank you, Christian, it's nothing to do with the man's poetry. (Beat; snide) Though no doubt he found plenty of things to do in the trenches other than fight.

Laughter from CHRISTIAN, his MATES, and a good few of the class. MR LYTHAM's quietly pleased.

> CHRISTIAN: (Directed at NATHAN) Sir, they all said, here comes Owen! Backs to the wall!

More laughter.

> MR LYTHAM: (*Still* smiling) Thank you, Christian, now if you look at the Preface of 1918, 'My subject is War, and the pity of War, the poetry is in the pity...'

Last lines OOV, as DONNA shoots a look across at NATHAN. He doesn't look at her, just faces ahead, silent. Burning up.

8/8 EXT. SCHOOL YARD, DAY 19 1250   8/8
NATHAN, DONNA, CHRISTIAN

NATHAN delving in his bag, sorting through books, angry, just assuming that DONNA's listening.

> NATHAN: Cos I can leave! Soon as I'm sixteen, I'm leaving school! If me and Dazz get that flat, I'll get a job in the Village, Dazz did that, I'll get bar work, I'll get anything, they never ask your age, Dazz said. He had trouble at school, he told 'em to shove it. He said you can report teachers for that sort of thing –

During this, on DONNA. CHRISTIAN's walking towards them, staring at her. A cold, powerful, sexual stare, his eyes going up and down her body; a look that says, I can have you, any time I like. DONNA's profoundly unsettled by the look, pulls her blazer across her chest, lacking her usual fire. CHRISTIAN passes by, looks back. DONNA finally explodes, upset.

> DONNA: Had a good look, then?

NATHAN turns to look, having missed it all. CHRISTIAN ignores him, just looks at DONNA. And sneers. CHRISTIAN walks on.

> NATHAN: What's that about?

DONNA: ...nothing.

NATHAN: What's he doing, was he looking at me?

DONNA: It's not always you.

Pause, NATHAN lost. DONNA recovers her composure, says simply;

DONNA: Did I tell you? Gary's moved in.

Big silence. NATHAN knows that's serious. Chastened:

NATHAN: When did that happen?

DONNA: Mum asked him, last week. Moved in, weekend. (Beat) Like you care, it's all Nathan and Dazz, Dazz and the flat and the Village. Me, I could be bleeding from the eyes.

Pause.

NATHAN: Sorry. (Pause) So how's it going?

DONNA: He's okay. (Pause. Quiet) Keeps walking out the bathroom naked.

Hold the pause, the full story bottled in that silence, DONNA for once unable to meet NATHAN's eye. Then she just stands, brisk, light again.

DONNA: Sally Watson's bought them shoes, that's ten of 'em now, it's a conspiracy.

She walks off, NATHAN grabs his things, for once having to follow her.

8/9 INT. THRIVE, DAY 19 1520   8/9
STUART, SANDRA, SECOND SECRETARY

STUART with SANDRA and NS SECRETARIES, other ACCOUNT DIRECTORS, lots of laughter, the best office story ever, STUART centre-stage. As noisy as NATHAN's classroom, but with the opposite effect.

SANDRA: Drove it straight through the window! They've been shouting all sorts! They said we're suing for damages, put me through to Mr Burton!

SECOND SECRETARY says 'What did Burton say?'

STUART: He said fuck 'em!

SANDRA: He did! He said we'll counter-sue, and we'll tell the papers what your man said, you're up against a PR company now! Yes!

During this, the phone rings, SECOND SECRETARY answers, says to STUART: 'Lisa Levene, says it's urgent'. STUART grabs it.

> STUART: What's happening?

8/10 EXT. ROMEY'S HOUSE/INT.ROMEY'S CONSERVATORY, INTERCUT WITH THRIVE, DAY 19 1521   8/10
LISA, ROMEY, LANCE, MR JORDAN, MRS LAKE/STUART, SANDRA, SECOND SECRETARY

LISA's on her mobile, in the garden, on the pretext of having a cigarette outside. Her POV: in the conservatory, ROMEY, LANCE and two Home Office people, MR JORDAN and MRS LAKE. It's like watching a silent film.
We can see that JORDAN's insisting, LANCE arguing.

> LISA: They arrived half an hour early, just turned up, walked in, no smiles, no cup of tea, straight down to business, it's looking good.

> STUART: I'll put you on the mobile. (Puts down the phone, presses *21*mobile number#, calling out:) Sandra! Cancel this afternoon, I'm going out.

> SANDRA: Going out where, ram-raiding? Get me a stereo!

His mobile rings, he answers, grabs his keys, stands, hurries out.

> STUART: What have they said?

> LISA: It's confidential, they asked me to leave the room. According to Lance, I'm the babysitter.

> STUART: Shit, hold on –

He runs back to a desk, opens the drawer, pulls out a brand-new teddy bear.

> STUART (cont.): Have they got the letters?

> LISA: They've got something – oh *yes*!

JORDAN has been quoting from a sheaf of A4 documents, but LISA's reacting to the fact that LANCE stands, angry, grabs the papers. JORDAN stands also, demanding them back, ROMEY telling LANCE to calm down.

8/11 THRIVE CORRIDOR/STAIRS INTERCUT WITH ROMEY'S HOUSE, DAY 19 1522   8/11
STUART/LISA, ROMEY, LANCE, MR JORDAN, MRS LAKE

STUART, with teddy bear, belting through the corridors, down the stairs.

> STUART: What's happening? What the fuck is happening? Lisa!

JORDAN's just tried to grab the papers, LANCE swings round. And punches him. ROMEY leaps up, pulling LANCE back, as JORDAN lunges forward to punch him back. MRS LAKE's on her feet, shouting at them to stop.

    LISA: *Fantastic!*

LISA clicks off the phone, runs to the house, on that action, hard CUT TO –

8/12 EXT. THRIVE, DAY 19 1523   8/12
STUART

STUART's in the jeep, the phone having gone dead on him.

    STUART: Lisa! *Lisa!*

He throws the phone down, guns the engine.

8/13 EXT. ROMEY'S HOUSE, DAY 19 1540   8/13
STUART, ROMEY, LISA, LANCE, SIOBHAN, MR JORDAN, SUZIE, MRS LAKE

Calmer now, a leisurely pan across two police cars and an ambulance now outside ROMEY's house. Then revealing STUART's jeep arriving B/G, as F/G a dazed PC is led to the ambulance, another PC arguing with SIOBHAN, SUZIE at her side, ROMEY standing there, distraught, LISA with her.
    On the jeep door as STUART steps out; a cascade of tiny glass chips.
    STUART walks forward, clutching the teddy bear. ROMEY sees him, heads for him, full temper, LISA following. Voices raised in suburbia.

    ROMEY: Was it you? *Was it you?*

    STUART: What? (Holds up the teddy) I was driving past, I bought this for Alfred –

    ROMEY: Someone told them, Stuart, was it you?

    STUART: Told them what?

ROMEY sees LANCE being led out of the house, handcuffed, with two more PCs. ROMEY runs to him (LANCE is glowering but defeated, knowing he's blown it). Stay on LISA and STUART. LISA's calm; in a crisis she's twice the bastard STUART is.

    LISA: Quite a temper, our friend Lance. Punched the man from the Home Office. And then punched the arresting officer. I think his application for a visa is officially null and void.

ROMEY calls across, as LANCE is put in the police car.

    ROMEY: Lisa! Go with him, he'll need a solicitor –

LISA goes to ROMEY, STUART trailing behind.

    LISA: I can't, I'm involved, they wouldn't allow it –

ROMEY: He needs you –

LISA: I'll get you someone, I'll phone the office –

ROMEY: (Turns on STUART again, furious) Of *course* it was you! You've never liked him, you never wanted him in that house –

STUART: I don't know what you're talking about.

The police car drives off, ROMEY despairing.

ROMEY: They knew. They knew the wedding was a fake, they had my *things*. From the *house* –

She breaks off as a PARAMEDIC leads MR JORDAN to the ambulance, MRS LAKE following. JORDAN's broken his nose, blood all down his front.

ROMEY: Mr Jordan, who told you? Who gave you the letters?

MR JORDAN: Not allowed to say. But the next time you see Nathan Maloney, tell him thanks a bunch.

ROMEY: Nathan…?

JORDAN and MRS LAKE get into the ambulance, the doors slam.

CUT TO – the ambulance driving off, clearing to reveal ROMEY, standing there, bewildered. She's helpless, shocked, begins to cry. LISA goes to her. And LISA gives STUART a fleeting glance; even she's ashamed, now.
STUART's feeling sick – not for LANCE, but hating seeing ROMEY like this. He turns, wanders back to the jeep. And there's only one person he can talk to, one person he needs. He gets out his mobile, presses a stored number.

8/14 INT. HARLO'S, VINCE'S OFFICE, DAY 19 1543   8/14
VINCE

VINCE at his desk, his mobile on the work-surface. It rings. He's saving stuff on his computer, reaches for the phone while still using the mouse –

8/15 EXT. ROMEY'S HOUSE, DAY 19 1543   8/15
STUART, ROMEY, LISA, SIOBHAN, SUZIE

STUART thinks better of it, shuts down the phone. Stands there, exhausted.

8/16 INT. VINCE'S OFFICE, DAY 19 1543   8/16
VINCE, ROSALIE

VINCE: Hello…?

But the mobile's dead. The phone screen tells him who called. STUART. On VINCE. Wondering what that means.

ROSALIE: It was your tie.

She's standing in the doorway, quiet. Her dignity is worse than her temper.

> ROSALIE: There was a man on *Changing Rooms* last night, he was wearing the same tie. We were laughing at your tie.

VINCE just smiles, nods, awkward. Beat.

> ROSALIE: I've not said anything. In case you're wondering. If you're ashamed, then… that's up to you.

> VINCE: I'm not ashamed.

> ROSALIE: You're not exactly proud, Vince. (Beat. She hands him a folder) That's from Carter, he wants it back Monday.

> VINCE: Yeah, thanks.

She could go, but she hesitates. A sad smile; because she *did* fancy him.

> ROSALIE: It's not that bad. The tie.

> VINCE: Yeah, didn't cost much, bargain, I got it from –

She doesn't wait for him to finish, turns and walks away, fast. On VINCE, relieved, but still sorry for ROSALIE. He looks at his phone screen. STUART.
   He clicks it on. Now it reads: CAMERON. He presses send. And for the first time this episode, he smiles, saying:

> VINCE: Hiya.

8/17 EXT. HAZEL'S HOUSE, DAY 19 1800   8/17
STUART, ROMEY, LISA, HAZEL, BERNARD

BERNARD's tinkering with his motorbike right outside the front door as the jeep pulls up, STUART driving, ROMEY and LISA as passengers. HAZEL appears at the front door even before BERNARD calls out (there's been a phonecall to warn them).

> BERNARD: Hazel. We've got lesbians.

> HAZEL: And I'm all out of herbal tea. (Calls inside, sharp) Nathan!

8/18 INT. HAZEL'S KITCHEN, DAY 19 1810   8/18
NATHAN, STUART, ROMEY, LISA, HAZEL

On NATHAN, facing STUART, ROMEY and LISA. A courtroom. HAZEL sits slightly apart (staying for NATHAN, *in loco parentis*). NATHAN aims it all at STUART, and it's accurate, NATHAN subtly – not giving himself away to ROMEY, LISA and HAZEL – enjoying it, at first.

> NATHAN: You treat that baby like a toy, like you don't care. And Lance, he'd take over, he'd be the dad, and you'd do nothing.

But I *know.* I know what you're like, you love him and you'd
never say. So I said it for you.

ROMEY: Lance is going to be deported!

NATHAN: I don't care.

ROMEY: (Tired, disgusted) Jesus Christ.

NATHAN's stronger – even ashamed – at STUART.

NATHAN: I don't give a toss about Lance, look at the rest I've
done. Left my family, and all of it, Donna and that. Just for you.

ROMEY: Keeps coming back to you, Stuart.

STUART: How was I to know?

ROMEY's strong, on the attack. Getting through to STUART. *And* NATHAN.

ROMEY: It is your fault, it's all your fault! Cos you just… *shag*!
You keep going, every night, and you never look back. Just look
back, Stuart, look at what you've done, look at *him.*

STUART's on the rack, now, the plan going wrong as he cops the blame. And
usually, he'd just laugh, but he's weaker, now, like his timing's gone.

STUART: I didn't know. Romey, if I'd known, I'd have…
I dunno.

ROMEY: And I chose you as the father.

Said with danger, maybe a threat that she'll do something about it. STUART
unnerved. He looks at LISA. Who looks away; like she might not keep her promise
to defend his rights. Nasty moment saved by:

HAZEL: You chose Lance as a husband, and look at him.
Slightest bit of trouble, out come the fists. D'you want a man like
that living with your kid?

ROMEY's already thought of this, but HAZEL's the first to say it out loud.

ROMEY: …maybe not.

8/19 EXT. HAZEL'S HOUSE, NIGHT 19 1840   8/19
STUART, HAZEL, ROMEY, LISA, BERNARD

In B/G, ROMEY and LISA getting into the jeep. (BERNARD's still at his bike,
ignoring it all.) STUART's heading down the path, stopped by:

HAZEL: You all right, then, stranger?

She's in the doorway, smiling. The only one who wants nothing out of him.

STUART: Yeah. Thanks for that. Just sort of…dunno. (Shrugs,
sad smile) Keep waiting for the punchline.

On STUART, bring in VINCE's voice immediately on the cut –

8/20 INT. CITY CENTRE ART GALLERY, NIGHT 19 2100   8/20
VINCE, CAMERON, STUART, SANDRA, STRIKING MAN

A formal function, waitresses carrying round canapés and wine. Not too full; the
impression that the evening's going to be boring. Just the sort of thing VINCE
needs to kick against, and send up, as he and CAMERON walk around. A chance
to see how much VINCE makes CAMERON laugh.

VINCE: Nooo, I'm not complaining, I like art, I'm good at art.
Those pictures of dogs playing poker, I love 'em. And Magic Eye
pictures, fantastic. I saw one once, it was a duck, you looked for
long enough and there was a duck. Brilliant. Worth millions.

CAMERON: I know it's dull, I've just got to stay for the speeches.

VINCE: No, fine. Me and art, we're like that. Art Garfunkel,
Bright Eyes. Burning like fire. Now there's a film, apparently
those rabbits weren't real. Fooled me.

Interrupted by:

SANDRA: Hiya, not seen you in ages, catch you later –

She's busy, carrying brochures, strides past. VINCE and CAMERON watch her as
she crosses the gallery. Towards STUART. He's at work, smiling, shaking hands
with gallery representatives. SANDRA reaches him, says 'look who's here' and
indicates VINCE and CAMERON.
    STUART gives them a nod, they nod back, then STUART turns away, goes
straight up to a STRIKING MAN, shakes hands. The smile. Even at a distance, it's
clear that STUART's copping off.

CAMERON: All right, let's go.

VINCE: Don't be daft. I can be in the same room.

VINCE and CAMERON are ostensibly studying a painting, turn back to it. But it's
a little dance of looks as VINCE sneaks a look at STUART. STUART's talking away
to STRIKING MAN. On VINCE; that old pang. Jealousy. But still wishing he was
there. CAMERON looks at VINCE, VINCE's eyeline darts back to the painting.
CAMERON glances at STUART, then back to the painting. Beat. Then VINCE
looks at STUART again.
CUT TO – STUART and STRIKING MAN.

STUART: We could go to Canal Street.

STRIKING MAN: What, and then go back to yours?

STUART: Sure.

STRIKING MAN: Mariner's Court, yeah?

STUART: ...yeah.

STRIKING MAN: (Still smiling, cold) I've been there. I must've made such a big impression.

STUART: Right! Right, yeah, course you have, yeah –

STRIKING MAN: (Turns away, dismissive) Nice to see you again.

STUART follows him. Just a few steps, but a pursuit is so unlike him, clumsy.
  Intercut with VINCE, the one person who can spot the smallest change in STUART's manner. STUART's aware of this; that's what's throwing him.

STUART: So, listen, what? D'you want to go, d'you want to, uh – ? Let's go, let's have a drink.

STRIKING MAN: Forget it.

STUART: We'll go back to mine.

STRIKING MAN: Just fuck off, okay?

STUART: Come on. (Steps in, smiling) I bet I was good.

STUART goes to take STRIKING MAN by the arm, a casual gesture. VINCE's POV: STRIKING MAN gives STUART a shove, steps back.

STRIKING MAN: I said fuck off, all right? What part of that don't you understand?

STRIKING MAN walks away. The gallery carries on as normal (only a couple of extras looking across, amused). But STUART knows VINCE and CAMERON have seen this, tries to shrug it off, grabs a drink, goes back to hand-shaking, trying so hard to be cocky.

CAMERON: Pathetic.

Hold on VINCE.

8/21 EXT. CANAL STREET CAR PARK, NIGHT 19 2330   8/21
STUART, NATHAN

Late night, men going home in B/G STUART's pissed as he heads for the jeep. He hauls himself in, tries to get the key in the ignition, misses. Then he gets it in, starts it up, stalls. He starts giggling. He's about to turn the key again when a hand comes in, grabs it.

NATHAN: Let's get a cab.

8/22 INT. VINCE'S FLAT, BATHROOM, NIGHT 19 2340   8/22
VINCE, CAMERON

VINCE is scrubbing away in the bath, CAMERON's in his boxers, brushing his teeth. And fed up of VINCE's conversation.

> VINCE: He's all bloody image. We're in Babylon once, we're off our heads, and Alexander's going mental, so we ended up dancing on a podium. Y'know, like twats, we looked stupid, so what? And Stuart! He just walks away, like we're dirt.

> CAMERON: I got those brochures. For Australia.

> VINCE: Oh, right, yeah, great. (Beat) Expensive.

> CAMERON: I can pay.

> VINCE: Well, yeah. We'll see. And this bloke at Mardi Gras, right, Stuart's been out all weekend, he's had ketamine and God knows what, and he sees this bloke, he says I'm having him –

CAMERON storms out, slams the bathroom door. On VINCE. Not a serious reaction, just oops. Stay on VINCE, noises off, CAMERON OOV stomping away, slamming another door, then mugs and things being slammed about. Then the sound of the door opening again, footsteps storming back to the bathroom, stomp stomp stomp – CAMERON shoves the door open again, stands there, angry.

> CAMERON: I love you.

He goes again, slams the door, footsteps stomping away. On VINCE. *Now* it's a serious reaction. Bad news.

8/23 INT. STUART'S FLAT, NIGHT 19 2350   8/23
STUART, NATHAN

STUART's got his head in the sink, running water, sobering up, NATHAN watching him, wary. STUART looks up, shakes his head like a dog, heads for the bedroom.

> STUART: Right, d'you want sex? S'pose I owe you a favour, come on then.

> NATHAN: I didn't do it for a shag.

> STUART: (His only hint of self-loathing) Nathan. It's all I've got to offer.

> NATHAN: How many men's had sex in here?

> STUART: Twenty-seven million.

Both laugh a little.

NATHAN: I was just on tap. That's all I was, on tap, you don't even *like* me.

Beat.

STUART: You're not so bad.

NATHAN: Really?

STUART: Let's just say, you're not the twat I thought you were.

NATHAN: Is that all?

STUART: That's all.

NATHAN: Yeah, well. One day.

STUART: (Laughs) Oh yeah.

NATHAN: Between you and me, I've got a plan, I'm going to be gay *forever*.

Pause. Then quietly:

STUART: Ten years' time, I'll be pushing forty. You'll be twenty-five. Jesus.

NATHAN: (Smiles) I can wait.

NATHAN looks across the room; a single Vince-Warhol print (decoration from the party) is still propped up, K9 in front of it. NATHAN quieter.

NATHAN (cont.): I thought Vince was so useless. I thought, he's mad, how come he hasn't shagged him? Hasn't even tried? (Smiles) He's not so stupid. (Beat) I'm off, I've got school.

NATHAN walks towards the door. STUART tries to keep it casual.

STUART: Have a coffee.

NATHAN stops, looks at him.

NATHAN: What for?

STUART: I don't know, what does anyone have coffee for? It's just coffee.

NATHAN: I'd better go.

STUART: We could watch a video.

NATHAN: Not porn.

STUART: It's not always porn. (Beat) Stay for a bit.

NATHAN: D'you want me to?

STUART shrugs.

NATHAN: D'you want me to stay?

STUART: Don't mind.

NATHAN: D'you *really* want me to stay?

Beat.

STUART: Yeah.

NATHAN: (Grins; not malicious, happy) Who'd've thought? Stuart Alan Jones. Begging me to stay.

STUART: If you think that's begging, you'd better not find your-self homeless.

And both smile.

8/24 INT. STUART'S FLAT, NIGHT 19 0030 · 8/24
STUART, NATHAN

STUART and NATHAN on the settee, the light of the TV flickering, sound low. They're close, but not intimate-close, and STUART's fast asleep. Like a kid.
     NATHAN looks at him, then gets up carefully, so as not to wake him. He takes the remote, switches off the TV, heads off.
     But halfway across the flat, he stops, looks at the Vince-Warhol print. On NATHAN: the trouble he's caused, the things he's done to fuck VINCE off. NATHAN makes a decision, moves across, fast. He picks up K9. Then hurries out.

8/25 INT. VINCE'S FLAT, DAY 20 0830 8/25
VINCE, CAMERON

VINCE is hopping about the flat, in a rush – and the rush helps him avoid CAMERON. CAMERON's in a dressing gown, eating toast, calm.

VINCE: I'm going to be late, where's that folder? The blue folder, shit, the traffic, this time of day – right, I'm off, you all right? You've got the keys, careful with the door, it needs pulling, see you –

He goes to give CAMERON a quick kiss, but CAMERON stops him.

CAMERON: You don't have to say anything back.

VINCE: ...yeah. (Twice as manic) God I'm late, right, the door needs pulling – I've said that, haven't I? Bye!

And VINCE runs out.

8/26 EXT. VINCE'S FLATS, DAY 20 0832 8/26
VINCE

VINCE hurries out, hassled, so deep in thought that he's a good few steps out before he sees: K9. Perched on top of the Mini's roof.

8/27 INT. THRIVE, DAY 20 1030 8/27
STUART

STUART's mobile rings, he looks at the screen. It says VINCE. STUART lets it ring for a good few seconds. Then answers.

    STUART: What?

8/28 INT. VINCE'S OFFICE, INTERCUT WITH THRIVE, DAY 20 1030 8/28
VINCE/STUART

VINCE on his mobile. Awkward.

    VINCE: Thought I'd better say thanks. For K9.

On STUART, working it out: NATHAN, K9, VINCE. The silence makes VINCE blunder on.

    VINCE: I mean, he's great, and... I know the circumstances were
    a bit, sort of – but he's great. Or it's great, whatever. He, I think
    Tom Baker says he. So. Thanks.

    STUART: Any time.

    VINCE: Better go.

Awkward pause, neither of them saying goodbye. Then VINCE hangs up.
    STUART puts his mobile down, picks up some paperwork. Then puts it down again. He looks at his mobile.
    CUT TO – VINCE, now hammering away at his computer. But he keeps glancing across at his mobile, on the desk.
    CUT TO – STUART.
    CUT TO – VINCE.
    CUT TO – STUART. He makes his mind up, grabs the phone, presses send.
    CUT TO – VINCE. The second the mobile rings, he grabs it, like lightning.

    STUART: What you doing for lunch?

8/29 INT. VIA FOSSA , DAY 20 1320 8/29
STUART, VINCE

STUART and VINCE sit together, having a sandwich and a pint. VINCE has been trying to be hostile.

    VINCE: Rosalie's not going to say anything. But I've still got to look
    at her, I've got to spend every day telling her what to do, and...

STUART holds the silence. No apology. Then:

> STUART: How's Cameron?

> VINCE: He's great, yeah. Wants me to go on holiday, Melbourne, sounds good.

> STUART: The poor sod. Give him six months, he'll be able to name all the Doctor Whos. In order. (Pause. Then fast) William Hartnell, Patrick Troughton, Jon Pertwee, Tom Baker, Peter Davison, Colin Baker, Sylvester McCoy.

> VINCE: What about Paul McGann?

> STUART and VINCE: (Together; an old joke) Paul McGann doesn't count.

Both smiling, more relaxed. Pause. And then VINCE can get back to what's nagging him.

> VINCE: It's all right, though, me and Cameron, it's okay. (Can't stop himself going on:) It's a bit of a love job, actually. Says he loves me, how's things with you, how's Alfred?

Pause, STUART not replying, just looking at VINCE, knowing VINCE wants to say more. And it works. VINCE more honest:

> VINCE: It pisses me off, though. The first one to say 'love', he's in charge. Puts him in charge. I dunno, it's all a bit… grown up. (He expects STUART to laugh at that. But STUART just watches him) You're supposed to ask. If I love him.

STUART leans in, direct, knowing VINCE so well, cutting through the chat. And from this point on, we're on CUs, the background, the sound, falling away, just STUART and VINCE at the centre of the world.

> STUART: You can't. You can't even respect him. He loves Vince Tyler, so that makes him stupid. The moment he said it, it all just died.

> VINCE: (Evasive, weak) No, s'nothing like that.

Long pause, VINCE suffering; STUART's absolutely right. Defenceless:

> VINCE: *Me*, though. I can't be the best shag he's ever had, he's Australian. I don't even know if I'm a good kisser, how d'you know if you're a good kisser?

> STUART: You just know.

> VINCE: Fuck off. (Both laugh. Pause, then:) It's not as if I've ever… done anything.

STUART: You've done nothing, Vince. You go to work, you go for a drink, you sit and watch cheap science fiction. Small and tiny world. What's so impressive about that, what's there to love?

VINCE: ...yeah.

STUART: It was good enough for me.

Hold the silence, both eye-to-eye. Heart-stopping. Then break out of the CUs, back to normal, STUART grabbing his jacket, about to go, casual.

STUART: I'm late, got to go. And tell him what you like, you're in charge, not him, tell him – tell him he's lucky. See you around.

VINCE: We could do this again.

STUART: D'you think?

VINCE: Just lunch. No harm in it.

STUART knows if it goes any further, he'll pull VINCE back to his side.

STUART: Naah. (Grins) Sorry, Vince, but my world's *huge*.

STUART walks off. On VINCE, watching as STUART walks away, being obscured by extras passing to and fro. Going, going... gone.

8/30 INT. NEW UNION, NIGHT 20, 2200   8/30
NATHAN, DONNA, DAZZ, HAZEL, BERNARD, ALEXANDER, CAMERON, CHRISTIAN, NEW UNION HOST, CATHY MOTT

Busy, music, life. It's karaoke night, NEW UNION HOST leading proceedings on stage, punters singing. NATHAN and DONNA walk in.

DONNA: D'you think Hazel would let me stay? Not permanent, just tonight, Gary's got his mates round, it's like a bomb's hit Chester Zoo –

DAZZ descends upon them.

DAZZ: Here they are, Wallace and Gromit, hiya. (A kiss for NATHAN) Have you heard, I've got a job, I'm doing bar work at Substation South, it's in Brixton, it's fantastic, I'm going down Saturday, I'm all packed.

NATHAN: ...what about the flat?

DAZZ: Oh I'll be all right, I've got friends in Camberwell, I'll shack up with them – oh my God, Steven Polack, back in a minute -

DAZZ hurries away. On NATHAN. He just looks at DONNA, shame-faced. She looks at him, solemn. Then she snorts with laughter, loving it, and NATHAN starts to laugh. He's been such a twat.

CUT TO – VINCE, with HAZEL, BERNARD and ALEXANDER.

>ALEXANDER: Police cars, two broken legs, lesbians screaming, Lance packed in a crate and shipped out the country, your mother had a front-row seat.

>VINCE: You never said!

>HAZEL: Well, I don't see you these days. (With a slight edge) No, you're Mr Grown Up now, it's all dinner for two. Don't you worry about us, we're still here. Still having a laugh – (Suddenly louder) Now don't say that about Cameron, I think he's lovely, that's not fair, Vince, he's a nice man.

Another routine VINCE recognises. He turns round, and CAMERON's just arriving (HAZEL, BERNARD and ALEXANDER laughing).

>VINCE: Hiya, I was just coming round – (To HAZEL, who's still laughing) You're on form.

>HAZEL: When am I not?

CUT TO – DONNA, NATHAN just coming back with drinks. But DONNA's all electrified, enjoying the drama.

>DONNA: Don't look, by the pillar, next to the red shirt.

He sneaks a glance across. It's CHRISTIAN HOBBS with a 17-year-old girl, CATHY MOTT. She's beautiful. CHRISTIAN's all smiles and attention, a completely different boy out of school. The model boyfriend.

>DONNA: That's Cathy Mott, that is, he's done all right, she's top of the list. Year 12.

>NATHAN: What they doing *here*, though?

>DONNA: Think about it, stupid. He's out to impress, Canal Street, it's New York to Year 12. Like he's so cool, the tosser.

8/31 INT. NEW UNION, NIGHT 20 2205   8/31
VINCE, CAMERON, NATHAN, DONNA, DAZZ, HAZEL, BERNARD, ALEXANDER, CHRISTIAN, STUART, NEW UNION HOST, CATHY MOTT

VINCE and CAMERON at the bar, getting drinks, a quiet word. CAMERON's at ease, smiling. In charge.

>VINCE: I had to see Hazel, I owed her a tenner –

>CAMERON: I thought you'd go to ground. My fault, I always get a bit heavy.

CUT TO – NATHAN and DONNA. NATHAN can't take his eyes off CHRISTIAN, burning up. And now, CHRISTIAN sees him. CHRISTIAN's thrown for a second, but won't give himself away to CATHY (who's talking away). And he actually smiles at NATHAN. Like they're friends. NATHAN turns away, to DONNA, boiling.

> NATHAN: Smiled at me! Bastard *smiled* at me!
>
> DONNA: D'you want to go?
>
> NATHAN: What's the point of staying here?

DONNA turns to go, not seeing, as NATHAN does: STUART. He's right across the pub, well out of sight of VINCE's group, just saying hello to some blokes, moving on, finding no one he really wants to talk to. STUART looks round, sees NATHAN.
Eye-contact. On STUART, then NATHAN, as in 1/9, connected across the distance. Keep the moment of suspension going, as though NATHAN suddenly sees everything clearly. NATHAN turns to look at CHRISTIAN (who's now so attentive to CATHY). NATHAN looks at the stage. He looks across at VINCE and CAMERON, now back with HAZEL, BERNARD and ALEXANDER.
And then he looks back at STUART. It's like NATHAN grows in height. Inspired.

> DONNA: You coming, then?
>
> NATHAN: What, like I've been driven out? What's this place for, Donna, what's it *for*?

CUT TO – ALEXANDER with VINCE, CAMERON, HAZEL and BERNARD.

> ALEXANDER: So I'm stood there in Battersea Power Station,
> Turbine B, wearing nothing but me Tommy Hilfiger pants, then
> lo and behold, he comes back in –
>
> HAZEL: Oh blimey, it's little Jimmy Osmond.

Their POV: NEW UNION HOST is leading NATHAN on to the stage, saying, 'Settle down, there's a young lad here wants a go, so give him a chance'.
NATHAN's at the mike as the karaoke music starts up. Reaction shots, DONNA on her own, VINCE, CAMERON, HAZEL, BERNARD, ALEXANDER watching, and across the room, CHRISTIAN and CATHY MOTT turning to the stage, CATHY recognising NATHAN from school.
NATHAN misses his intro, stands there, scared, but determined. Then he ignores the music, talks into the mike.
The Union falls into silence *slowly* throughout this.

> NATHAN: Right, cos, I just want to say...

He's still nervous. But then, NATHAN's POV: STUART stays distant, away from VINCE's group, but he steps into the light, watching NATHAN, fascinated, smiling. Which is all NATHAN needs.

> NATHAN: Cos that boy over there. Blue shirt, white T-shirt, dark
> hair, with the blonde girl, him. (On CHRISTIAN as people start
> to look. The karaoke music stops) I'm in school with him, right.
> His name's Christian Hobbs. And Christian Hobbs, d'you know

what he does? He finds a boy, and if that boy's a bit quiet, if he's a bit different, Christian Hobbs kicks his head in. He kicks them and he calls them queer. That boy there. He beats us up cos we're queer.

And only now, we've reached 90% silence (never 100%), the Union staring at CHRISTIAN. Hold the silence, eyes drilling into CHRISTIAN.

Then BERNARD stands, stronger than we've ever seen him.

BERNARD: Oy, Sunny Jim! That's your cue to fuck off out.

During all this, CATHY MOTT's been humiliated. She grabs her coat, about to go. CHRISTIAN automatically goes to follow, she turns, hisses 'Piss off!' CATHY walks out, CHRISTIAN turns back to look at NATHAN. Furious. But now NATHAN's smiling. He looks so much older.

NATHAN: Plenty more I could have said, Christian. And *that's* a favour.

CHRISTIAN turns and goes, seething, but also scared.

Beat, as the moment fades. No applause; instead, NEW UNION HOST takes over, says 'That was a public service announcement, now let's dance'.

Disco music starts, and the normal pub atmosphere returns as NATHAN steps off the stage, and now it's just the gathering of VINCE, CAMERON, HAZEL, BERNARD and ALEXANDER who clap – sending it up a bit – their enthusiasm calling NATHAN over. On VINCE. Admiring NATHAN for once.

NATHAN reaches HAZEL's table as DONNA runs over, hugs him.

ALEXANDER: He's here, he's queer, I'm buying him a beer!

NATHAN: Hazel, I was thinking, I mean I hope you don't mind, and it's been great and everything, but… I think I might move back home.

HAZEL: Oh bugger it, that's the rent money gone.

But she leans over the table and gives him a kiss, delighted.

ALEXANDER: I'm filling up, look at me, I'm moist – can I have his room?

DONNA: (Gleeful; he's coming home) You're dancing, you are!

Music takes over, full volume, as NATHAN and DONNA run over to the dance floor, take centre-stage, fling themselves round like lunatics, laughing. Favouring NATHAN; the light's bouncing off him, he's radiant.

On STUART, still watching, unseen. He looks across at the gathering of VINCE, CAMERON, HAZEL, BERNARD, ALEXANDER, as HAZEL stands, grabbing hold of BERNARD, her voice carrying across.

HAZEL: Shake a leg, Bernie! Let's show 'em!

HAZEL and BERNARD go to dance. STUART's smiling. Missing them. Then STUART just turns and walks away, melts into the crowd. CUT TO – NATHAN and DONNA, dancing, watching HAZEL and BERNARD.

> NATHAN: Forty years' time, that's us.

> DONNA: That's me with the moustache.

And NATHAN and DONNA laugh like kids, loving it.
> CUT TO – VINCE, CAMERON, ALEXANDER watching NATHAN.

> VINCE: Fifteen.

> CAMERON/ALEXANDER: Yeah.

> VINCE: Bastard.

> CAMERON/ALEXANDER: Oh yeah.

On NATHAN, incandescent. So completely young. Scene dissolves, with some part of that atmosphere – as incidental music? – carrying over sc. 8/32–33.

8/32 INT. HARLO'S, DAY 21 1000   8/32
VINCE, MARCIE, ROSALIE

VINCE, carrying the mood of 8/31 with him, happy, smiling, walks down one of the aisles towards MARCIE, gives her a blue folder. ROSALIE's in B/G, in earshot, at work.

> VINCE: Marcie, can you take that to wages?

> MARCIE: What did your last slave die of?

> VINCE: A good beating. It's for Simon Carter, d'you know him? Black hair, sort of Fox Mulder look, he's got the best arse in the shop. Put in a word for me. I've always fancied him.

MARCIE gobsmacked.

> VINCE: Run along.

And she does. VINCE gives ROSALIE a smile, saunters back the way he came. King of his domain.

8/33 EXT. NATHAN'S HOUSE, DAY 21 1600   8/33
NATHAN, JANICE, DONNA, GARY

NATHAN and JANICE are getting out of the car, NATHAN with his bags. DONNA's across the street, with a little French flag. NATHAN looks at her.

> DONNA: Well someone had to get the flags out.

> NATHAN: That's France, though.

DONNA: S'all we had, it came with the cheese. I wasn't going to spend money.

NATHAN: See you later.

JANICE: Maybe tomorrow, you've seen enough of him, Donna. My turn.

NATHAN winks at DONNA, goes in. DONNA's grinning, fit to burst.
    The 8/32–33-good-mood evaporates now, as a voice cuts in: 'Donna, you left that bloody door open?' She looks back at her house, the front door open. A glimpse of GARY. Big, hard, ugly. DONNA's smile dies. GARY slams the door, she looks round to see NATHAN's front door closing shut.

8/34 INT. MALONEYS' HALL/KITCHEN, DAY 21 1601　　　8/34
NATHAN, JANICE, ROY, HELEN

JANICE leads the way down the hall as HELEN cannons into NATHAN, yelling his name. He lifts her up, carries her into the kitchen. Stops dead. ROY MALONEY's there, awkward, embarrassed. JANICE awkward too – she didn't tell NATHAN this, in case he took off again.

JANICE: Your dad's just popped in, thought we could all have tea. It's only pizza, mind, I'm not cooking.

NATHAN: …you staying?

ROY: Let's wait and see. I think so.

Pause, neither quite knowing what to do. ROY's never met NATHAN on adult terms before. And so, stuck, he offers his hand. NATHAN responds, they shake hands, feeling like this is daft. But for all the difficulty, both smile.

8/35 INT. MALONEYS' KITCHEN, DAY 21 1630　　　8/35
NATHAN, ROY, JANICE, HELEN

Pan across the table, pizza boxes empty, to find ROY and NATHAN at the sink, washing up. More relaxed, now, normal father/son edginess.

NATHAN: I'm still going out, though. To the Village.

ROY: Not on school nights.

NATHAN: And I'm not going to change, you know that, don't you? Cos it's not a phase, I'm not growing out of it. I'm going to be gay forever –

ROY's been looking round; he can see, at a distance, JANICE, with HELEN. ROY moves closer into NATHAN.

ROY: You've made your mind up, and it's obvious there's no stopping you. It's Helen I'm worried about, she's ten years old, she's a child. I don't want her head filled with notions.

NATHAN: Like what?

CU ROY, right in NATHAN's face: rage and fear in his eyes.

ROY: As far as Helen's concerned, the anus is for shit. Got that?

And ROY walks out. On NATHAN, struck dumb. Pull out on him, just standing in the kitchen, suddenly young again. The house around him seems small and dark.

8/36 INT. BABYLON, NIGHT 21 2300   8/36
STUART, ALEXANDER

Full, music blasting away, boys dancing. High on a lonely perch, STUART stands alone, looking down. ALEXANDER's down below, calls up.

ALEXANDER: Hello, sugarface, you all right?

STUART: (Opens out his arms) My world's so fucking huge.

And he doesn't mean it for a second.

8/37 EXT. VINCE'S FLATS, NIGHT 21 2301   8/37
VINCE

VINCE running up to the Mini, on his mobile.

VINCE: I'm late, I had to buy them a drink at work – (Opens the Mini's door) Christ, you heard the door on this?

8/38 INT. RESTAURANT, NIGHT 21 2301 INTERCUT   8/38
WITH EXT. VINCE'S FLATS
CAMERON/VINCE

CAMERON at the restaurant bar, on his mobile.

CAMERON: Yeah, I'll take it to the garage. Get a move on or we'll lose the table.

VINCE: (Swings the door to and fro) Listen to that! Bernie can fix it.

CAMERON: I wouldn't trust Bernie, I'll take it to the garage.

VINCE: I'll do it.

CAMERON: Oh yeah, like you're going to get that door fixed in your flat?

VINCE: I will!

CAMERON: It's like waiting for a kid to tidy his bedroom. I paid for the bloody thing, I'll take charge of it.

And we're on CU VINCE as he just stops dead, so many things falling into place, like a massive thud in his head. Hold on him. He's holding his breath.

> CAMERON: Vince…? You still there?

> VINCE: …how many Doctor Whos can you name?

> CAMERON: What d'you mean?

> VINCE: All the actors who played Doctor Who. Name them.

> CAMERON: I don't know!

> VINCE: Just try.

> CAMERON: Well. Jon Pertwee. Tom Baker. Um…

> VINCE: Is that it?

> CAMERON: What does it matter?

> VINCE: Any more?

> CAMERON: That bloke with the white hair.

> VINCE: William Hartnell, any more?

> CAMERON: The vet. What the hell does it matter?

Hold on VINCE: it matters so much.

> CAMERON: Vince…?

> VINCE: Sorry, what? It's breaking up. We're breaking up, sorry –

He clicks the phone off. He looks at the Mini. He can't believe his own mind.
   He throws the keys inside the Mini. Holds the lock down on the door, shuts it, locking the keys inside. Then he steps back from the Mini, scared of it.
   Then he runs down the road, off into the night.

8/39 INT. NATHAN'S BEDROOM, NIGHT 21 2302   8/39
JANICE

JANICE knocks on NATHAN's door, goes in with a mug of tea.

> JANICE: Knock knock, your sister's been saying…

The room's empty. On JANICE. Suddenly scared, she slams down the mug, goes to the wardrobe, flings it open. Empty.

8/40 EXT. STREET, NIGHT 21 2303   8/40
VINCE

The main road into town from Fallowfield, busy. VINCE is like a mad thing, trying to wave down a taxi.

8/41 INT. MALONEYS' HOUSE, NIGHT 21 2303   8/41
JANICE

JANICE runs through the house, down the stairs, to the kitchen, terrified.

>   JANICE: Nathan? Nathan!

8/42 EXT. STREET, NIGHT 21 2304   8/42
VINCE, HOMELESS MAN

VINCE is practically out on the road, waving at uncaring taxis. A HOMELESS MAN comes up to him.

>   HOMELESS MAN: *Big Issue?*

>   VINCE: Yes it is!

8/43 EXT. NATHAN'S HOUSE, NIGHT 21 2305   8/43
JANICE

JANICE, in a complete panic, runs across the road to DONNA's house, rings the bell, hammers on the door.

8/44 EXT. CANAL STREET, NIGHT 21 2305   8/44
NATHAN

Tight shot on NATHAN, with his holdall, running down the street. Grinning.

8/45 EXT. DONNA'S HOUSE, NIGHT 21 2306   8/45
JANICE, GARY

JANICE stands in the doorway. GARY returns, says, 'She's not in her room'.

8/46 EXT. CANAL STREET, NIGHT 21 2306   8/46
NATHAN, DONNA

Wider on NATHAN running. Revealing DONNA at his side, with her holdall. Both laughing as they run, top-speed, exhilarated.

8/47 EXT. NATHAN'S HOUSE, NIGHT 21 2306   8/47
JANICE, ROY

JANICE running back to her house, as ROY runs out, furious.

>   ROY: My bloody wallet's gone!

8/48 EXT. CANAL STREET, NIGHT 21 2307   8/48
NATHAN, DONNA, TAXI DRIVER

A taxi's pulled up, NATHAN and DONNA by the door. NATHAN offers the DRIVER nine twenty-pound notes, from ROY's full-of-cash wallet.

> NATHAN: Will that get us to London?

DRIVER says, 'Should do, yeah, what part of London d'you want?'

> NATHAN: Slap bang in the middle.

NATHAN throws his holdall into the taxi, gets in. Then realises that DONNA hasn't followed, looks at her. She's hesitant, a bit scared.

> NATHAN: You coming?

Beat. Then DONNA smiles.

> DONNA: This had better be good.

And she jumps in. The taxi drives off, London-bound.

8/49 INT. BABYLON, NIGHT 21 2308   8/49
STUART, HARVEY

STUART's on the dance floor. He sees a good-looking bloke, smiles, and the man smiles back. He's wearing the same clothes from episode 3. It's HARVEY.

8/50 EXT. STREET, NIGHT 21 2308   8/50
VINCE, HOMELESS MAN

VINCE is still trying to flag down a taxi, but at the same time, he's following the HOMELESS MAN down the road, calling out, loud:

> VINCE: It is, it's dinner for two! Sod that! Who says you have to grow up? I'm not getting married, I'm not settling down, I'll be like a twat when I'm sixty! A twat and happy!

> HOMELESS MAN: Could you leave me alone, please?

8/51 INT. BABYLON, NIGHT 21 2309   8/51
STUART, HARVEY

STUART's some distance away, in direct eye-contact with HARVEY now. STUART turns on the grin, the sex. HARVEY grins back.

8/52 EXT. STREET, NIGHT 21 2310   8/52
VINCE, HOMELESS MAN

VINCE the same, flagging taxis, following HOMELESS MAN.

VINCE: And I *know*, all right? Nights with Stuart, they're shit, half the time. But I don't care! I love him!

A taxi stops, he runs to it, opens the door, then tells the taxi driver to hold on and runs back to the HOMELESS MAN. Up close, intense.

VINCE: Unrequited love. It's fantastic! Cos it never has to change. It never has to grow up. And it never has to die.

HOMELESS MAN: I said that, and look what happened to me.

VINCE: Don't spoil the moment.

VINCE runs back to the taxi, jumps in, the taxi roars away, disappearing off towards the centre of town.

8/53 INT. BABYLON, NIGHT 21 2316   8/53
VINCE, STUART, HARVEY, HAZEL, BERNARD, ALEXANDER

(Music: 'It's Raining Men', *the* gay club track: slow build before the chorus covering the meeting, then exploding out into the dance.)
STUART moves over to HARVEY. No words, just a smile between them, maybe some intimate gesture, then they turn, to move on to the dance floor. But in turning, STUART sees, standing behind him, centre of the floor:
VINCE. Looking so cool, so much in charge.
They look at each other. VINCE sizes up STUART, confident. STUART's wary. But STUART shifts so his back's turned completely to HARVEY. HARVEY's pissed off, walks away. STUART doesn't even notice; he's just turned down a shag for VINCE.
VINCE and STUART circle round a little, lions marking out their territory, creating a space, others dancing on the edges.
VINCE grins, then points at the podium, centre of the dance floor. STUART shakes his head. No way.
VINCE points at him: *you*. At the podium: *there*.
STUART gives a helpless smile.
Then STUART runs, VINCE runs, both leaping up on to the podium in the same second, as the music goes wild, into the chorus. And both start dancing, mental, happy, laughing. Spotlights slam down on them. They're looking like twats, and not giving a toss.
Run credits over this, VINCE and STUART at the centre. And dancing in the crowd below them, ALEXANDER.

End on VINCE and STUART.

A small and tiny world, but they're slap bang in the middle.